A WOMAN'S COURAGE

A
WOMAN'S
COURAGE

S. Block
with Maria Malone

ZAFFRE

First published in the UK as an ebook in 2020 by
ZAFFRE

This paperback edition first published in the UK in 2021 by
ZAFFRE
An imprint of Bonnier Books UK
80–81 Wimpole St, London W1G 9RE
Owned by Bonnier Books
Sveavägen 56, Stockholm, Sweden

A CIP catalogue record for this book is
available from the British Library.

ISBN: 978–1–78576–567–4

Also available as an ebook

1 3 5 7 9 10 8 6 4 2

Typeset by IDSUK (Data Connection) Ltd
Printed and bound in Great Britain by Clays Ltd, Elcograf S.p.A.

Zaffre is an imprint of Bonnier Books UK
www.bonnierbooks.co.uk

This book is dedicated to all those who helped bring
Home Fires *to page and screen, and all its*
readers and viewers

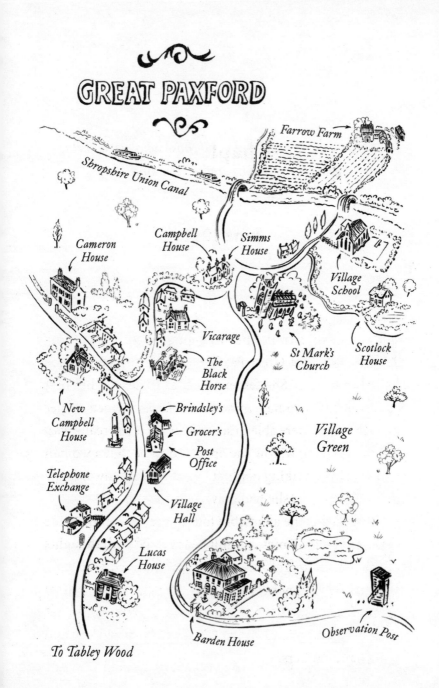

Chapter 1

June 1941

Pat Simms sat in the front pew of St Mark's, parish church of Great Paxford, straight-backed, hands folded in her lap. She felt exposed, as if, despite her best efforts, those who had come to pay their respects to her husband, Bob, were able to see her for what she really was: not the grieving widow she appeared to be, but a woman on the brink of taking her first tentative steps towards the glorious freedom she had craved for so long.

She gazed at the altar, oblivious to the consoling words of the Reverend James, her mind crammed with thoughts of the life she might now have, a future filled with possibilities unfolding before her. At last, the chance of real happiness. A small sigh escaped from her lips. At her side, her good friend, Erica Campbell, reached out and put a hand on hers.

It seemed as if barely any time at all had passed since the funeral of Erica's husband, Will. On that occasion, the church had been packed, a measure of the high regard in which the villagers had held their doctor. The turn-out for Bob, Pat noted, was smaller but nonetheless respectable. Many of those in attendance were friends of hers from the WI. Most, if not all, Pat guessed, were there to express support for her, rather than for Bob, who had made almost no effort with anyone in the village. The one exception, of course, was Joyce Cameron, who had been genuinely fond of him.

At the signal from Reverend James, Pat got to her feet to deliver the eulogy. She had agonised over what to say, lost count of the number of versions written and discarded before arriving at a form of words she felt were appropriate.

Words that would not stick in her throat when the time came.

She chose to focus on Bob's work, the success he had achieved through his writing, and the passion for what he rather grandly referred to as his 'calling'.

'When he died, Bob was busy working on another book,' she began. 'I can honestly say his dedication and commitment to his craft were nothing short of exceptional.'

Once she had spoken about his books, she spoke of the war, the character he had shown in coping with the debilitating injuries suffered while reporting on events at Dunkirk almost exactly a year earlier. On she went, choosing her words with care, saying only that which was indisputable, while keeping to herself the painful truth about a man who, behind closed doors, had been cruel and brutal, given to violent outbursts.

She kept her eyes on her notes as she outlined the efforts Bob had gone to in order to provide the house they had only recently moved into, pausing briefly as the memory of the two of them arguing on the night he died came back to her. For a second or two the text seemed to shift and separate on the page. She hesitated, not daring to meet the gaze of those facing her, afraid her audience might be able to read between the lines of each sentence she uttered and judge them inadequate. She imagined someone jumping up to challenge her, asking her what had really happened, and what she really felt.

But, of course, nobody did. Why would they? She was among friends and they believed her, felt for her.

She wondered what they might say if they knew the truth.

Sarah Collingborne sat near the front of the church with her sister, Frances Barden. The make-up of the congregation made Sarah reflect on the many women in the village who were now, one way or another, without their menfolk. Certainly, the toll the war was taking on the community was considerable.

Sarah's own husband, Adam, had chosen to leave his post as vicar of St Mark's in order to serve as an army chaplain, and had then been captured at Dunkirk. At least she knew he was alive, and she held fast to the hope he would, one day, return. She glanced sideways at her sister.

Frances was alone, too, in a way – widowed when her husband, Peter, was killed in a car crash. On her other side sat Noah, Peter's son by another woman, whose existence Frances had only found out about after Peter's death. She had adopted the little boy, but Sarah knew Frances missed Peter, and missed the vision of him she had believed in before his death brought his secrets to light.

In death our secrets, however carefully we conceal them, have a habit of revealing themselves, thought Sarah, *often in ways no one would ever have predicted. Perhaps we can only hide our true selves for so long.*

Sarah gazed at Pat, who was speaking with remarkable composure. Sarah was one of the few people who knew about the beatings and bullying to which her friend had been subjected throughout her marriage. Over the years, Pat had become expert at creating the impression that all was well, even when the opposite was true.

She looked pale, Sarah thought, her face more lined than a week ago, the tell-tale smudges beneath the eyes indicative of sleepless nights. She was a little thinner, too, the coat she had on swamping her. Pat was composed on the surface, perhaps – but what was she feeling inside? As Sarah took in her words, she could not help thinking how unfair it was that Bob should be laid to rest with dignity, his reputation unsullied. Yes, he was the writer, the man of letters his wife spoke of, but he was also so much more.

So much *less*.

Sarah watched her friend as she paid tribute to a husband she had not loved: a difficult balancing act, indeed. It was what Pat *didn't* say that struck Sarah as significant; no mention of her love for Bob, nor the sense of loss one would expect her to be feeling now that he was gone. Instead she harked back to the past, recalling how the two of them first met, Bob an aspiring novelist, Pat working for a publisher.

It was safer ground than the here and now, and a clever way of suggesting all was well between them without saying anything that wasn't actually true. Sarah understood. It was all a front. Pat simply doing what had become second nature to her over the years.

Teresa Lucas had been in two minds about whether to attend the funeral. Since her husband, Nick, had resumed his duties as a fighter pilot, she had been overwhelmed by anxiety, afraid that he would lose his life. A funeral, she knew all too well, would only make her feel even worse.

Given the nature of Nick's job, where death was an occupational hazard, Teresa had become almost primed for the worst thing to happen. Pat's situation, however, could not have been more different. Bob was at home, facing nothing more dangerous than a typewriter, which made his death all the more shocking.

It seemed wrong, somehow. Against the order of things.

Did that make it worse? Teresa wondered. Was loss not simply loss?

She chose to sit near the back of the church, close enough to the door that she could slip out unnoticed if she felt unwell. In recent days, Teresa had discovered just how debilitating the early stages of pregnancy could be. Morning sickness was something she knew about, of course – or so she'd thought, anyway. What she had been blissfully unaware of was that powerful waves of nausea could occur, with precious little warning, at any hour of the day. So-called 'morning' sickness was, she had come to realise, a misnomer.

For the best part of a week, Teresa had kept very little down, almost everything she ate sending her dashing to the bathroom to be sick. She felt hollow, light-headed. Nothing tasted right. Even a simple piece of toast spread with jam, or a dash of milk in her tea at breakfast, would somehow turn her stomach. The air inside the church felt stale, the scent of flowers unpleasant. She wondered what her chances were of making it to the end of the service without incident.

Other than Nick, the only person who knew she was pregnant was Great Paxford's GP, Myra Rosen, seated a few rows in front, who had assured her the sickness was normal and would pass. When, though? Teresa wondered. And what about the child she was carrying? How could it possibly grow when its mother was barely eating?

She had not yet become used to the idea of having a baby. Only a few months had passed since she and Nick were married, and she felt she was still learning the ropes when it came to being a wife, making mistakes her husband knew nothing about. When she thought about her friendship with Annie and how she had recently allowed it to tip over into something more, her morning sickness became tinged with queasy guilt.

What madness had possessed her to betray Nick at the risk of losing everything?

She blinked rapidly, grateful to have come to her senses, and made a vow to herself to be a good wife in future. A *faithful* wife. No more infatuations. No more deceit. The Teresa of old was gone for good.

Soon, she would be a mother. The thought of it terrified her. While she knew she was good with children, and had been an excellent teacher, motherhood was an entirely different prospect. She felt in no way qualified, and had no experience of babies. What was meant by *maternal instinct*? What if she wasn't up to it?

No. She *had* to be.

The doubts she had about herself and her own abilities did not extend to Nick. He would, she felt certain, know instinctively how to be a wonderful father. *As long as he gets the chance*, she thought. *Dear God, please keep him safe. I will be a good wife and mother, if only you keep him safe.*

Teresa brought her thoughts back to Pat. She had last seen her at a WI meeting and had intended to ask about the new house, until the air-raid siren sounded and sent everyone to the shelter. From that moment on, Teresa's only thoughts were of Nick and whether he was among the pilots sent up on that night's op.

She could not bear to think of Pat returning home that night to find her husband dead. It seemed beyond cruel.

Teresa marvelled at Pat, so calm and dignified, her voice steady. Either she was coping supremely well or, more likely, she was in a state of shock. What would the future hold for her now? Alone, stuck inside a big house she had barely had time to get to know, all semblance of the life she had imagined suddenly gone.

Teresa swallowed hard.

We none of us know what lies ahead, she thought. *Anything can happen. Almost always, when we least expect it. No matter what we tell ourselves, all we can know with any certainty is that* nothing *is certain.*

Joyce Cameron dabbed at her eyes with a hanky. It had come out of the drawer pressed and pristine that morning and was now damp with tears. It was not like Joyce to allow herself to be overcome by her feelings, or to express them in public. In most things, she was the epitome of the stiff upper lip, the type to confront whatever life laid at her door and get the better of it. *Chin up*, she would tell herself. What else could one do?

The year before, when a Spitfire crashed onto the village and Joyce was among the casualties, she had remained stoical, thinking herself fortunate to have sustained only minor injuries, aware of how much worse things could have been. In some ways, the crash had changed her life for the better; Pat and Bob, whose home was destroyed, had come to live with her on a temporary basis. As Joyce recuperated, Pat took on the role of housekeeper and Bob settled at his typewriter.

In a short space of time, Joyce had grown immensely fond of her lodgers. She had enjoyed their company, and felt privileged to witness first-hand the long hours Bob spent hunched over the typewriter, bashing away at the unwieldy keys, sustained by cups of tea or a sandwich consumed at his desk – all in the cause of producing the exhilarating, page-turning prose Joyce knew him to be capable of. It was this talent of his that had enabled Pat and Bob to eventually move into their own home, a large property in a remote spot some distance from the village.

Joyce had been happy for them, of course, but at the same time she had been sad to see them leave, knowing how keenly she would miss their company.

'I envy you, Patricia,' she'd said, as they prepared to move out. 'You really have it all. A clever and talented husband, a wonderful marriage. My dear, you deserve every happiness.'

She had intended to give them a few days to settle in to the new place and then pay a visit, but somehow she had been distracted by matters closer to home; various household tasks she had been meaning to see to for a while. Trivial matters, she now realised. Nothing that could not have waited.

She had never gone to the new house, and now Bob was dead. She could not quite take it in.

A couple with so much to live for, their future snatched away by the most terrible tragedy.

We think we have all the time in the world, she thought, *believing the worst will not happen to us. And yet we can lose what we hold most dear in the blink of an eye, our lives turned on their heads without any preamble. How can that be right?*

Finding herself welling up once more, Joyce reached for the damp hanky and pressed it into service.

Pat made her way back to her seat dry-eyed, the handkerchief in her bag unused, still folded into a neat little square. She caught only some of what Reverend James was saying: 'Death will be no more. Mourning and crying and pain will be no more.' Had she suggested that particular reading? She couldn't remember. The arrangements for the funeral had been made in something of a daze. Erica, who had been through it all herself so recently, had done most of the work, with Pat simply nodding her assent to whatever was suggested. She had been dreading the occasion, knowing she would find it an ordeal, something to get beyond.

'For those words are trustworthy and true,' said Reverend James.

Trustworthy and true. Pat bent her head, feeling all eyes on her. It was naïve to assume she was surrounded only by well-wishers. In a village like Great Paxford, there was always talk, a twisted pleasure to be derived from malicious gossip. Perhaps already some were speculating on Bob's unexpected death, hinting that it was not just sudden but *suspicious*. Mrs Talbot came to mind. She had always been sharp-tongued, quick to judge, not one to hold back when it came to tittle-tattle.

Pat wondered if this was how it felt to be on the stage, a character playing a part. If ever there was a time to give the performance of her life, this was it. For her own sake – and for Marek, who was now away fighting. His words to her before he had left, urging her to find a way of enduring in his absence, were what now kept her going. *Be strong. Survive.* She stole a glance at Erica, the only person who knew about her secret love, and felt a prickle of guilt.

I am about to bury my husband, and it is my lover who occupies my thoughts.

In the days that followed Bob's death, Pat had felt as if she were in enemy territory, picking her way through a desolate landscape, bombs exploding around her, bullets screaming past her head. If she were to survive, she knew she could not afford to put a foot wrong.

It was what she held onto when the police questioned her about Bob's death. A fall, she had told them. An accident, while she was out for the evening. Bob, who was unsteady on his feet, his bad leg prone to giving way under him, must have lost his balance at the top of the stairs. It was the only explanation. Borne out, it appeared, by the rug that lay crumpled on the landing.

The police officers had been sympathetic, concerned for Pat, never so much hinting at any wrongdoing on her part.

'A dreadful thing,' the detective had told her. 'Is there anyone you could stay with for a few days? It might be too much for you, being alone in such a big house after . . .'

She had caught sight of them earlier at the back of the church, the detective with greying hair and kind brown eyes, and the younger man in uniform, who had made her cups of strong tea with generous amounts of sugar. Pat wondered if their presence at St Mark's meant they had not yet finished with her, and her stomach cramped in alarm.

No, she had no reason to be afraid. It *was* an accident. Nobody thought otherwise.

She closed her eyes for a moment, the events of that fateful night coming once more into sharp focus. Bob bearing down on her, about to deliver another beating. Knowing she must stand up to him or forever be his prisoner. What she had done was an act of self-preservation.

I did not kill my husband. I did not push him. He lost his balance.

She blinked.

I have blood on my hands.

Grainy images came to her of the seconds before Bob fell, and she heard again the sickening crack as his head hit the polished wooden floor of the hall, saw herself sidestep the rug he had slipped on and slowly descend the stairs.

She had done nothing as he took what might have been his final breath. She had felt not guilt but relief. What did that make her? She had hated him, wanted him dead.

Well, she had got her wish.

She rose for the final hymn. 'Abide with Me'. Another choice she did not remember making.

As Bob lay dying in front of her, she had made no attempt to save him. She had not called for help, not telephoned for an ambulance. Instead, she put on her make-up and got ready to go out. She had coolly stepped around her husband's lifeless body and shut the door on him, gone to the WI meeting as if nothing was amiss.

Everything that followed had been a lie.

A sudden stab of fear caught at her. She could never escape what she had done in those final moments. What she had *not* done. It was something she was going to have to live with.

Whether it was a secret she could bear, and what damage it might do as it gnawed away at her, time alone would tell.

Chapter 2

A FEW DAYS AFTER THE funeral, Sarah Collingborne
was back at St Mark's for the Sunday morning service. As the church began to fill up, she was struck once
more by how changed the congregation was since the
outbreak of war. Most of the younger men had joined
up and gone to fight. Some would not be coming back.
Others were missing, their fate unknown. 'Missing' at
least meant there was still hope. Sarah's heart went out
to those families who had received nothing more than a
sparse few words on a telegram and who now existed in a
kind of limbo, praying and hoping for news. Good news.
She considered herself fortunate.

Adam was alive.

He was able to write.

She felt inside the pocket of her skirt for his letter.
Since its arrival, she had carried it everywhere, even placing it on her bedside table at night, then sleepily reaching
out in the dark once or twice to tuck it under her pillow.
There was comfort in keeping it close, she found, keeping

it to herself. She had told no one about it, not even Frances, who sat beside her, focused on Reverend James as he delivered a reading from *Romans*: '. . . although the body is dead because of sin, the spirit is alive because of righteousness . . .'

Sarah's fingers tightened around the envelope. In all conscience, she could not keep it to herself, although she had been tempted to, fearing that once she shared Adam's letter, the power of his words and the connection she felt to them would somehow be broken. And yet it would not be right to behave as if she had heard nothing from him when there were others in the village beside herself who keenly felt Adam's absence.

They deserved to know what news there was. Each week, they gathered to pray for Adam's safe return. They missed him, just as she did – his kindness, his good sense, that way he had of getting to the heart of things. If he were here – and oh, Sarah wished he were – he would be working tirelessly to bring some sense of peace to those in need.

And yet it was her news, and part of her was reluctant to share it, to share him, with her neighbours.

What remained of the service passed in a blur, Sarah lost in her own thoughts until she felt a nudge and glanced up to see Frances giving her a curious look. From the altar, Reverend James beckoned her forward.

Sarah made her way to the front of the church, sensing a change in the atmosphere, one or two murmurings of disquiet. It was strange how the air could feel suddenly different when charged with anticipation. She looked out at the sea of anxious faces now gazing at her, and swallowed. The last time she had stood up in church to speak was when she had learned of Adam's capture.

Almost a year had passed since then. It seemed even longer.

She decided to plunge straight in. 'As you're aware, the Reverend Collingborne is being held in a German prisoner of war camp. This week I received a letter from him which I'd very much like to share with you.' She registered the looks of concern that passed among those facing her and sought to reassure them. 'It appears from what he's able to say that he is well and coping with his situation.'

At once, the tension seemed to evaporate. She took the letter from her pocket and pulled it free of its envelope. Adam's neat handwriting covered both sides of a single sheet of paper. She had studied the words so many times, poring over each one, searching for hidden meaning, that she could almost have recited them from memory. *My beloved Sarah*, Adam wrote. Three precious words she was not willing to share. Her eyes went further down the page.

'"Conditions here are really not so bad",' Sarah began. '"I am sharing my quarters with some decent chaps who have a way of making light of things. There is a good deal of laughter, what might be termed 'black humour'. The place itself is bearable, the guards watchful, but I have received no ill treatment and am able to continue with some of my chaplaincy work. Most of us are in reasonable spirits. We have enough to eat and we do PT almost every day after breakfast to keep fit. For some, however, the mental strain of captivity is proving to be the most distressing aspect of confinement".'

Sarah paused to look up, and saw one or two heads nod in agreement. Alison Scotlock, a friend from the WI, whose husband, George, was lost in the Great War, caught her eye and gave an encouraging smile. Seated in the row behind were the Brindsleys: Miriam, cradling Vivian on her lap; Bryn, one hand resting lightly on his daughter's ankle; and David, their eldest, who'd survived the sinking of his merchant ship and was now back home. For a long while, he had been 'missing'. It had been a dark and difficult time for his parents, who somehow managed to stumble through each day until their son's return breathed life into them once more.

Sarah inhaled and continued: '"More than anything I look forward to the day when I will return. Never in my entire life have I longed so much for home. A great deal must have changed since I last saw you. I cannot help but think that many among the congregation at St Mark's must now be in need of love and support. So many separations, so much loss and suffering. In this time of turmoil and great uncertainty there cannot be a single soul who is not, in some way, affected. All any of us can do is manage as best we can, one day at a time. In spirit, at least, I am very much with you. With *all* of you. Great Paxford is where my heart lies".' Sarah skipped the next few lines, which were for her eyes alone. She gazed at the faces in front of her and registered expressions of relief. A few smiles. '"You are all very much in my thoughts and prayers at all times. If that brings even a small amount of comfort, I give thanks to God".'

She folded the letter, replaced it in her pocket and went back to her seat. Frances put a hand on her arm. 'Very nicely done,' she said. 'You really are full of surprises.'

As the church emptied, Sarah was approached by several people eager to speak to her.

Alison Scotlock appeared at her side. 'That was really very touching,' she said. 'Adam doesn't feel so far away anymore. So like him to be thinking of others.'

'And still managing to do some good in the parish, even though he's not even here,' Miriam Brindsley said. 'Let him know we're grateful for his news, won't you, and that he's very much in our prayers.'

Sarah nodded. 'I will, of course.'

'See how happy they all look,' Frances said, as they trailed away. 'A few well-chosen words and you've managed to deliver a real tonic to the village.'

'*Adam's* words,' Sarah said.

'He does have a way of saying the right thing, whatever the moment requires,' Frances said. 'And, as ever, his sense of timing is impeccable. Truly uplifting. Had you noticed the atmosphere in church before you got up to speak? It was . . .' She frowned, searching for the right word. '*Flat,*' she said at last. 'Mind you, that might have something to do with your husband's rather pedestrian stand-in. I do feel for Reverend James. I've no doubt he means well but he does tend to be . . .' Frances left space for Sarah to supply whatever adjective she felt was most suitable.

Dull, Sarah thought. *Uninspiring.* She had always found Reverend James a poor substitute for Adam. It was as if he were attached to the parish in only a half-hearted kind of way – not quite committed or fully engaged.

And yet, what chance did the poor man have, following in the footsteps of someone like Adam, filling in on a temporary basis until he was shunted to another parish where the congregation might well be less than enthusiastic about having him? It was not the most comfortable position for anyone. She had never before considered that her own presence must serve as a constant reminder that the rightful vicar of St Mark's was absent. In church, as she'd delivered her news and the atmosphere had changed, Reverend James must surely have been aware. It was almost as if the parishioners were half-hearted in their feelings towards *him*. Perhaps she was being unfair to find him lacking, given what he was up against.

'I'd say you've managed to put a collective spring in our step,' Frances told her.

'Not me – *Adam*.'

Frances gave her a searching look. 'Well, you certainly caught me unawares. I had no idea you'd even heard from him, and I shan't ask why you decided not to tell me. I'm sure you had your reasons.'

Sarah wasn't sure she could explain. It had been a small act of rebellion, perhaps. She had wanted him all to herself, if only for a short time. She had known when she married Adam that there would always be an element of having to share him, that others would lay claim to his time and energy, sometimes at inconvenient moments. He was never off duty; he would never turn away anyone in need. She loved him for it. And yet, she also knew (and had been at pains to point this out to Adam) that she would never be a typical vicar's wife. She didn't share her husband's faith, for one thing. For another, she could never see herself hosting genteel gatherings at the rectory or making house calls on parishioners. But Adam had never minded or sought to change her. Each accepted the other for who they were.

She gave Frances a helpless look. 'I honestly don't know why I didn't tell you.'

'It doesn't matter,' Frances said. 'It takes courage to open oneself up like that, and I'm very proud of you.'

Gwen Talbot emerged from St Mark's, pausing for a moment to adjust the angle of her hat, a straw affair decorated with a tired-looking floral arrangement, before heading their way. 'I won't be a moment,' Frances said, making a swift escape before Mrs Talbot, a prickly character, could reach them.

Sarah had long suspected that Gwen Talbot disapproved of her, that she considered her unsuitable. She wondered if Mrs Talbot might be about to say something regarding the rights and wrongs of a vicar's wife interrupting Sunday worship to air his personal correspondence. Behaviour unbecoming, perhaps. Inappropriate. It would be just like her to be the one person to find fault.

Sarah braced herself and forced a bright smile. 'Mrs Talbot,' she said. 'How nice to see you.'

Gwen Talbot nodded. 'And you, Mrs Collingborne. We don't often see you in church on a Sunday.'

Sarah refused to let her smile slip. It was true; she wasn't a regular, especially since Adam had been gone. Gwen Talbot wouldn't be the only one to have noticed – but she would be the only one to say so.

'It was very good of you to let us know about the Reverend Collingborne,' Mrs Talbot went on. 'We're all very concerned. And yet, I can't help thinking that the ones being held with your husband are fortunate in a way. There'll be some, especially the younger ones, having a hard time of things. Just boys, some of them – too young to be at war, if you ask me.' Her voice showed signs of cracking. Gwen Talbot's son had joined up and recently returned to the village wounded. 'What you said . . . the letter. Your husband's right about what he called "mental strain". What's going on inside can be harder to deal with sometimes than anything.'

Sarah guessed that Mrs Talbot was talking about her son. Since his return he had kept to himself, and Sarah had barely seen him around the village.

'I don't suppose you find it easy,' Mrs Talbot went on, 'managing on your own.'

Sarah didn't. And yet she knew she was better off than many. 'I count my blessings,' she said. 'Adam is safe, and that's the main thing.'

'You'll just want him back. Soon as.' She reached up and made another adjustment to her hat. It was past its best, the brim starting to fray, Sarah saw. 'Whenever I've needed support in the past I've not had to ask twice, not where the vicar's concerned,' Mrs Talbot said. 'He's always been one to put the needs of others first, your husband. I'd be most grateful if you'd let him know I send my best wishes and that I keep him in my prayers.'

Sarah thanked her and said she would. She watched the straw hat bob away, feeling somewhat thrown. This conversation was not what she had expected at all.

As the congregation dispersed, Sarah had the feeling her eyes had been opened in some way, as if she had seen another side to Gwen Talbot. An altogether softer side.

It got her thinking.

Chapter 3

PAT HAD INTENDED TO go to church, thinking it would do her good to be among people. The new house, so far from the village, made her feel isolated – precisely what Bob had hoped for when he bought it. Before they moved in, there were signs her husband was on the way to becoming a changed man, more likely to bring her a morning cup of tea in bed than raise a hand to her – almost considerate.

Against her better judgement, she had allowed herself to hope that their move might signal a new beginning: happier, more peaceful times, an end of his constant belittling. No more beatings.

For years, her marriage to Bob had been akin to walking on the most delicate of eggshells, which constantly gave way beneath her. His lack of success had fed into his anger. He saw himself as a gifted writer, and yet for years he'd been forced to do the kind of work he considered beneath him. It had made him resentful. He felt unacknowledged, unappreciated. Underpaid. When his first novel, intended to set him on the path to the literary career he felt he deserved, made

little impact and generated none of the wealth he had anticipated, Pat bore the brunt of his rage and frustration.

As they got ready to move, however, things had shown
definite signs of improvement. His latest novel was doing
well and he seemed altogether more content, less prone to
fly into a fury. He had even begun to show remorse for his
previous behaviour.

But the spirit of cautious optimism in which she moved
into the new house proved all too brief.

She only had herself to blame. She had become com-
placent, dared to think she was safe when she was not.

Bob had caught her out.

After the funeral, her friends from the WI had rallied
round. 'Come and stay with me,' Erica had said. 'I can't
stand to think of you alone in that big house in the middle
of nowhere. Especially after . . . everything that happened
there.' Erica looked concerned. 'It's filled with the wrong
kind of memories now.'

She was right – the house had its ghosts. One ghost,
anyway.

'It's kind of you, but there are things I need to sort out
there,' Pat had said. It was at least half true. There were Bob's
belongings, and the sale of the house. She was due to meet
with the solicitor to find out how she stood financially. 'And
I want to make sure I'm able to cope on my own.'

She didn't see why she wouldn't manage. Being married
to Bob had lent her a certain resilience, made her stronger
than perhaps she seemed.

'I know how glad I was to have company after Will died,' Erica said. She'd had her girls, Kate and Laura, and, lodging with her, Myra Rosen, who'd taken over as the village doctor.

'I need to face up to things,' Pat replied. 'I need to be independent. I'm on my own now and I have to learn to deal with it.'

She told herself that she would not be alone forever, that Marek would survive the war and come home to her. As yet, she had received no reply to the last letter she had sent him – but she told herself not to worry. She could not even be sure her letter had reached him. If it had, he would have found some way of responding, to let her know he was safe and thinking of her.

In the days following the funeral, she was busy getting ready to move again. She arranged to put the house back on the market. She removed Bob's things from the wardrobe in the bedroom they had shared and put them into the spare room. She would think of something useful to do with them now that clothes rationing had been introduced. She would have to start going through the papers in his study soon, too.

For the next few days, she saw no one.

When Sunday came, she was up early. She put on the pale blue print dress Marek liked and applied face powder sparingly, wondering if make-up might soon be in short supply, like so many other things. She peered into the cracked little mirror propped up on the dressing table and teased a comb through her hair. *I look better*, she thought. *Less anxious. No longer a woman in fear of her life.*

The moment she stepped from the bedroom onto the landing, her mood changed, and she was transported back to the night when she had stood in the very same spot as Bob loomed over her.

'You don't need friends. You only need me. Now get back in the bedroom until I say you can come out.'

She closed her eyes for a moment.

What was it Erica had said? *The wrong kind of memories.*

Shaken, she made her way downstairs and into the kitchen, no longer in the mood for church, not sure she could face the friends she knew would be looking out for her. She sat at the table in her blue dress, sun streaming through the back window, dust motes floating in the air. The teapot and her cup from breakfast were still out, and she poured what was left and took a drink even though it was almost cold. From a shelf on the wall next to the range came the sound of a clock ticking. *Just go. Don't let him hold you back*. If she set off right away she could still be in Great Paxford in time for the service.

She got to her feet and went into the hall, automatically sidestepping the spot where Bob had lain.

Where he had died.

When she reached the front door, something held her back.

Knowing what she knew, had she any business going to a place of worship?

Chapter 4

THE VILLAGE WAS BATHED in sunshine, one or two enormous clouds dotted against the sky. In recent weeks, much to everyone's relief, the German bombing raids seemed to have come to an end, and fewer people were leaving their homes in Liverpool and making their way into the countryside each night to seek sanctuary. On such a glorious summer day, under a brilliant blue sky, it was almost possible to imagine there was no war.

Sarah made her way out of the village, past the Observation Post, Adam's letter still in her pocket. She had been overwhelmed by the kindness of the congregation, and felt as if their good wishes had suffused her with energy. Once at home, she was too restless to read or listen to the wireless, and the darning that lay in her sewing basket held little appeal. She considered getting out into the garden and doing some tidying there, but quickly dismissed the idea, putting on a pair of comfortable shoes instead and setting off for a long walk.

Some time later, she stood in front of Pat's yellow door and pressed the bell. So much had happened since she first visited the house with Frances and Alison, less than three weeks before. Then they'd stood on the doorstep, knocked and got no reply – despite hearing the unmistakable sound of typewriter keys being struck within. They had persisted, ringing the bell, rapping on the door, even calling through the letterbox – but to no avail. All the while, the relentless hammering carried on. It was enough to set your teeth on edge, Alison had remarked, astonished that such a racket could yield anything remotely creative.

Finally, they'd given up and gone away.

Now the front door opened and Sarah smiled. 'Hello, Pat. I wondered if you might like some company?'

'Sarah.' Pat was surprised to see her. The house was out of the way, six miles from Great Paxford – not what might be called well-situated for visits of a spontaneous nature.

'I'm sorry to turn up like this without any warning,' Sarah said. 'We missed you at church this morning, and it's such a lovely day that I felt like walking. And I wanted to see how you are. Am I interrupting?'

'Not in the least.' Pat smiled. 'Come in.'

After the heat outside, the hallway felt delicious and cool, if a little gloomy. 'We can sit in the garden at the back, if you like,' Pat was saying, as she headed off along the narrow passageway. 'The front doesn't get the sun until later in the afternoon.'

Sarah hung back. Facing her was the staircase, a wide sweep leading to the rooms above. It was steep, with no landing halfway. Nothing to break a fall. Her gaze dropped to the floor, the stained floorboards that were so highly polished they gave the impression of being wet. Almost like a deep, dark pool. She imagined taking a step forward and slipping, fighting for breath. *This was where it happened.* A shiver ran down the back of her neck.

When she looked up, Pat was at the end of the corridor, watching.

'I'll make tea,' she said. 'Come through when you're ready.'

They sat at an old wooden table in a shady spot in the garden. Tiny birds with bright red heads and elaborate plumage darted in and out of a horse chestnut. 'Goldfinches,' Sarah said. 'What is it you call them when there's a group like that?'

'A charm,' Pat said, not taking her eyes off a bird that hung almost upside down on a flimsy branch. 'It seems the right word. They're the prettiest little birds.'

At the funeral, Sarah had thought her friend looked thin and worn out, as if she had not slept. It was not surprising, given what she had been through. Already, in the space of a few days, she seemed much better.

'I see the *For Sale* sign is up,' Sarah said.

'I don't want to stay here any longer than I have to,' Pat told her. 'Not now.' There were too many memories. The wrong type.

'I think you're right to move. As soon as you're able.' Sarah studied Pat, who suddenly seemed miles away. 'How are you?' she asked gently.

'I'm fine, coping. It's just . . .' Pat was quiet for a moment. 'I wonder, is it true what people say about secrets? That they always come out sooner or later?'

At Bob's funeral, Pat had done all she could to portray him as a decent man, a good husband, when nothing could have been further from the truth. Sarah understood. Having covered for him for so many years, the last thing she would now want would be for his cruelty towards her to become widely known.

'I think we're entitled to keep certain matters to ourselves, to have a degree of privacy when it comes to personal matters,' she said. 'So, in answer to your question, no, I don't think secrets need always surface.'

Pat nodded. 'I blame myself for Bob's death. If it wasn't for me—'

'You mustn't think like that,' Sarah interrupted.

'I made him angry, more than you can imagine. *Me*. Almost everything I did put his back up: working at the Exchange, the things I said, what I didn't say, my clothes, the books I chose to read.' She gave a helpless shrug. 'It's as if everything about *me* sent him into a fury. I was a constant source of irritation. I can't help thinking that if only I'd been different, perhaps he'd still be alive.'

'I don't follow . . .'

'That night.' Pat took a breath. 'He didn't want me to go to the WI meeting . . . I insisted. The last conversation we had was an argument.' She stared at the ground, unwilling to look Sarah in the eye.

Sarah knew from Adam's work in the parish that Pat was not the only woman in Great Paxford to suffer at the hands of a violent partner. Some had confided in him, hoping their vicar might be able to offer advice on how best to change their ways – 'become better', as one woman put it – so that their husbands no longer felt compelled to beat them black and blue. Adam had done all that he could to assure these women they were in no way to blame.

'Bob treated you very poorly,' said Sarah. 'He made your life miserable. He might as well have put a chain around your neck. That's not love, Pat, and I don't believe there's anything you could have done to placate him. It wasn't *you* that made him violent, it was *his* need to control you. I can't begin to understand what made him like that, but one thing I am certain of is that you weren't the cause. He was a bully. That's all there was to it.'

Pat didn't look up. Sarah followed her eyes to where a ladybird was making its way over the stone path.

'I can only imagine what you've put up with, the treatment you've endured over the years,' Sarah said. 'But Pat, it's over now. You're no longer shackled, and that's a good thing. You can move back into the village and be among your friends. Imagine – no more having to rush home because Bob's waiting, one eye on the clock. If you run into a friend, you can stop and chat if you feel like it.' Sarah hesitated. She wanted to get this right. What would Adam have said if he were here? After so many years with him, had some of what she thought of as his vicar's wisdom rubbed off on her?

'Even if your life together wasn't happy,' she went on, 'it doesn't mean you're not grieving. And I know you're feeling guilty, too – not that you have any need to. We don't have long on this Earth and what time we have is filled with uncertainty. No one expected Bob to die when he did – least of all you – but that's what happened. It's what God or the Universe or however you want to think of it had in store for him.' A friend of hers in Oxford was fond of saying, *When it's your time, it's your time*, and Sarah happened to think they were on to something. 'I don't know much,' she said, 'but I do know life is for living, especially now, when we're at war.'

Pat looked at her. 'I was going to come to church today, but I just couldn't face it.'

Sarah took the letter from her pocket and pressed it into her friend's hand. 'It's from Adam. I shared it with the congregation this morning. There were some bits I skipped, but . . . well, I don't mind if you see them. Go on, read it.'

When Pat finished with the letter, she handed it back with a pained smile. 'Here I am, wallowing in my own troubles, and I hadn't even asked about Adam or how you're managing without him.'

Sarah smiled. 'I'm managing well enough, really. It's extraordinary how much comfort a few lines can bring.'

Pat nodded.

'It might sound trite, but it feels as if there's a piece of him that's *present* now, somehow. As if he's with me, under my skin . . . tucked inside my heart.' She laughed. 'Does that sound ridiculous?'

Pat smiled. 'Not at all. I know exactly what you mean.'

It was how she felt about Marek.

Chapter 5

FRANCES BARDEN HAD THE air of a woman on a mission. Something about the tone of her voice, the almost imperious tilt of her chin and the determined gleam in her eyes gave it away. They were all familiar signs to those who knew her.

She was impeccably turned out as ever, in a silk blouse and elegant trousers, her copper hair fashioned into complicated curls. Frances was a commanding figure, and she approached her role as chair of Great Paxford's WI with the utmost dedication; no one doubted that Frances was the right woman for the job – not even Joyce Cameron, who had once coveted the position herself. Frances was inspiring, a natural leader who saw it as her mission to elicit the very best from her ladies. She had a reputation for making stirring speeches, urging the membership to aspire to great things – and, invariably, they responded. Her contagious 'can do' attitude was precisely what was needed during such challenging times. She was energetic, relentless, driven to press constantly for ideas that would keep the branch and its members fully occupied working for the greater good. At times her enthusiasm was utterly exhausting. 'We are *doers*, ladies, and there is always more that can be done,' she was fond of saying, prompting Sarah to point out how much she was beginning to sound like Mr Churchill. Frances took this as a great compliment.

The country was at war. It was not a time to take things easy.

Frances was inordinately proud of the achievements of the WI. The soup kitchen at St Mark's, set up to offer a hot meal to the nightly trekkers coming to escape the Liverpool bombings, was a fine example of members pulling together. A shelter had also been created in the village hall for families driven from their homes. The actions of the WI had ensured order and harmony in what might have otherwise been a chaotic time. They had defused the tension between those seeking refuge and villagers opposed to their presence. It was not *too* dramatic, Frances felt, to believe that for a time at least, the peace of the entire community had been at risk – and they had been the ones to fix it. Frances felt immensely proud of all the branch had achieved.

Now, though, the bombing had abated, and the people of Liverpool no longer felt the need to escape their city each night. A few stragglers continued to arrive, but the numbers had dwindled to such an extent that the soup kitchen was no longer felt compelled. A vacuum now existed – and Frances felt compelled to fill it.

'I was thinking, ladies,' Frances said, addressing the committee members gathered in her dining room, 'that we could do with finding a new project, something . . . significant.'

Erica sent an uneasy look in the direction of Sarah. All those on the committee were accustomed to the sometimes overly ambitious schemes dreamed up by their chair. Often, Frances struck precisely the right tone and tapped into the general mood, but occasionally her ideas veered towards the downright impractical. At one stage she'd been keen for members to make and deliver lunches each day to farmworkers – a mammoth task which had not taken off.

Before anyone had a chance to speak, the door opened and Pat appeared, slightly out of breath. 'Sorry I'm a bit late,' she said, pulling out a chair at the end of the table next to Erica. 'I cycled and it took longer than I expected.' She shrugged off her cardigan.

'On behalf of all of us, welcome back,' Frances said. 'Without wishing to dwell too much on all that you've endured – and still will for some time to come – you're among friends. Anything we can do, you need only ask.'

There were murmurings of agreement around the table and Pat nodded, grateful to be with friends who had some understanding of what she'd suffered at Bob's hands. It never ceased to amaze her that, given Bob's reckless and at times brutal character, there were many in the village who had never managed to see through her husband. In general, allowances had been made for him. Bob Simms was *unusual*, after all. He was a *writer*, in a world of his own. The consensus seemed to be that he was not so much *rude* as in possession of various authorial quirks.

Among those who subscribed to this view was Joyce Cameron. Ordinarily formidable and not one to suffer fools, Joyce had been completely taken in – mesmerised, almost – by the simple act of Bob sitting at the typewriter bashing away at the keys, as if that in itself signified both creative genius and innate goodness. Joyce had been in a better position than anyone to observe Pat and Bob at close quarters when they lodged with her – and yet, for reasons Pat was unable to fathom, she had failed to spot anything untoward. Bob's sarcasm, his brusqueness and lack of patience went unnoticed. Joyce held him in the highest esteem and since his death had kept asking Pat in sorrowful tones how she was coping without him.

She was coping perfectly well. Bob's death, shocking though it was, was a welcome release.

He was her jailer and now she was free.

Pat smiled at the women surrounding her, counting herself lucky to have such good friends, women who would go out of their way for her. *Anything at all, you only have to ask.* She was overwhelmed by their kindness.

And there was another feeling too, a deeper one, a prick of guilt. She was not the grieving widow most of them thought her. She did not deserve their kindness.

'We've missed you,' Erica said.

'I'm glad to be here,' Pat replied. 'Although some might think it too soon to be out gallivanting—'

Alison gave a wry smile. 'A WI committee meeting hardly constitutes gallivanting.'

'Unless people think a "committee meeting" is cover for something else,' Steph Farrow teased. 'A secretive gathering conducted behind closed doors, discussing who knows what? We could be up to anything!'

Frances raised an eyebrow. 'Hardly.'

'Our meetings are among the few occasions I have to ditch my farm overalls and put on a dress and some make-up and look half presentable,' Steph said. 'Remind my Stan what he sees in me.' She smiled. 'I ran into Gwen Talbot one day when I was on my way here and she had the cheek to ask where I was off to "all done up".'

'What did you tell her?' Sarah asked.

'I said I had a date. Which was true – a date with you ladies. Her eyes nearly popped out of her head.'

There was laughter around the table.

As Pat had pedalled through the village, rejoicing in her new-found freedom, a cool breeze on her face, she had been aware of several pairs of curious eyes on her, as if people were surprised to see her out. It was her first proper outing since the funeral, and it occurred to her that the mere act of riding a bicycle might be considered inappropriate by some – frivolous, even. Until she moved back to the village, however, it was simply the most practical means of getting about.

'No one can expect you to avoid all company,' Sarah told Pat.

Frances agreed. 'Stuck on your own, miles from anyone. The house is lovely, I'm sure, but rather out of the way.'

Pat nodded. 'I suddenly felt the need for company,' she said. 'I was listening to *In Your Garden* yesterday and found myself chatting away to Mr Middleton.'

Sarah smiled. 'I frequently converse with the wireless.'

'I used to talk to Boris,' Alison admitted, smiling at the thought of her old dog. 'And I found him to be a very good listener, too. He had an intense look of concentration about him, as if he hung on every word I said. I convinced myself he really understood.' She gave a wry smile. 'Although, thinking back, I suspect his keen expression was geared more towards getting a treat than anything else.'

'I was half expecting Mr Middleton to say something directly back to me.' Pat shook her head. A month had passed since Bob's death, during which time she had kept to herself and had little company. 'It made me realise being cooped up for too long isn't healthy. The new house *is* lovely, but it's not quite home.'

It never would be either. The sooner it was sold, the better. She had received good news the day before when she met with the solicitor who was handling Bob's will. Everything was now hers, he told her. And when the figures were presented to her, she was taken aback.

It turned out that Bob's writing was rather more success-ful than he'd led Pat to believe. His latest novel had racked up respectable sales – on top of which, the destruction of their former home had yielded a substantial payment from the insurers. Pat learned that he had not needed to borrow in order to buy the new house, that she now owned it outright. She was, suddenly, quite well off. There was no need to wait for the house to sell, when she could move back to Great Paxford as soon as she liked into a rented property.

'Well, we're very glad to have you back in our midst,' Frances said.

'And I have an idea for a project,' Pat said. 'I was thinking we might take on clothes rationing.'

The idea of clothing coupons, unexpectedly announced on 1 June, Whit Sunday, had been met with a good deal of grumbling. In a wireless broadcast, the President of the Board of Trade, Oliver Lyttelton, seemed to equate patriotism with being badly dressed. 'We must learn as civilians to be seen in clothes that are not so smart,' he said.

Not everyone shared his enthusiasm.

'Families with growing children will find it more difficult than most, I imagine,' Pat went on. 'Perhaps the WI could organise some kind of event in the village hall. We could ask for donations of items people no longer need, or don't fit – things that still have some wear in them.'

'A jumble sale?' Frances asked, her eyes narrowed.

'*Like* a jumble sale, but a good deal smarter,' Pat said, aware that Frances would be after something a little more ambitious. 'No piles of clothes on trestle tables for people to rummage through. I thought we could improve on that. We could have everything on rails, if we can get hold of some – shirts and blouses, trousers, skirts, knitwear. And an area for shoes – children's feet grow so fast. I've often heard parents complain that they're having to replace shoes that are practically brand new because their child has suddenly grown out of them. We could charge a modest amount, too – not so much that it would put people off.'

'Just children's clothing?' Erica asked.

Pat hesitated. 'Well, no, although I think that would be a priority.'

'I think it's a wonderful idea,' Sarah said.

'We could urge people to donate unwanted knitwear, and anything past its best can be unpicked and the wool salvaged,' Alison suggested. 'Put to good use for the items we're knitting for our servicemen.'

Frances suddenly had a zealous look about her. 'This is really marvellous, ladies.'

'Lots of us have things at home we're never going to wear, some in perfect condition,' Pat said. She was thinking of the outfit she had worn on her wedding day and which had hung in the wardrobe ever since – the turquoise dress and matching coat, shot silk, the kind with a sheen that caught the light, bringing out different colours in the fabric. She had found it in a haberdasher's in Manchester and made it up herself without using a pattern. All that work for a single outing. Someone else could perhaps benefit from it now. 'We could have a stall for accessories, too. Scarves, belts, jewellery . . . anything people don't want anymore.'

'What about menswear? I still have George's things,' Alison said. She blushed, as though ashamed to have been so sentimental. 'I've never quite got round to doing anything with them, but now they could go to a good cause.'

'This is your chance,' Frances said. 'I can donate some of Peter's, too.'

'I'm sure I read somewhere about a woman who had taken one of her husband's suits and remodelled it into a rather smart two-piece for herself,' Sarah said.

'We could think about running a series of classes to teach people some of the basics of dressmaking,' Pat said. 'I used to do a bit, going back a few years now.' Her mother was a seamstress and Pat had acquired some of her expertise. When she was younger she'd made a lot of her own clothes and had got rather good at altering things: changing a neckline, shortening sleeves, adding trim to hemlines to adjust the length. With a little imagination, it was amazing what could be achieved. 'Perhaps we could get a sewing circle going,' she suggested.

'I'd be happy to do some darning,' Steph said. 'I seem to be endlessly fixing holes in Stan's and Little Stan's socks and work clothes. I've become quite the expert now that I can't do so much on the farm.'

The women nodded. A recent heart attack meant that Steph could no longer tackle any of the heavy manual work, and they all knew how much she missed it.

As they began to draw up a plan of action, Frances felt a glow of satisfaction. Once again, she had issued a clarion call and the response was nothing short of remarkable. By the end of the week, Alison and Erica would have notices up around the village advertising the WI sewing classes. Pat had agreed to come up with a structure for the sessions to ensure that any of their members keen to bring their sewing skills up to scratch would have the opportunity. Even those starting from nothing would emerge having learned something worthwhile. The whole thing would culminate in an ambitious clothing sale which Pat suggested they call 'Fashion on the Ration'.

'We could have done with Teresa here,' Alison said, as the meeting broke up. 'She has a good eye for style.'

'She sent word to say she's a little under the weather,' Frances said. 'Something she ate, she thinks, nothing serious.'

Sarah hung back to speak to her sister after the others had gone. 'What did you make of Pat?' she asked Frances.

'Bright, full of life. Better than I've seen her in a long time. Without wishing to seem unkind, I can't help thinking Bob's death could well be the best thing to have happened to her.'

'She always seemed to carry an air of anxiety before,' Sarah said. 'It's gone now – did you notice?' It was as if Bob was a weight that had dragged her down, and without him she was lighter, unencumbered. 'We knew things were bad at home for her, but it makes me wonder if it was even worse between them than we ever suspected.'

'Do we ever really know what goes on between two people in private?' Frances sighed. 'Pat was remarkably loyal to Bob. She didn't complain. She never admitted to any of us how badly he treated her. We worked it out ourselves over time.'

'Do you think it was really loyalty that prevented her from telling us?' Sarah asked. 'Or was she simply too afraid to confide in anyone?'

'Both, I suspect,' Frances said. 'She might have been embarrassed, too, perhaps. She had all kinds of reasons to say nothing, I'm sure. Perhaps she hoped that things would settle down.'

Something came back to Sarah – a session at the telephone exchange when Pat had arrived for work late and a little breathless. Bob had brought her tea in bed that morning. His behaviour had become kinder, more considerate, she'd told Sarah. He had even cooked for her. Sarah found it suspicious; in her experience, a leopard rarely changed its spots. Pat, however, seemed to think he was genuine.

'Before they moved house, she did say he was hugely improved,' Sarah said. 'As if they were about to start afresh. A new home, a chance to put the past behind them.'

And then, before they'd had time to settle into their new life, Bob was dead.

'Well, she seemed in good spirits today but I'd be surprised if in the coming months she doesn't have some setbacks,' Frances said. 'She will be bound to have her ups and downs. We need to remember that when it comes to putting on a brave face, she's an expert. It's what she's been doing for years, after all. Let's keep a close eye on her, without being too intrusive.'

Sarah nodded. 'We'll make sure we're there whenever she needs us.'

Chapter 6

Teresa Lucas fought to suppress the wave of nausea that swept through her. 'It doesn't feel . . . normal,' she said. 'I can't help thinking something must be seriously wrong – that I'm properly ill.'

'I do assure you, it's quite normal,' Dr Rosen said. Teresa opened her mouth to object. 'Unpleasant, of course, but it will pass.'

'When?' Teresa heard the desperation in her own voice.

'In time. Women react differently to pregnancy, so it's impossible to be exact but I'd expect to see an easing of symptoms by about twelve weeks. Fourteen, perhaps.'

'*Fourteen weeks*! There'll be nothing left of me by then.' She was keeping so little down – almost anything she ate sent her dashing to the bathroom to bring it back up again.

'Try to stick to foods that don't make you sick. Simple things. Dry toast. A plain biscuit. Sometimes, it's the smell of cooking that can trigger an episode, so be aware of the things you can't tolerate and do what you can to avoid them for now. You must ensure you keep your fluid intake up. Water will help. Small sips, often.'

Teresa sat motionless, turning over in her mind what she had been told. 'Nothing can be done?' She was incredulous. 'I simply have to put up with it?'

'I'm afraid so. As I said, it's normal. It *will* pass.'

'And the baby?' Teresa swallowed hard. 'How can a child possibly thrive when its mother is barely eating?'

Dr Rosen smiled softly. 'You mustn't worry,' she said. 'Many mothers experience what you do, especially in their first pregnancy, and their babies are perfectly healthy. Try not to focus on it. You won't help yourself by fretting.'

Teresa left the surgery a little comforted, but still feeling unwell. She walked slowly in the direction of the village's main street, but at the junction she hesitated. She had been intending to shop for groceries, but simply thinking about food caused her stomach to spasm. The door to the butcher's was open and Miriam Brindsley emerged and began sweeping the path in front of the shop. Last year, she had given birth to a daughter, Vivian. A surprise, Miriam had said – the most wonderful blessing. She hadn't even known she was pregnant until Dr Campbell confirmed it. Miriam looked up from her sweeping and gave Teresa a wave. Teresa smiled back, thinking with a pang that Miriam couldn't have suffered any of this dreaded morning sickness. If she had, she wouldn't have needed a doctor to tell her she was pregnant.

Perhaps things were different with a second baby.

On an impulse, instead of heading home, Teresa turned in the opposite direction. The air was fresh, the sun breaking through after the earlier downpour. A walk might make her feel better. As she passed St Mark's, she caught sight of what looked like the back of Erica Campbell's head, disappearing out of sight. Visiting Will's grave, no doubt.

Seeing Erica served as a sharp reminder to Teresa that she had much to be thankful for. She did not need to look far to see loss and suffering all around. Much of it was down to the war, of course, but not all. Lung cancer had cut short Will Campbell's life; in what seemed to be no time at all he had gone from being a busy GP to a man in serious decline, and the pioneering treatment he'd received had not been enough to save him.

Teresa paused for a minute, looking up at the church, conscious that behind her lay the remains of what had been the homes of the Campbell family and of Pat and Bob Simms. Both properties had been destroyed when the Spitfire crashed onto the village. *On our wedding day*. She and Nick, surrounded by friends, the celebrations in full swing, a few yards away. A miracle, Teresa thought, that no one had been killed on the ground. There but for the grace of God . . .

She kept walking, enjoying the fresh air in her lungs, starting to feel almost like her old self again. She was no longer fighting the urge to be sick, which was a distinct improvement.

Since discovering she was pregnant – the moment itself marked by violent retching – Teresa had quickly learned just how debilitating the early stages of her condition could be.

Whenever she had thought in her younger years about how it might feel to be pregnant, she had pictured herself glowing. *Blooming*. More recently, she had allowed herself to dream about the beautiful moment when she broke the news to Nick that their first child was on the way. Instead, Nick, the wing commander at Tabley Wood, had found out when he returned from the base unexpectedly one day and discovered her on her knees in the bathroom, her head over the toilet bowl.

She allowed herself a wry smile. It was nothing like she had imagined, and yet the distinct lack of romance had done nothing to dent his delight.

Teresa continued to the outskirts of the village and, as she grew nearer Alison's house, she decided to pay an impromptu call. When she had first come to Great Paxford and was teaching at the local school, Teresa lodged with Alison, and the women had become good friends. Teresa trusted her.

She was the only one who knew about her past.

The front door was open, and Teresa called a greeting and came inside, just as Alison emerged from the kitchen in an apron, wiping floury hands on a cloth. The smell of cooking made Teresa's stomach churn in protest.

'I was passing and thought I'd drop in,' Teresa began, 'but I can see you're busy.'

'Wrestling with that trusty standby, a Woolton pie.' Alison frowned. 'Which may or may not be improved with the addition of a little Marmite. I can't help feeling I'm taking a risk there.'

'It will be lovely, I'm sure. You always know how to get the best out of a dish.'

'Have you time for a cup of tea?' Alison asked.

Teresa shook her head. 'Not for me, thanks, but you go ahead.' She noticed the fresh flowers on the windowsill, the cloth on the table in the front room: two places set. 'Are you expecting company? I shouldn't hold you up.'

'Not for a little while.' Alison took off her apron, hooked it over the kitchen door and gestured with a smile for Teresa to sit down. 'How are you? I feel as if I've hardly seen you since the funeral, and we didn't get a chance to talk properly then.'

'No, I went straight home afterwards. Any news of Pat?'

'She came to the committee meeting, and she does seem to be coping well. The house is up for sale – she says she's moving back into the village.'

Teresa nodded. 'Good. She'll be better off once she's got her friends close by again.'

Alison got to her feet. 'I just need to check something,' she said and disappeared into the kitchen.

Teresa heard the sound of a drawer opening, something clattering onto the counter. 'Who are you entertaining?' she called out. 'Anyone . . . *special*?' She already had a shrewd idea who the guest was likely to be.

Alison came back into the room, her cheeks flushed. 'If you must know, I've invited John for something to eat.'

John Smith was one of the trekkers who'd been coming to the village to avoid the bombing raids on Liverpool, a regular at the soup kitchen run by the women of the WI. There, he and Alison had become friendly – something Alison, who went to great lengths to guard her private life, was reluctant to admit to.

'All I can say is that it's about time,' Teresa said, with a laugh. 'I've always thought he's a lovely man, and it's obvious how much he likes you.'

'It's just a meal,' Alison told her. She sounded almost prim. 'Nothing more—'

Teresa laughed. 'Honestly, Alison, it's *me* you're talking to! You don't need to make everything sound so formal. I know you like him – and why wouldn't you?' Alison seemed about to object, but Teresa kept going. 'Where's the harm in enjoying the company of someone you get along with? Especially now, when nothing feels certain or lasting and everything can change in a moment. You need look no further than Pat.'

Or Erica, so recently widowed. Or her daughter, Kate, whose own husband was killed within weeks of her wedding, before they'd even had time to move into their first house. Or Frances, whose life had seemed almost charmed until her husband, Peter, died in a car crash.

'I really don't want to be the subject of gossip,' Alison said.

'Of course not – but when happiness is in such short supply, find it where you can, I say, and hang onto it.' She smiled. 'You might as well simply enjoy spending time with John, and if one day the friendship you have leads to something more . . .'

'I've tried to imagine myself out for a stroll with John,' Alison eventually said. 'Attending social occasions, simply as *friends*.' She shook her head. 'Imagine how that'd be received.'

Teresa hesitated. She knew that some of the village had had a hostile reaction to the arrival of the trekkers, particularly those who, like John, had black skin. Having grown up in Liverpool, Teresa was fairly used to people with a different skin colour – but she knew well enough that a small village would be altogether more narrow-minded in its outlook.

'I think it's better to keep things as they are.' Alison sounded firm. 'A discreet friendship, nothing more.'

Teresa hesitated. 'I remember when I met Nick – it was obvious what a good man he was, funny and decent and kind, and yet I held back. I'm not sure I quite believed things could work out between us. *You* were the one who encouraged me. Had you not, I might easily have let something wonderful slip through my fingers.' She looked at Alison earnestly. 'I would hate to see you miss out on what could be a really lovely friendship, at the very least. Why not give it a chance and see how things work out?'

Alison didn't answer. The wireless was on low in the background, and at the mention of a communiqué from the Air Ministry regarding action over France the day before, both Alison and Teresa turned towards it.

'Fighters of the RAF were again over the Channel and Northern France in strength,' the announcer began. 'Blenheim aircraft of the Bomber Command, which accompanied them, bombed the marshalling yard at Hazebrouck, which handles the traffic to the Channel ports. Many German fighters were encountered and heavy losses were inflicted on them. Our fighters destroyed thirty of the enemy aircraft. A number of others were severely damaged by our fighters and by our bombers. One of our aircraft – a fighter – is missing.'

'You can see why I worry so much,' Teresa said. 'Someone, somewhere, will have received bad news about their loved one.'

Alison nodded. 'How is Nick?'

'I wish he wasn't flying – but he's a pilot, it's what he does. I try not to worry too much.' In truth, her anxiety was crippling at times, keeping her awake at night, invading her dreams once she did manage to sleep. She was haunted by the image of the Spitfire lying broken in the village, with its pilot, a boy surely too young to be flying, lifeless in the cockpit.

It had become the enduring memory of her wedding day.

Sometimes she didn't know what made her feel more ill – the morning sickness, or the fear.

'Nick's an excellent pilot,' Alison said.

Teresa nodded. 'If that was all that mattered, I wouldn't worry.' She hesitated. For a moment, she thought about telling Alison she was pregnant, explaining how that was adding to her fears, how she worried about their child growing up without a father, about her trying to raise a baby on her own – but she and Nick had agreed to keep the news to themselves for the time being.

Instead, she steeled herself and said brightly, 'We both know how rare it is to find someone special.' She was thinking once more of John. 'A connection, if you like. Somebody you trust, who accepts you as you are. That's why I'd urge you to keep an open mind.' She hesitated. 'I'd be hard pressed to tell you what love is, but I do know how it *feels*. And I'm sure you do too.'

Alison pursed her lips. 'Not everything works out in the end.'

'But some things do. Sometimes you just have to follow your heart and hope for the best.'

Once Teresa had left, Alison spent the rest of the morning working, sorting through a substantial mound of papers. Bills and receipts, various dog-eared scraps comprising illegible jottings and figures she had not found easy to decipher. She took off her spectacles, rubbed at her eyes and straightened up, feeling a twinge of discomfort in her back. The small pull-down desk on her writing bureau was most certainly not designed for office work.

She gazed at the mess in front of her, which had been delivered the day before in a series of envelopes. *Needs a bit of sorting out,* she was warned. It turned out to be quite an understatement.

When she had first trained as a bookkeeper, she thought of it as an occupation in which order reigned supreme. Precision was needed – logic, which was what she found appealing. Alison enjoyed filling columns with figures, dealing in numbers, knowing there was a correct answer. Everything was certain, clear, black and white. It was once you strayed into grey areas that problems ensued; she knew all about that.

And yet, at times, it felt as if what she did demanded a huge element of interpretation, particularly where some of her older, long-standing clients were concerned. A few, the ones whose books she had been doing for a number of years and knew well, were in the habit of gathering up every bit of paper they could find and thrusting it at her in the hope she would make sense of it all. On occasion, it felt as if she were engaged in a complex puzzle, searching endlessly for a single elusive piece of evidence which, when discovered, would create further problems: the ink long since faded, the handwriting unreadable. She thought with a weary sigh of the dust-covered receipts written in pencil – *pencil!* – which came to her once a year from the cobbler whose books she maintained.

Increasingly, her work involved a degree of querying to ensure she was on the right lines. In her younger days, when she had less patience, Alison would have been frustrated by all the toing and froing. But now, for the most part, she found a sense of satisfaction in solving such puzzles. Earlier, she had examined under a magnifying glass the untidy scrawl on the back of a single receipt, wondering at its significance. Just as she was on the point of conceding defeat, she double-checked her sums and worked out where it fitted. Triumphant, she had put it on the relevant pile and written the final figures in the ledger.

Order restored.

She went out into the garden to cut a few of the pink roses that grew wild and wound themselves through the hedge. It had been raining hard this morning, but now the sun was getting out and the air smelled of mint and wet grass. She breathed it in. In the past, on such a day, she'd have pulled on her stout shoes and taken Boris to the woods for as long a walk as he could manage. Towards the end, that had not been very far. He had reached a point where he seemed to stop enjoying the woods altogether, preferring to stick to the lanes or root about in the garden. It was less demanding, she supposed.

She had not yet got used to being without him.

In recent years, Boris had been her steadfast companion, a loyal best friend. He made her feel less alone – and yet, at the same time, she felt that he had an acute understanding of her loneliness. She wished that dogs had longer lives; it seemed deeply unfair that Boris managed just short of eleven years before passing quietly away.

She blinked away tears. There was no shame in feeling sad, she told herself, even about a dog. And Boris had been so much more, whatever anyone else might think. The important thing was not to wallow when others were going through so much. She thought of Pat, Erica, Frances – all now widowed. And there was Sarah, so anxious about Adam. Seeing her in church putting such a brave face on things had touched Alison.

In many respects, she felt fortunate, one of the lucky ones. She missed Boris, but these days she felt content in a way she had not for some time.

John arrived with a posy of fragrant sweet peas just as she was tidying her work away.

'They're lovely,' Alison said. 'I've got some like these in the garden.'

John smiled. 'Ah, well, they're not just in the garden anymore. They've managed to find their way under the hedge and now they're climbing up the other side. There's quite a display. I hope you don't mind that I picked a few.'

'Of course not. You're meant to cut them, I think – it keeps them flowering.' Smiling, she went into the kitchen and found a vase to put them in.

John leaned against the doorway. 'Something smells good,' he said.

She looked up. 'Nothing more exciting than a Woolton pie, I'm afraid. I couldn't come up with anything more exotic.'

'It sounds good to me,' he said. 'Nothing beats home cooking.'

John loved to cook himself, but there was no kitchen in the hostel, and he mostly made do with sandwiches from the café down the road these days. There wasn't always a choice and sometimes he wasn't quite sure about the filling, which was more often than not some kind of strong-smelling spread that the woman serving called 'bloater paste'. It was fish, she said. John liked fish, but this was nothing like any fish he had ever tasted. This was . . . well, he wasn't sure what it was. The odour was quite overpowering. He ate it anyway. When you were hungry you couldn't afford to be choosy.

Alison put the flowers to one side and checked the contents of the oven. 'I think this is done,' she said, lifting the pie dish out. The pastry was beautifully browned and crisp, the smell utterly delicious. John had skipped breakfast, and he was ravenous.

'We can eat, if you're ready,' Alison said, draining potatoes and cabbage. She tipped gravy from a pan into a china boat. 'I'm not sure about the sauce, it seems a little thin,' she said, peering at it.

John felt his stomach rumble. Thankfully, Alison didn't seem to notice.

'How are things in Liverpool?' she asked as they sat down to eat.

'Not too bad,' he told her. 'It's more peaceful anyway, now that the bombing's stopped.'

'Do you think that's an end to it?'

'I hope so. There's not much left for them to destroy. The place is in pieces.'

He had been to look at the spot where his old house once stood, almost the entire row of terraced houses on one side of the street now reduced to rubble. In its midst, two of the properties were somehow still standing. At one end of the row a family had moved back into their ruined home, he saw, even though it was completely open at the front. The woman who lived there, someone he had said hello to once or twice, explained that they would rather stay and make do as best they could. She had managed to salvage a few things, she said; the pantry had not been completely destroyed, and she had retrieved some tinned goods from under a pile of rubble. The problem was she had nothing to cook on. She offered John a tin of custard powder, but it wasn't any use to him; he had no means of cooking either.

'You must be relieved, not having to trail out here every night,' Alison said.

John nodded, although the truth was that he missed the food and shelter the women of Great Paxford's WI, Alison among them, had provided for those seeking to escape the bombing. For a while, he had been able to count on at least one bowl of hot food a day and a comfortable place to sleep. 'Things are certainly much quieter,' he conceded.

She smiled. 'I'm glad it's not so bad anymore.'

In some ways it was worse, he thought. But he only smiled and said, 'This pie is delicious, by the way. It's got a really good flavour.'

'Marmite. I wondered if it might help.' She watched as he finished his meal. 'Have you lost weight?' she asked.

He had hoped she wouldn't notice. 'I don't think so, maybe a little. I do a lot of walking these days.'

'Here, you finish this,' Alison said, sliding what was left of the pie onto his plate.

'It's too much,' he protested. 'Keep a little back for yourself for later.'

She shook her head. 'I still have soup from yesterday.'

'Well, then, thank you. I'll do my best.' He made himself eat slowly, savouring every bite. As he did so, he looked up at her and smiled. It was something, really something, to know someone as kind as Alison. Tomorrow he would be relying on whatever delights his local café had to offer.

Chapter 7

Bryn Brindsley locked up the shop, took off his white coat and went through to the kitchen where Miriam was putting out their tea: stewing steak in rich gravy, light herby dumplings and the loaf she had baked earlier, cut into thick slices. Now that she had the time, she made bread every day, and it went down a treat with Bryn and David. Miriam suspected she could make twice as much as she did and it would still get eaten. At least flour was not in short supply – not yet, anyway. David dipped a crust into his gravy and bit into it.

'This is great, Ma,' he said, between mouthfuls. 'We should open a bakery. Take over next door. Butcher and baker.'

'And be up half the night toiling over hot ovens?' Miriam replied.

'I'm teasing,' David told her.

'I saw Mrs Collins earlier, packing up the last of their things,' Miriam said. The couple who ran the greengrocer's next door had decided to shut up shop and head to Scotland to sit out the war. 'They're off tomorrow, first thing.'

'They'll be missed, no doubt about it,' Bryn said. 'There's always been a fruit and veg shop in the village. Don't suppose people will be happy when they can't get their shopping locally.'

'Told you we should expand,' David said, giving his father a wink. 'Get that bakery up and running. Now that Ma's got time on her hands . . .'

Bryn smiled at Miriam. It was sheer joy for them to see David like this. Playful, teasing. This way of life they had once taken for granted – work, easy conversation when they sat down to eat together at the end of the day, the sense of being a close family unit – it was finally coming back. Miriam had not understood how highly she prized the everyday ordinariness of their lives until the war snatched it from them. Even before David went to sea, as soon as he'd said he wanted to enlist, she had sensed it being torn from her grasp. Now he was back at work in the family butcher's shop and a good deal happier than he'd been for a long time.

'I've been thinking,' David said, 'about the shop and some changes we might make.'

Miriam and Bryn exchanged a look.

'Things are running pretty smoothly most of the time,' David went on. 'Even when we've got a few customers in together I make sure no one's kept waiting too long.'

'You're very smart when it comes to spinning plates,' Bryn said.

'There's a few who like to chat, seem to enjoy the company. They don't want to be served and out double-quick, but the ones behind don't want to be held up either.' David grinned. 'But I think I've found a way round that.'

Another smile passed between Bryn and Miriam. Once or twice they had noticed how David invented a reason for a customer who was inclined to talk to step to one side briefly while he got on with serving whoever else was waiting. He went out of his way to be tactful: 'If you wouldn't mind giving me a moment, Mrs So-and-So, I'll just see to these ladies before I deal with your order.' Managing to keep everyone happy. It was a rare gift, Miriam thought.

It was mostly women who shopped at Brindsley and Son, and David, always courteous, impressively efficient, proved popular. Like his father, David kept a sharpened pencil behind one ear and used it to tot up even the most awkward of sums with accuracy and surprising speed. Customers, used to seeing scribbled (sometimes incomprehensible) workings-out on the paper bag in which their meat purchases came, were now given a neat itemised receipt. It was a small difference, perhaps, but one that was noticed and appreciated. Word went round about the improvements David was making. 'That boy can keep a conversation going and make out the bill at the same time without a single slip-up,' Joyce Cameron – something of a stickler – was heard to remark. Even hard-to-please Gwen Talbot took a shine to him. The heroism he'd shown when his ship was torpedoed, returning to the blazing vessel again and again to pull bodies clear, had earned him enormous respect.

Miriam couldn't help but feel proud.

It hadn't been long after his homecoming when she realised she was no longer required behind the counter. 'Surplus to requirements,' she had told Bryn, amused. 'All I seem to do is fetch whatever's needed from the back as and when David says. Without a word being said I've ended up as some kind of' – her eyes widened – '*junior* assistant.' They both laughed. 'I'm back where I started,' she said, 'when we first met.'

Bryn had raised an eyebrow. 'We both know you were in charge from day one,' he told her.

It had become obvious that David could manage the shop perfectly well without an assistant, junior or otherwise, and, increasingly, Miriam left him to it. She occupied her time checking on Bryn, nipping between the shop and the house to keep an eye on Vivian – until, finally, a few weeks ago, she had suggested stepping back, doing the odd few hours as and when required.

'I could spend more time with Vivian,' she'd told Bryn.

It seemed to Miriam that her daughter was changing and growing each day. She smiled and murmured and cooed, sometimes seeming deep in a world of her own. Miriam longed to know what went on inside her daughter's head. Soon, she would be on her feet, taking her first steps, and then talking. It would happen so fast, and Miriam didn't want to miss any of it. Bryn was only too happy to agree.

And David was delighted to assume more responsibility. He was doing as much as he could in the shop, although the lifting he'd once managed with relative ease was now beyond him, and Bryn had to carry the heavy carcasses. There was nothing to be done; the damage to his back was so severe it would never heal. But despite that, David was taking over more and more of the work, and was constantly coming up with small changes in the shop. His enthusiasm for the business, for life in general, was clear.

Now, Miriam got to her feet. 'Let me just check on Vivian and then we'll have afters,' she said. She had made rice pudding with a thick brown crust. It was a favourite of Bryn's, who made a point of scraping every bit of caramelised skin from the edge of the bowl.

Upstairs, Miriam peered into the cot at her sleeping daughter and smoothed her nightdress, admiring the delicate knitted cardigan that had come from Bryn's mother. Yellow, the colour of sunshine, perfectly complementing Vivian's cheerful disposition. She was an easy baby, no trouble at all, going down for her nap each afternoon on the dot of three o'clock without complaint and at night sleeping a good six hours. On occasion, Miriam would tiptoe across to her cot to check on her, only to find she was awake, chirping softly to herself, gazing at the mobile suspended above her, utterly contented. It was rare for her to cry. David had been a good baby too, although Miriam remembered more sleepless nights, more pacing up and down in order to get him to settle. She now put his restlessness down to her own lack of confidence as a new mother. For another minute or so she watched Vivian.

Two perfect children.

Miriam and Bryn could not quite believe their good fortune.

When she thought back, it seemed extraordinary that Vivian was here at all, let alone was so placid and good-humoured. Every time she looked at Vivian, the images came flooding into her mind – the first moment she had seen her daughter, the Spitfire crashing through the doctor's surgery moments later, the bricks and rubble crushing them down. She had thought Vivian was going to die. That was her first thought, before she thought of Bryn, of herself; it seemed so cruel for this little life that had just come into the world to be taken away so soon.

And Vivian might have died had it not been for Dr Campbell. He had shielded her from the explosion with his body, and they had all managed to get out alive.

Miriam smiled, shook the memories away. She had every reason to be happy. David was home; Vivian was everything she could have asked for. Miriam knew in her heart the Brindsleys were blessed, that for reasons she was unable to explain they had somehow been singled out for special treatment.

What had happened with David only confirmed it, as far as she was concerned. When his ship went down and weeks turned into months without news, there had not been the smallest shred of hope for her and Bryn to hold onto. Some – most – would have given up. Not Miriam. She clung to the belief that one day her son would be home.

And now he was.

We're survivors, all of us.

She went back downstairs, where Bryn and David were still deep in conversation.

'I can manage on my own almost all the time, even when it's busy,' David was saying.

'What about on ration day?' Miriam asked, as she served up the pudding. 'There's always a queue, a few grumblings if people have to wait too long. I can give you a hand, keep things moving.'

'I've already thought about that,' David said.

Bryn nodded. 'Go on then, son.'

'You're right, it's our busy day, but I've come up with something that should save people having to queue as long.'

Bryn glanced at Miriam.

'It's just an idea,' David said, but his voice was eager. 'When you think about it, there's nothing complicated about the ration system. Everyone gets so much, an allowance based on the household. It's fixed and less than people are used to, so whatever they're entitled to, that's what they want. I've been keeping a note of who gets what. It's always the same from one week to the next.' He waited for a reaction.

'Well, yes, I suppose so,' Bryn said.

As Miriam watched this exchange, she thought how different things were now in comparison to how they'd been when David first got home. His experiences in the war had left him scarred in more ways than one, and he had taken out his frustrations on those closest to him. At times it had seemed to Miriam that she was engaged in her own daily battle against the invisible aggressor that occupied her son. At night, unable to sleep for worrying, she had sometimes said as much to Bryn. 'Give him time,' he'd say. 'Things won't get better overnight – we have to be patient.' But of course she had worried. Her deepest fear was that David blamed them in some way for what had happened. Bryn always insisted she was wrong. 'He's taking it out on us because he knows he can, that no matter what he says or does we love him, we always will.' He would hold her in his arms and tell her things would come right. 'He'll get through this, we all will.'

And day by day, Miriam had begun to believe him. Over time, David had grown happier, all the signs pointing to him being more settled. Bryn now took on most of the butchery work; the cold store, where he could be heard whistling as he sawed and sliced, had become his domain. But there was no doubt that David was now in charge in the shop.

'I was thinking how much easier ration day would be if I got things ready in advance,' David said now. 'I could make up the rations and have them waiting when the customers come in. Everything labelled – name, amount – in alphabetical order so you put your hand straight on it. The customer hands over the coupons, they get their allowance.'

'It would take a bit of work getting things organised.' Miriam sounded doubtful.

'I've thought about that,' David said. 'I've already got a record – names, coupons. If the allowance changes, I can easily amend the figures. So, on ration day, I make an early start.' He looked at Bryn. '*We* make an early start. Crack of dawn. Work together, getting enough bacon sliced, while I make up the orders. We open early, too. At least a few of our regulars will come in first thing. There's nothing to it. It means a bit of extra effort beforehand but I don't mind that. I reckon it'll go like clockwork and everyone will be a lot happier.' He smiled. 'What do you reckon?'

'I reckon you might be on to something,' Bryn said.

David nodded. 'Thanks, Dad. Now that's sorted, I'll have a think about next door.'

Bryn looked puzzled. 'Next door?'

'Taking over the Collinses' place and turning it into a bakery for Ma.' Miriam's jaw dropped open in surprise. 'I'm *joking*, Ma.' He laughed. 'Can't believe you fell for that one. Although, come to think of it, it would be an awful shame to leave it standing empty . . .'

Chapter 8

SARAH DECIDED TO CALL on Teresa before doing her shopping. She hadn't seen her since Bob's funeral, when she'd been sitting on her own at the back of the church. Afterwards, there had been no sign of her.

As Sarah rang the doorbell, she looked up at the house. Its curtains were closed, and for a moment she wondered if Teresa was out.

At last the door opened, revealing Teresa, with the heavy-eyed look of someone who had recently roused themselves from sleep and was not yet properly awake. Her blouse was creased, her dark hair on end, a single strand plastered to her pale brow.

Sarah had never seen Teresa look anything less than immaculate. She wasn't sure she had ever seen her without her trademark red lipstick.

'I'm ever so sorry,' she said. 'I didn't mean to disturb you, but Frances said you've not been feeling well, and I thought I'd drop by to see if you needed anything.'

'Oh. That's kind, thank you,' Teresa said. 'Do come in for a minute.'

Sarah followed her into the front room, where Teresa drew the curtains and let in some light. On the settee, cushions were piled up at one end, a crocheted blanket thrown aside. Teresa straightened things up, plumping the cushions, shaking out the blanket and draping it over the back of the settee. It seemed obvious she had been having a nap, and Sarah felt a stab of guilt for having woken her.

'I really didn't mean to disturb you,' Sarah said. 'I won't stay.'

'Oh, I don't mind. Sit down for a minute.' She attempted a smile. 'It's good of you to come.'

Whatever was ailing Teresa seemed to have knocked her sideways.

'I can make tea if you'd like some,' Teresa offered, as they sat down.

'I won't, thank you. Let me make some for you, though.'

Teresa made a face. 'I can't face it. Just the thought turns my stomach.'

Sarah looked concerned. 'Is it some kind of food poisoning?'

Teresa shook her head; she looked utterly washed out.

'How long have you been feeling like this?'

'Off and on, a few weeks.' Teresa caught Sarah's concerned look. 'You've caught me at a particularly bad moment. I'm not always so . . . gruesome.' She got to her feet, peered at her reflection in the mirror and made a half-hearted attempt at a smile. 'Heavens, I look as if I've been dragged through a hedge backwards.'

'Have you seen the doctor?' Sarah asked.

Teresa looked away. 'I'm perfectly well,' she said, hesitantly. 'Really, there's nothing to be worried about.'

Sarah studied Teresa for a moment, her paleness, her tiredness, the slight shift in the way she held herself.

A sudden thought hit her.

'Oh!' she said. 'You're not . . . ?'

Teresa flushed, and Sarah knew at once she had guessed correctly.

'You're pregnant,' she said, her eyes widening.

Teresa broke out into a proper smile. 'Well . . . we haven't told anybody yet.'

'Oh, but . . . that's wonderful. Congratulations! You must be thrilled.'

Teresa returned to her place on the settee. She closed her eyes for a moment. 'I am – or, rather I would be, if I didn't feel so awful. Morning sickness. I never imagined it could be quite so debilitating. As for the "morning" bit – that's something of a sick joke, if you'll pardon the pun. I am being ill at all hours of the day and night.'

'It sounds dreadful, but . . . it's normal, isn't it? I mean, nothing you need worry about?'

'So I've been told. All I can say is it doesn't *feel* normal. I can barely eat, I can't even face cooking – Nick's having to eat in the mess at Tabley Wood.' She winced. 'At least he's guaranteed a decent meal. I do my best, but I wouldn't

71

call myself the world's most accomplished cook, nowhere near. Anyway, Nick's so delighted at the prospect of being a father he doesn't mind that I'm in no fit state to feed him at home. It won't be for ever. Soon, I'll be back to turning out one of my trusty stews. But, for now . . .'

Sarah smiled. 'I'm so pleased things are working out for you,' she said. 'You deserve it, both of you.'

She thought back to Nick's arrival in the village. The new wing commander at Tabley Wood, drafted in to replace his married predecessor, who had been hurriedly moved on following the scandal over his affair with young Laura Campbell.

Nick had stayed at the vicarage initially with Sarah and Adam. What Sarah felt for Nick had been . . . complicated. The spark between them had been undeniable. Dangerous. She could easily have fallen for him. There was a moment she would never forget when she came close to risking everything. Her marriage. Adam.

'I haven't told Alison yet,' Teresa said, 'so would you keep it to yourself for now?'

'Of course.'

There was another pause, and then Teresa spoke again. She seemed keen to have someone to confide in. 'I'm not sure I'm ready to be a mother. The idea of it terrifies me.'

'You'll be wonderful, I'm sure.'

She nodded, unconvinced, and yawned. 'Sorry, I'm wiped out. Anyway, enough about me. What about Adam – any word from him?'

Sarah told her about the letter she'd been tempted to keep to herself, and how pleased she was to have shared it with the congregation at St Mark's. 'I toyed with the idea of not telling a soul, not even Frances – I'm not even sure why. Something to do with how much I miss him, I think, and wanting – in ways I can't even explain – to keep him to myself.' She glanced at Teresa. 'Selfish of me, I know, when his parishioners are every bit as anxious for news as I am.'

Teresa nodded. 'It makes sense to me.'

'The odd thing is how much better I feel now. People have been so kind, and I suppose it's brought home to me the extent of the love there is in the village for Adam.' Sarah smiled. 'I feel almost overwhelmed – supported, I suppose. I don't think I'd properly appreciated until now that it's not just my *husband* being held in a prison camp, it's our *vicar*. It's not only difficult and upsetting for me, but for the entire community.' She thought for a moment, trying to put into words what had been going round her head. 'It's made me feel as if I want to do more.'

'In what sense?'

'Oh, I don't know – open my eyes to what other people are going through. See where help is needed and do what I can.' *Be more like Adam.* She smiled. 'Do I sound like some dreadful do-gooder?'

Teresa shook her head. 'Not at all. Adam would be proud.'

Chapter 9

PAT WAS BUSY PACKING, emptying the bookshelves in the front room and placing everything carefully into chests, getting ready to leave the house she had moved into only three months before. As she worked, she thought back to the rainy April day that she and Bob had taken possession of what was intended to be their dream home. Bob in a rare good mood, talking about a new beginning, Pat almost believing him.

Almost.

She stopped what she was doing for a moment, remembering Bob hobbling from room to room on his bad leg. 'Doesn't it feel good to have a place of our own again?' he'd said. 'No one breathing down our necks the whole time. No more having to put up with that nosy old bat watching my every move.'

Joyce. Joyce, who worshipped Bob.

'Not a minute's peace. How I managed to get anything done with her wittering on at me I'll never know. *Oh, Mr Simms, what an absolute privilege to witness an artist at work.*' Pat had been about to speak up in defence of Joyce, but Bob hadn't finished. 'No neighbours listening through the walls, sticking their noses into our business.'

The Campbells. Erica and Will, who had been good friends to Pat.

'I could hardly breathe in the midst of all that. Good riddance to the lot of them. If I never set foot in Great Paxford again, it'll be too soon.'

Pat had stayed quiet, watching the rain beat against the windows, the removals men hurrying in and out, trailing dirt into the hall.

Pat would not have chosen somewhere so big. The rooms and their high ceilings seemed to dwarf the modest amount of furniture they had, and she suspected it would be impossible to heat the place in winter. Not that Bob had asked for her opinion. By the time he told her he'd found somewhere suitable, the sale was already going through.

'Thought it would be a nice surprise for you,' he'd said, pleased with himself.

Not that it mattered now. In a few days, she would be gone. She had found a cottage to rent in Great Paxford, a little place not far from the village school. She intended to move within the week, impatient to get away.

She need never see this place again.

She reached for a stack of hefty tomes and put them to one side – a series of numbered volumes to do with military campaigns that she remembered Bob sending away for, proudly lining them up on a shelf like soldiers in their smart green jackets embossed with gold. They were expensive looking, more for show than anything. After all, since when was Bob interested in the Napoleonic wars? As far as she knew, he had not so much as leafed through them, let alone actually read any of the books. Well, they were of no interest to her and she had no intention of keeping them. Perhaps a reference library might consider taking them.

As she packed away the last few books, one fell open and an envelope with her name on it fluttered out. Bob's handwriting. She stared at it, her breath caught. For a while, when they first started seeing each other, Bob had often written to her. A few lines on scraps of paper that he would slip into her bag or inside the pocket of her coat for her to find once they had parted. Sometimes it was a simple *Love you, B*, on the back of a cinema ticket. Or a few lines begging her to save him from what he called the misery of his freezing garret. That had always made her smile, since his lodgings comprised a warm and comfortable room on the ground floor of an elegant house where the landlady fussed endlessly over him. *Only you can rescue me from this living hell*, he would write, tongue firmly in cheek. It was Bob's way of letting her know he wanted them to be together. Within weeks of their first meeting he asked her to marry him and, though she was taken aback at the speed of his proposal, she'd found herself saying yes.

When she thought back to those days, it seemed a lifetime ago, an entirely different world. When had things changed? Certainly once they were married, the gestures she had found so endearingly romantic ceased. For a while, she'd continued to check her pockets and under the pillow, anywhere she thought a scrap of paper might be hidden. When she dropped hints and said how much she always loved getting one of his notes, Bob seemed non-plussed, a little put out, even – as if she was being critical of him. Why on earth would he write, he wanted to know, now that they were under the same roof and could have a conversation whenever they needed to?

She never mentioned it again.

Now she picked up the envelope and stared at the familiar, almost flamboyant handwriting, not sure she wanted to read whatever lay inside. Perhaps she should simply tuck it back inside the book it had fallen from, or throw it away – bury it with the kitchen waste. A voice inside her head warned against raking up the past.

And yet, she couldn't help her curiosity. She took the single sheet of paper from its sheath.

I am writing this on the train, it began. Pat felt her heart rate quicken. *I'm on my way to Bradford (shades of Wigan Pier). Opposite is a man sucking noisily on a pipe. I have never studied pipe-smoking at such close range and find it fascinating, the rig-marole involved to get the thing in a fit state to light, only to take a few puffs before it's out again. Not much smoking being done and a good deal of ash*

deposited on the front of a perfectly good suit jacket!
As you can see, I have time on my hands. And so, my
dearest Patricia, in the spirit of being productive and
writerly I have decided to compile a list of some of the
things I love about you:
*   That smile of yours.*
*   Your eyes, the colour of forget-me-nots.*

She felt suddenly dizzy. *My dearest Patricia ... the things I love about you.* She pushed the letter back into its envelope. Some things were too painful.

As she steadied herself, she had the feeling that Bob was close by – watching, gloating, enjoying her discomfort, still managing to knock her off-balance when she least expected it.

No, she had no desire to be reminded of how things had once been between them. It was the past. *Over.* The romance that had swept her up once seemed so misleading now; he had used flattery and a few well-chosen words to reel her in. And she had been foolish enough to trust he was the man he appeared to be.

She closed her eyes for a moment. *The sooner I'm out of this house, the better.* She went into the kitchen and pushed the letter deep inside the bin.

She was still packing when the doorbell went, startling her. She glanced at the clock and remembered that Erica had said she would call and help with any chores that needed to be done.

'There's not very much to do,' Pat said as she showed her in. They stood in the front room, surveying the boxes.

'How long before you move out?' Erica asked.

'Not long. Only a few more days. I'm just waiting to hear back from the removals people.'

Erica nodded. 'It's fortunate you don't have to wait for this place to sell first.'

'I'm not sure I could stand to.'

They went into the kitchen and Pat filled the kettle to make tea. The back door was open and Erica stood on the step, watching a blackbird peck about in the border. 'It's a lovely spot,' she said. 'Peaceful. It'll make someone a lovely home.'

Pat sighed. 'I thought things might be different here,' she said. 'New house, new start. Bob was full of it. I can't remember the last time I'd seen him so buoyant.' She glanced at Erica. 'The move seemed to mean so much to him. I think he genuinely believed that once we got here and were free of all the distractions he disliked so much – other people, mainly – things would somehow be all right. Better, at least.'

'Can a man like Bob ever change?' Erica asked.

'That's something I constantly I asked myself. I *hoped* so, but I was always cautious.' She hesitated. The letter had shaken her, and it seemed to help to talk it out. 'He could be very charming – plausible, I suppose. Look how easily he took in poor Joyce. All those months living at close quarters and she suspected nothing. In her view, he was wonderful, a good husband.' She sighed again. 'He knew how to put on a front when it mattered, present the right face.' *We both did.* 'It may sound strange but when he was at his worst, at least I knew where I was with him. Any show of kindness made me wonder what he was up to. I learned to never quite trust him. It wasn't safe.'

'Oh, Pat, I wish I'd been able to do more.'

'No one could have done anything, and he knew it.'

Erica reached out and gently touched her arm. 'It's over now. You're free. That's the important thing.'

Was she, though, or would Bob continue to haunt her? Would he find a way to punish her for hating him? For loving Marek?

Pat looked up at her friend. 'The night he died, we'd had an argument. He didn't want me to go out, even though I hadn't seen a soul for weeks. He forbade me, and . . . well, it was one of the few occasions I defied him.'

Erica frowned. 'It sounds . . . almost as if he was holding you hostage.'

It was. That was exactly how it was.

'He was upset, as you can imagine,' Pat said. An understatement. 'I don't regret going, I just wonder whether he would still be alive if I hadn't.'

If I'd stayed with him, summoned help. If I'd done the right thing. Instead of leaving him to die.

Erica said, 'He'd been drinking, hadn't he? It could have happened whether or not you were here. You mustn't torment yourself.' She paused. 'I would never wish what happened to Bob on anyone, but he's gone and there's nothing you can do to change it.'

Not now. But, at the time, perhaps . . .

'We tend to want all the answers,' Erica continued. 'When someone dies we're always left with questions, all those what ifs.'

What if . . . I had called an ambulance?

'You could drive yourself insane. You *mustn't*.'

Pat felt a sudden urge to tell Erica everything, to swear her to secrecy. She was loyal; she had told no one about Marek. Pat knew she could trust her. 'If I told you,' she began – but then the shrill whistling of the kettle on the stove interrupted and reality sank back in. She shook her head, took a breath. 'You're right, I can't change what happened.'

'Then let it go,' Erica said gently.

Chapter 10

INSPIRED BY THE WI committee meeting, Alison had decided to sort through her clothes, and a pile of unwanted items now lay neatly folded on the bed in the spare room. At last she had dealt with George's belongings. For too long she had held onto them as if they were part of him, but now she could see that they were just 'things'. Her memories would stay in her heart for all time. As she went through everything, she had also found a number of perfectly good garments she had forgotten about, among them the embroidered blouse and pleated skirt she now had on for the first time in years. She ran a comb through her hair and checked her reflection in the full-length mirror on the back of the wardrobe. The new outfit made her look quite different, and for a moment her confidence wavered. She was expecting John, and didn't want him to think she had made more effort than usual just for him.

Even though Alison had been unwilling to admit as much to Teresa, she knew she was growing extremely fond of John. He was kind, respectful. They never ran out of things to say to one another. He made her laugh. It was true what Teresa had said about finding a connection, something that rarely happened. She had felt it with George, and never thought she would need to find it with anybody else. They were going to spend their lives together. Everything had been planned out.

And then the Great War came.

Like so many others, she'd had to forge a future that bore no resemblance to the one she had once envisaged. It had not been easy. George had been her world. His confidence and optimism had rubbed off on her, but once he was gone she became altogether more subdued. It was likely that she would be on her own from now on, she had decided. She had better get used to the idea.

Alison had always thought of herself as a practical person, the kind of woman to cope with whatever life had in store for her. But at times, over the years, she had been lonely. Boris had made a difference, true – but still, sometimes she craved human company. What she would have given sometimes for someone to have breakfast with, a companion thoughtful enough to bring her a cup of tea while she worked. Someone to talk to even when she had nothing very interesting to say. Simple companionship. Being part of a unit, part of a team. Those were the things she missed most of all.

Having Teresa stay with her had made an enormous difference. Alison had found herself looking forward to her lodger arriving back each afternoon with stories about her day at school and the sometimes hilarious exploits of the children. For a while, the house had felt more alive. Teresa's presence had made Alison aware of how serious she had become. It was not easy, after all, to find things to laugh about on one's own. She missed Teresa dreadfully. The house was an altogether more joyful abode with another person in it.

Not that she had much to complain of. She'd had a good life. And at least she had found love with George, even if he was taken from her too soon. She had memories of him to treasure, moments of joy that would never leave her. Not everyone was as fortunate; she knew very well that there were some who would never know what it was to love and to be loved.

But now, perhaps, she had a second chance, something she would never have thought possible. She didn't think she could be misreading the situation – after all, she saw the way John looked at her. She knew very well that it was her alone he made an effort to come and see, that he had no reason to leave Liverpool now that the bombing had stopped.

No reason, apart from her.

She wandered into the garden, and was met with the scent of lavender and mint, the gentle humming of bees at work as they went from one flower to the next. She stopped for a moment, watching a bumble bee as it lumbered about. Another landed on the sleeve of her cardigan and rested for a moment. She was so busy watching the bees she didn't notice John arrive.

'Good day to you. Not interrupting, am I?' he said, tipping the trilby hat he always wore.

Alison smiled. 'Not at all – the bees just caught my attention. The lavender's alive with them.'

He made no move towards the garden. 'Aren't you coming in?' Alison asked.

'In a minute. I've something to show you first.'

Alison gave him a curious look.

'I hope you're going to like it,' he added uncertainly.

He bobbed briefly out of sight, reappearing a moment later with a skinny dog on a makeshift lead. The dog, a terrier of some kind, had coarse brown and white hair. It gazed in Alison's direction. 'Come and meet a very special friend of mine,' John told the dog, giving a slight tug on its lead. The animal trotted obediently up the path beside him.

Alison was perplexed. 'You have a dog?'

'I found her, wandering in the city, looking lost.' He bent and scratched the dog's head. 'Shared a bit of food with her, and next thing you know she followed me home. I'm guessing she was on the doorstep all night, because when I came out this morning there she was, waiting. Jumped up soon as she saw me.'

'She must belong to someone.'

'Seems to think she belongs to me now, don't you, girl?' The dog gave him what might have been interpreted as a hopeful look. 'I asked around, but no one knows whose she is. Might be her family moved on and left her behind. In the street I found her, half the houses have gone. Bombed out. I don't reckon she's got a home now.'

'But you can't keep her – how can you?'

John smiled. 'That's just it. I was thinking . . . maybe the two of you might get along. Company for one another. She's a good dog – walks on the lead, comes when you call her. Can't see she'd give you any trouble.'

The dog flopped down on the path and closed its eyes, its chin resting on the toe of John's shoe. Alison hesitated. She did not enjoy being put on the spot. It was not so much the idea of another dog she objected to; rather that she seemed to have no say in the matter. As if John, in that gentle and courteous way of his, was backing her into a corner.

Even as the thought came to her, she knew she was being unreasonable. She loved dogs. She missed Boris. John knew that, and had thought she might like the company, had come with the dog as a kindness.

Still, the glow she had basked in all morning in anticipation of his visit all but evaporated.

She imagined heads turning as John made his way through the village with the dog. Speculation as to where he was headed. Her name being mentioned. She felt a sharp prickle of humiliation at the thought.

'You're assuming rather a lot, thinking you can foist a stray on me without warning,' she said. She sounded sharper than she had intended.

John looked taken aback. 'No, that's not . . . I meant no offence, Alison. I was thinking of you. I hoped you might be pleased.'

'I wish you'd at least had the *decency* to ask before simply arriving on my doorstep with a mongrel on the end of a bit of string.' John seemed to flinch. For her to imply he was anything less than decent was, she knew, grossly unfair.

'If I've overstepped the mark, I'm sorry.' He sounded bewildered. At his feet, the dog sighed and turned onto its side. 'Of course I wouldn't presume to . . . I think you know how much I respect you, Alison.'

They gazed at each other. It was the closest they had come to falling out – and over something trivial. Alison took a deep breath, and thought of what Teresa had said. The last thing she wanted was to fall out with John, but somehow the thought of accepting the dog, of what that might mean between them, seemed almost too much. 'I'm just not sure I want another dog,' she said, softening her tone. 'Boris was a one-off. I doubt that any dog, even one as good-natured as yours seems to be, can replace him.'

He nodded. 'I can take her back.'

Alison hesitated. 'Look, come inside.' She turned back towards the house, glancing over her shoulder to make sure John was following. The dog came after him.

'I didn't intend to be so sharp,' Alison said, drawing up a chair at the kitchen table. 'As you've now seen for yourself, I'm not very good with surprises.'

The dog crawled under the sideboard, looking up at them from its hiding place.

John gave her a long look. 'I thought you knew me better than to think I was the kind of man who'd use a friend.'

Alison sighed. She could see she had hurt his feelings. 'You did the right thing rescuing the dog and bringing her here.' She wondered how many others would have done the same. Liverpool had suffered dreadfully. Lives lost, homes destroyed. She could understand why a pet might be abandoned. Most strangers would have left it to scrabble around and survive as best it could. But not John. He had stopped and shown kindness – and she had taken him to task for it.

'The dog can stay,' she said softly.

He gave her a wary look. 'Are you sure that's what you want? I wouldn't want you to feel you've no choice.' He hesitated. 'If it comes to it, I could take her to a shelter.'

Alison was inclined to think the poor dog would not last long in such a place. She looked down at the creature, her soft fur and wagging tail. There was something about her keen expression that reminded her of Boris.

'I'm sure. I'd like to keep her.'

The following morning, Alison came down to find the little dog curled up on the chair once occupied by Boris. She stroked its head before going into the kitchen and filling the kettle. When she turned round, the dog stood in the doorway, looking up at her. Alison was used to Boris pushing his snout at her, letting her know he was hungry. The new arrival was still shy.

'I suppose you want breakfast,' she said. 'I'll have to see what I can give you.' She made a generous helping of porridge and ate hers while she waited for the remainder to go cold in the bowl Boris had once used. The moment she put it down, the dog began to eat, taking dainty little mouthfuls. Nothing like Boris there either, who used to attack his food as if he were permanently starving.

Alison sat at the table with a cup of tea, thinking back to the day before. It niggled her how sharp she had been with John. She had regretted it and softened soon enough, but things were still a little awkward between them when he'd left. He was a good listener – like George. No, she didn't want to compare him to George. She longed to explain it all, her horror of being the subject of gossip, her anxiety about her feelings for him, how people might view their friendship – but she couldn't say any of that without telling him how she felt, and that she could never do.

In the end, when she had begun a stumbling apology and attempt at an explanation, John had said: 'You know, Alison, you've no need to explain yourself to me, or to anyone. I only need to look at you to know there's nothing bad.'

She could say the same of him.

Chapter 11

SARAH EMERGED FROM HER shift at the telephone exchange into bright sunshine. She stood for a moment, feeling the warmth on her face. It was too nice a day to go straight home, she decided. Perhaps she could take a walk and get some air.

As she made her way through the village, she spotted Joyce Cameron on the opposite side of the street, striding briskly in her direction. Straight-backed, head held high, wearing a jacket with gleaming brass buttons, she had an almost military air. Her hat was angled to protect her face from the sun, and had a clutch of feathers sprouting from it. She raised a hand in greeting and Sarah crossed over to speak to her.

'What do you think of the gaping hole in our village?' Joyce asked.

Sarah was momentarily thrown. *What* gaping hole? she wondered. For a second she thought of the Spitfire crashing into the doctor's surgery, of buildings ripped apart. A knot of panic seized her. But before she had a chance to speak, Joyce gestured at the far side of the High Street. 'Our abandoned greengrocer's, now reduced to a shell. Is there anything that speaks of neglect more than white-wash on windows? An absolute tragedy, if you ask me, and not just because of the look of the thing, although that is bad enough. We have lost a valuable resource.' She sighed. 'It seems a great pity the Collinses felt compelled to run for the hills.'

'Not the hills, as such,' Sarah said. 'Edinburgh, I heard, to be with family until the war is over.'

Joyce tore her gaze from the offending windows. 'In troubled times, tempting though it may be to run away, I am yet to be convinced about this notion of pastures new providing sanctuary. It's something of a myth, I'd say. Better to hold fast to what you know.' She gave a wry smile. 'As I am able to testify from personal experience.'

Shortly after the outbreak of war, Joyce and her solici-tor husband, Douglas, had moved out of Great Paxford and gone to live in Heysham, not far from Morecambe, on the north-west coast, because it was considered safer. Weeks later, Joyce returned to the village. Alone. Her hus-band, she said, had stayed behind to pursue his ambition of becoming a Member of Parliament. Sarah had never been convinced by this explanation but, like everyone, would not have dreamed of challenging it, or seeking to press Joyce for further details. There was gossip, of course, but not even Mrs Talbot would have dared ask Joyce. She could be rather intimidating when she wanted to be.

'You've no regrets about moving back, then?' Sarah asked tentatively.

Joyce looked thoughtful. 'Do you know, you're the first person to have asked,' she said. 'But no. My only regret is leaving in the first place. I knew at once it was a mistake, and I'm glad I was in a position to put things right. In all honesty, I found the coast a rather gloomy place. It was somewhat depressing. There is a great deal of talk about sea air being good for you, but it did nothing for me. I would never have settled there.'

Sarah hesitated. This was the most she had ever heard Joyce speak on the matter, and she did not want to miss an opportunity. What if, after all, Joyce had only kept quiet about her reasons for returning because her friends had never asked? She glanced around, to make sure they were alone in the street. 'It must be very different, though, living alone?'

She caught Joyce's look of surprise and at once feared she had strayed into territory that was off-limits.

'Douglas certainly thought I wouldn't manage it,' Joyce said slowly. 'And it *is* different. But then, I would never go so far as to say that marriage, in itself, necessarily guarantees a greater degree of happiness than a solitary existence. It rather depends on the marriage, don't you think?'

'Yes, of course.' Sarah felt somewhat thrown off-balance. This was, she thought, one of the longest conversations she had ever had with Joyce. All their previous conversation had tended to lean towards the superficial – matters concerning the WI, or bland pleasantries on the subject of the weather. Sarah had at times found Joyce rather superior, something of a snob – especially so when Joyce and Frances were engaged in a tussle over who was best suited to lead the WI. Certainly, she had never felt inclined to forge a friendship with Joyce.

It was true that when Joyce returned to the village, Sarah had detected a certain vulnerability that was not there before. It was almost as if she had been left bruised by her seaside experience. No matter how she chose to dress things up, the fact remained that she and her husband had parted company, and that could not have been without its difficulties. Sarah had chosen not to get involved, telling herself she didn't know Joyce well enough to pry into her private affairs.

Was it possible that Joyce was not the impenetrable force she appeared to be; that beneath the somewhat brittle exterior was an altogether more thoughtful woman than Sarah had imagined? She knew well enough that everybody had a side they presented in public – an armour, a means of concealing weaknesses. This morning, Sarah felt she had been allowed a glimpse of what might well be the real Joyce.

'Of course, the position *you* now find yourself in is entirely different,' Joyce went on. 'You must feel your husband's absence acutely. To be separated not by choice but by circumstance is never an easy matter. There's something about longing that seems to cause a good deal of heartache, and of course the uncertainty . . . I am sorry, I didn't mean to pry. I only meant that I realise it must be hard. I hope it's of some comfort to know how many of us are thinking of the Reverend Collingborne.'

'It makes a great deal of difference.' Her gaze went to St Mark's in the distance, that had been a solid and reassuring presence for six hundred years. For many, it represented the heart of the village, a focal point where the community could gather and find comfort in one another. But like everything and everyone, it was by no means invincible. When the Spitfire crashed into the village, it had only narrowly avoided demolishing the church tower.

'Yes, the plane crash,' Joyce began, as if able to tap into Sarah's thoughts. 'When I survived, I made a promise to myself to make the most of life. From that moment on, I decided I would really live each moment as best I could.' She smiled. 'It's proving harder than I had thought. Do you know,' she went on, 'I so enjoyed having Pat and Bob to live with me. I was very sorry when they moved out. And now I feel an overwhelming sense of guilt.'

'But why?' asked Sarah softly. 'There is no reason for you to feel guilty.'

'I meant to visit them in the new house, but events overtook me.' She sighed. 'It was a valuable lesson, a reminder that nothing can be taken for granted. Procrastination is our enemy. We must do the things that matter while we can.'

Sarah had walked almost to the canal when she encountered Miriam pushing the pram. 'Got as far as the bridge before I found my way barred,' Miriam said. 'A pair of swans and their cygnets, basking in the sun. Didn't fancy trying to move them.'

Sarah peered under the pram hood at Vivian and was rewarded with a smile. 'I was thinking of going that way,' she said.

'You might be better sticking to the towpath.'

'Thank you.' Sarah smiled. 'Not working today?'

'Surplus to requirements.' Miriam raised an eyebrow in mock indignation. 'Bryn and David have got things running like clockwork between the two of them. I'm under strict instructions to steer clear.'

'On such a glorious day like this, I can't imagine you miss being stuck behind the counter.'

'Well, I won't complain about having more time with this little one.' Miriam bent to retrieve a knitted doll flung from the pram by Vivian. 'In some ways I *do* miss it, though. The shop's always been a good way of keeping on top of what's going on in the village and, behind the counter, I was in the thick of it. People told me all sorts. Now Bryn's mainly in the back, doing the heavy work, so he's out of touch, and it's down to David to let me know what's what.' She bent to retrieve the doll a second time. 'Seems he's more concerned with how we might make the business more profitable than passing on any nuggets of news that come his way.'

'I've noticed how much happier he seems these days,' Sarah said. 'More like his old self. It's all down to you and

Bryn. I can't imagine it's been easy for him. Well, for any of you.'

'Harder than I ever imagined,' Miriam said. 'All the while he was missing, I dreamed about him being back. Do you know, it became something of an obsession, the only thing that mattered. I had a vision of David walking back into our lives and making everything right again, the same as it always was. Just like that.' She smiled. 'Not for a moment did it cross my mind he would be so angry, so *changed* by what he'd been through. So *different*. When I think about it now, I can't believe I was so naïve as to think that things would be the same. We're none of us the same, are we? Not when there's a war on.'

Sarah thought of Adam, of how the POW camp might take its toll on him – on his physical well-being, on his mind. He was older than David, at least, better able to cope with whatever the war threw at him than a young boy. She hoped that was true. But what Miriam had said about getting her son back, thinking all would be well, had struck a chord. Sarah too constantly imagined Adam returning. It was the only thing, sometimes, that kept her going. It was her constant thought, his homecoming, their old world instantly restored, the happiest of reunions, smiles and laughter – everything bathed in a soft, burnished glow as life returned to what had once been 'normal'.

But what, she wondered, would be 'normal' in future?

She missed him so much, more than she would ever have believed possible. At times his absence caused her so much pain that she wondered if she was ill. Occasionally she took herself off to bed and fell into the kind of sleep that made her feel even worse. In the early hours she would panic and jump up, her heart pounding, unable to get her breath. Often, she could not imagine getting through even one more day. And yet somehow she did. She had to. For Adam.

'I suppose you must have needed great patience, allowing him the time he needed to adjust,' Sarah said.

'I can't even tell you how closed he was to start with,' Miriam said. 'We couldn't get a thing out of him. I was tiptoeing round on eggshells. Anything I said, he almost bit my head off. Same with his dad. We'd no idea what he'd been through and he had no intention of telling us. Not a word about how badly he'd been injured.' The shocking state of his back, those wounds that would never heal.

'He made it home. That's the main thing.'

'I always believed he would, even when it seemed hopeless. When no one else expected things to work out and Bryn thought I was going mad, I just *knew* we'd get him back.' She glanced at Sarah. 'And it's a joy to see him getting his teeth into the business, wanting to shake things up.'

'He's young and full of confidence. Ambitious, too, I expect.'

'Oh, you have no idea.'

The night before when they'd finished supper and Miriam was washing up, Bryn making himself comfortable in the armchair at the side of the hearth, David had again brought up the subject of the recently vacated premises next door and suggested they consider expanding the business. He made it seem casual, an everyday proposition, as if he was simply offering to help his mother dry the dishes.

'We're in a position to do it, financially,' he said, 'and it makes sense. The trade's already there – you should hear them all grumbling in the shop about the Collinses leaving them high and dry. It's a gap and we're best placed to fill it.' Not so much a *gap*, according to Mrs Cameron, as an *eyesore*. 'I've been through everything and we'll never have a better opportunity.'

Bryn, who'd been about to close his eyes for five minutes, was suddenly wide awake. 'What do we know about running a greengrocer's?' he asked.

'We know how to run a *business*,' David said, undaunted. 'It can't be any harder than running a butcher's. Different, that's all.'

That word again, Miriam thought.

Everything was *different*.

After they had said their goodbyes, Sarah kept walking until she reached the little bridge, still under the occupation of the swan family. Sarah was not afraid of swans. Their reputation for being aggressive and prone to unprovoked attacks seemed to her rather unjust. She found them graceful and intelligent – loyal, too. The idea of birds staying with their mate for life appealed to her. When she and

Adam were in Oxford, they had often walked by the river and watched the swans glide by.

'Hello,' she said, as she drew near to the little group. Five cygnets, as big as their parents, distinguished only by their soft brown and white plumage. The cob got to his feet and faced her while his partner snoozed, her head tucked inside a wing, apparently unconcerned. Sarah wondered how long this pair had been together. In Oxford, a pair known locally as Victoria and Albert had occupied the same nesting site for at least eight years.

'Don't worry about me,' Sarah told the cob as she edged past.

She was thinking about what Miriam had said. For the period that David was missing, Miriam's unwavering belief in her son's eventual safe return had been a cause for concern among her friends at the WI. It was as if she had retreated into a world of her own making, one with no basis in reality – or so it seemed to Sarah at the time. Now she had a better understanding of why Miriam had clung to hope so rigidly. It was the one thing she had, the only thing that kept her going.

Sarah felt the same about Adam. As if by virtue of sheer willpower, she could bring about his safe return. The only outcome she was prepared to contemplate. In that respect, she was not unlike Miriam.

Being without you is harder than I ever imagined, Sarah thought. *I have only the sketchiest idea of how you might be living, the hardships you may be forced to endure. I tell myself that no matter what, you'll come through this. We both will. We must. I tell myself that life will go on – somewhat changed, no doubt, but as long as we're together I will not mind. I will never mind anything again as long as I have you.*

On her way home, Sarah made a detour and called on Joyce. The conversation they'd had earlier was still on her mind. Joyce, usually so reserved, had opened up in a way that was surprising to Sarah, and she wondered if she might be even more forthcoming in the privacy of her home. It had not crossed her mind before that Joyce might be lonely now that she was on her own.

Sarah rang the bell with some trepidation, but Joyce seemed pleased to see her. She showed her into the front room, where a vase filled with flax and cornflowers, a few tea roses in their midst, caught Sarah's eye.

'What a lovely arrangement.'

'A little less formal than the ones I do at St Mark's, but at home one can afford to be rather more relaxed, don't you think?'

Sarah nodded. 'If only I had your skill.'

'Not so much skill as many hours spent practising,' Joyce said.

She went to make tea and Sarah sat in an armchair at the side of the hearth. The room was filled with the perfume of the roses.

Joyce appeared with a tray and poured tea from an elegant pot into matching china cups.

'I wish I managed to keep my house as neat as yours,' Sarah said.

Joyce smiled. 'I often think people underestimate the pleasure that order can bring. Do you know, your husband came to see me before we left for the coast. The house was in disarray, tea chests in every room. I made tea for him – only to discover the best china had already been packed away – it was terribly embarrassing. Not that our vicar minded; there is nothing snobbish about him.' She smiled. 'In that respect, he and I are not alike.'

'I didn't know he came to see you,' Sarah said, hoping Joyce would go on.

She nodded slowly. 'I think he sensed I was reluctant to leave, or at least that I was less enthusiastic than I might have been, even though I had said nothing. I had an inkling, you see, that things might not work out once I was free of the distractions that kept me so occupied here. I suppose I feared I might be left with little to do other than examine the state of my marriage and find it wanting.' She hesitated, as though she had already said more than she'd meant to. 'And I was proved right.'

Sarah nodded. She was not sure what to say. First Gwen Talbot, now Joyce Cameron. She was beginning to feel that she had known only a fraction of the pastoral work Adam undertook.

'It helped, our talk that day,' Joyce said. 'It gave me a sense of clarity. He has always been astute in his observations, your husband. He always knows where and when he is most needed. Compassion, I suppose you'd call it.' She looked at Sarah for a moment. 'I imagine you won't have to search too hard to find similar stories to mine. It is no wonder he is held in such high regard in the village.'

'I'm grateful to you for telling me,' Sarah said. 'I've always known that Adam has enormous reservoirs of understanding, a capacity to put himself in another's shoes. I don't think I've ever met anyone as selfless. You know, when he said he wanted to serve his country again, I was very much opposed to the idea. Not only because I feared for his safety, but because, selfishly, I didn't want to be left alone. But it was hopeless of course to even think I could change his mind. Later, I realised I didn't actually want to. It would have been like clipping a bird's wings. Adam could never be prevented from helping anyone.'

'I quite understand.' Joyce gave her an appraising look. 'You're more like him than perhaps you know.'

For a moment, neither one spoke.

'If there's anything I can do,' Sarah said, breaking the silence. 'One lone woman to another . . .'

'This war,' Joyce said. 'It changes everything, don't you think?'

'I sometimes feel as if the Earth is no longer quite so solid,' Sarah said. 'That the very foundations of our lives, the things we once took for granted, might collapse and crumble away to nothing beneath us, without any warning.'

Joyce nodded. 'I feel exactly the same.'

Chapter 12

Pat's move back to Great Paxford was accomplished with a degree of stealth. When friends enquired about a moving date, she kept things vague. 'Next week. It depends. Still one or two details to sort out first. Legal matters, papers that need to be signed.' She was fortunate to have so many offers of help and was grateful for them – but, finally, she had her independence. She wanted to prove – mainly to herself – that she could manage without an army of helpers.

For too long she had operated under Bob's direction, doing his bidding, taking orders. *Love, honour and obey.* He had never tired of reminding her she had taken a vow of obedience. Now she was in charge of her own destiny – a slightly grand way of putting it, perhaps, but it accurately summed up how she felt. For the first time in a long time she found herself in charge, in a position to make important decisions. She wanted to make sure she was still capable – starting with managing the move unassisted.

She had arranged with the removals people (the same ones who'd handled the move into what she now thought of as the old house) to pack the bulk of her belongings a day ahead of her actual move. The following morning, they arrived as it was starting to get light, loaded up and had her installed in the new cottage before most people were awake. As the van with its red and cream lettering made its slow progress through the centre of the village Pat saw only one familiar face: David Brindsley, arms folded, standing in front of what had been the greengrocer's shop. She was about to wave but he had his back to the road, eyes fixed on the empty property, seemingly oblivious to the lone vehicle that trundled along the otherwise deserted street.

Once installed in the cottage, Pat wandered from room to room, allowing her newly acquired good fortune to sink in. It was the first time she had taken possession of a home that was hers alone. The house was perfect; it had more than enough space, but it was not so large as to feel daunting, like the old house did. It was ideal for one, requiring only a modest amount of housework. *Good*, she thought cheerfully. *I have more important things to do with my time than clean.*

Upstairs, the main bedroom was a good size. It had fresh white paintwork, pale oak floorboards and a view of the garden at the back. A patch of what looked like wild meadow, daisies and buttercups amid a tangle of cornflowers, had taken over the far end of what was likely lawn at one time. There was a vegetable patch in need of urgent attention and, in one overgrown corner, she could just make out a cold frame through which tall stalks of something weed-like poked.

It wouldn't take her too long to fix it up. She looked forward to growing peas and beans, onions and carrots. Thanks to Mr Middleton's informative broadcasts, she felt sufficiently confident to tackle a modest kitchen garden.

She undid the clasp on the sash window and opened it as far as it would go, allowing in a breeze that made the curtains rise and fall. The room, with its buttermilk walls, felt airy and light. She made up the bed with crisp white linen and the patchwork quilt her mother had made as a wedding gift, which ever since had languished out of sight at the bottom of the blanket box after Bob took against it.

'I'm not having that tatty-looking thing on the bed,' he'd said, although his objections, Pat suspected, were more to do with the quilt having come from her mother than anything else, since the two of them didn't get on.

She began unpacking her clothes and putting them away. It didn't take long, because she didn't have much – but then, she didn't need much. She was safe, and she was at peace. By most standards, thanks to Bob, she was well off, too – it was the only good turn he had ever done her, even though he hadn't meant to. Pat did not care much for money, but it was something, still, to have enough to get by, to know she could be independent.

She carried Bob's clothes into the spare room, intending to donate anything of reasonable quality to the WI 'Fashion on the Ration' event. Someone would be glad of them.

Next she went into the bathroom with its gleaming white porcelain and polished brass taps. Everything was new, according to the agent. Pat placed a bar of coal tar soap in the washbasin and draped towels over the hook on the back of the door, noting with some satisfaction that the bath was enormous.

Downstairs, she shook out the rug given to her by her friends at the WI, the very one Bob had slipped on, and put it in front of the hearth. There was no sense in being squeamish. It was not the rug that had killed him, after all. In the kitchen, she put the last few plates into a cupboard and settled at the table, thinking she might write something for the Mass Observation project.

She had not managed to finish her last report, begun in secret at the new house while Bob was, she thought, too busy working to be concerned about what she was doing. That was how he'd caught her out, bursting in and ripping the pages from her hand, her words revealing the true extent of her loathing for him and her love for Marek. What followed was a brutal beating, worse than anything she had endured while they were living in Great Paxford, where there was a chance one of the neighbours might hear the commotion, where Pat's swollen face, her bruised and blackened eye, were harder to conceal. It was the very worst it had ever been. Such was his loss of control that she had thought he might kill her.

In the end, he was the one who lay dead.

* * *

Shortly before lunch, she went out for a walk. It was a comfort to be back in the heart of the village, not miles from everything and everyone she knew. Without thinking about where she was going, she found herself at St Mark's, at the side of her husband's grave. A mound of bare earth, marked only by a small bunch of dying larkspur. She supposed Joyce had put them there; on the day of the funeral she had been more upset than anyone, deeply moved by the eulogy in which Pat managed to say so little. Someone must have noticed, surely. Or was it enough to simply *sound* sincere?

She gazed at the burial mound. It amazed her, sometimes, that she had spared him – that she had kept up the pretence to the end. Even Joyce, who had seen them at close quarters every day until recently, knew nothing about the true state of their marriage. Pat had seen to that, covering for him, making out all was well. She wondered if Joyce would have held him in such esteem if she'd had the slightest idea who he really was. Would she have wept for him?

No. Pat knew she would not. Yet she had made sure Bob kept his reputation, despite all that he put her through. She saw to it that he went to his grave the respected man of letters he considered himself to be.

It was more than he deserved.

She bent to remove the rotting flowers. She would have to arrange a headstone soon. She had been putting it off, unable to decide on a suitable inscription. *Husband*

and Writer, perhaps, or a quotation, if she could think of something appropriate.

One thing she was certain of: there would be nothing to suggest love, or sorrow at his passing.

'Don't worry, Bob,' she muttered, 'I'll find a form of words you won't object to. The world will never know what you put me through.'

The sound of footsteps made her whip round. Joyce, a bunch of bright pink dianthus in her arms, was approaching. 'I was on my way to do the church flowers when I saw you,' she said. 'I didn't intend to interrupt a private moment.'

Pat shook her head. 'You're not interrupting. I was just about to leave. I've actually just moved back into the village, and I'm getting the new house organised.'

Joyce hesitated. 'I didn't realise you were moving. Can I help in any way?'

'That's kind of you, but there's not much to do. As soon as I get things straight, you'll be very welcome.'

Joyce nodded. 'I shall look forward to it.'

They stood in silence for a moment.

'I can't begin to imagine what you must be feeling,' Joyce said at last. 'Life can indeed be cruel at times, dangling happiness in front of us, only to snatch it away without notice. I just can't comprehend it. It seemed you and Bob had an abundance of riches in store. So much to live for.' She fixed Pat with a look of despair. 'It's the unfairness of it all I struggle with most. A new home,

Bob on the cusp of great things with his writing, the two of you so happy . . .'

You have no idea.

'I can't afford to dwell on what might have been,' Pat said. 'It doesn't help.' She glanced at Joyce. 'I don't mean to sound hard-hearted, but *wallowing*, harbouring regret . . . it seems *wrong*. Almost as though it would be lacking in gratitude for the life I have. After all, I'm still here. I have to do the best I can. If there's one thing Bob's death has taught me it's the value of appreciating the here and now. In the end, it's all we have.' She took a breath. 'And Bob wouldn't have wanted me moping about, being miserable, would he?' Sometimes it was easier to tell people what they wanted to hear.

'No, of course not,' Joyce said. 'I envy you your wisdom, my dear. You have great dignity. It's truly remarkable that you're coping so well.'

Pat gave a wry smile. 'I'm no different to anyone else. We live in uncertain times when no one can be sure what each day will bring. And there's so much loss, every-where you look. The *unfairness* you spoke of – it more or less sums things up, doesn't it? We all know there's nothing remotely fair about war and what it does. None of us need look very far to see examples of sacrifice and suffering, or lives cut short. And there's precious little we can do other than face whatever comes our way and manage as best we can.'

* * *

At home, Pat found she couldn't settle. Her visit to the grave and the encounter with Joyce had got her thinking, made her realise how much about herself she would forever have to keep inside. For years, so much of her life had been shrouded in shame and secrecy. The truth of how she had lived – well, some of it – was known only to a few close friends, but even they had no real idea. The visit to Bob's grave had reminded her how little even he knew about her innermost thoughts. He had shown precious little interest and she had rarely been able to be honest with him.

She sat at the table, pen in hand, a blank sheet of paper in front of her, mulling over what it was she wanted to say. Then, finally, she began to write.

There are things I wish I'd been able to tell you, Bob, and now I'll never have the chance. You made a point of silencing me. As far as you were concerned, my opinion was of no consequence. In our marriage you were the only one that mattered. I had no voice. For years, you made me feel that I was nothing. As if not one thing I could say or think or feel mattered. Everything you did was designed to diminish me. I can see that now. For so long I believed I was the problem, that there was something wrong with me, that somehow I provoked you because I wasn't a worthy wife. I truly thought that if only I tried harder, things would change, get better. They never did. I convinced myself you must have had good reason to despise me and, over time, came to believe it was because I was a disappointment. Not good enough. Plain, not pretty. Too dull, slow-witted. I could never hope to hold the interest of a man like you. A man like you.

I know differently now. The problem wasn't me . . . it was you.

You're the one who was damaged. I simply had the misfortune to get in the way.

Pat put down her pen. Her hands were shaking, her breathing hard. It eased something in her, to write like this, to be honest, somewhere, somehow, even if only to herself. And yet something about directly addressing Bob made her anxious, too, as though he might be hovering over her shoulder, able to read her words.

She had not quite come to terms with the fact that she was no longer in thrall to him. She was so unused to speaking out that a small part of her still feared it was dangerous, even on paper, away from prying eyes. It would take time, she realised, to get used to the idea that she was now free, free to let go of the guilt she still harboured at having left him to die. She was not quite there yet.

She stood up quickly, folded the paper and placed it out of sight in a drawer.

Chapter 13

THERE WAS A GOOD turn-out for the monthly WI meeting in the village hall. News that the branch intended to tackle clothes rationing had been greeted with enormous enthusiasm.

'Fear not, ladies,' Frances was given to saying, as she went about her business in the village, 'we've come up with a rather exciting initiative to beat the dreaded clothes coupons. All will be revealed at Thursday's meeting. Don't miss it.'

As a consequence, members packed into the hall, keen to find out more.

'You do realise you've got the whole village fired up,' Sarah said, as she and her sister entered the hall.

'Which was exactly what I intended,' Frances replied.

'Expectations are certainly running high.'

'I'm convinced we've tapped into something of concern to everyone,' Frances said.

Even Joyce, who had initially expressed disappointment that the WI committee had failed to come up with anything more imaginative than 'the usual jumble sale' swiftly changed her mind once she realised Pat was behind the initiative.

'I happened to be in Brindsley's the other day and the conversation was all about tackling alterations and carrying out repairs. One or two of the younger ladies were saying they wouldn't know where to begin.'

'I'm hoping this might be a chance to brush up on my "invisible" mending, which has always been a little too obvious,' Sarah said, with a laugh.

'Then you're a perfect candidate. I think several of our members will find sewing lessons extremely useful.'

Teresa arrived at the hall a minute or two before proceedings were due to get under way. She was feeling much better than she had of late – almost human again. To her great relief, for the first time in weeks, she had made it through an entire day without being overcome by sickness. Earlier, to Nick's delight, she had managed a sandwich without any ill effects. 'Success!' he'd declared, pulling her close and kissing the top of her head, as if she'd just done something momentous. 'Well done, darling, I'm very proud of you.' She couldn't help but smile. It seemed rather excessive given that all she had done was eat a sliver of cheese between two pieces of bread. Still, considering how unwell she'd been, it did constitute something of an achievement.

She found a seat next to Alison near the front of the hall.

'You made it,' Alison said, with a smile. 'I take it you're feeling better?'

'Hugely.' Teresa laughed. 'Like a different woman.'

Alison looked at her closely. 'You look much brighter, there's definitely some colour back in your cheeks. The last time I saw you, you seemed a little pale.'

Teresa nodded. 'I woke up this morning feeling transformed. I'm finally able to face food.' She gave Alison a meaningful look and lowered her voice. 'For the first time in ages I was free of the awful nausea that's been plaguing me.' She placed a hand gently on her stomach.

Alison's eyes widened as the penny dropped. She too spoke quietly. 'How wonderful. I can see why there's such a *glow* about you.' Her eyes shone as she reached over and gave her friend's hand a squeeze.

Teresa mouthed, 'Thank you, we'll speak properly later.'

The women stood for their customary rendition of 'Jerusalem'.

'*And did those feet in ancient time walk upon England's mountains green . . .*'

Frances felt a sudden swell of pride. The joy on the upturned faces as the women's voices rose, singing as one, never ceased to move her. For a time, when she and Joyce had been at loggerheads over the running of the branch, several of the members had stayed away. Now it was clear that any rift there once had been was truly healed, the women again united in a common cause.

'. . . *Till we have built Jerusalem in England's green and pleasant land.*'

As Frances began to address the meeting, the chatter in the room fell silent. 'It's wonderful to see such a good turn-out,' she said. 'As you know, ladies, we're facing a new challenge on the domestic front.' She gazed around the room. 'Clothes rationing has been introduced, something none of us much likes but must simply get used to.' There were one or two murmurs. 'It is not the worst thing in the world, admittedly, but it is still a source of inconvenience for many when times are already hard enough – especially those with children, who do seem to grow at a somewhat alarming rate.'

Frances knew this well enough from Noah, who was always rapidly outgrowing his clothes. It seemed to happen almost overnight. A perfectly good shirt or a pair of shorts were suddenly too small and in need of replacing. Everyone she spoke to assured her that all children were the same. She had mentioned it in passing to Claire, her housemaid, who had once worked for Joyce, only to find herself out of a job after voting for Frances in preference to her employer as chair of the WI. Frances had swiftly taken her on. Claire was young, in her early twenties, and Frances was fond of her. She was hard-working and eager to please and had made an excellent job of letting down the hem on a pair of Noah's shorts. She must have said something to her husband Spencer, Great Paxford's postman, who approached Frances a day or two later with a suitcase containing some of his own old childhood clothes.

'My mother was in the habit of keeping what she called my Sunday best outfits,' he said, sounding a little embarrassed. 'Said they might come in handy when I had children of my own. She hung onto everything. Some of it looks good as new. I've gone through what there is and sorted out a few things that might do for Noah.' Among the 'few things' was some of the most exquisite knitwear Frances had ever seen. A great deal of work had clearly gone into making the sweaters with their complicated cable patterns. She was greatly touched. 'You must keep them,' she had said, but Spencer was adamant. Noah, who worshipped Spencer, was much taken by the idea of wearing clothes that had once been his.

Frances concluded by saying, 'I'm going to let Pat explain what we thought we might do.'

Pat thanked Frances and stood up. She'd made a few notes so that she wouldn't forget anything, but as she looked around the hall, she felt a sudden attack of nerves. She slowly rested her papers on the table so that no one would see that her hands were shaking.

It was the first meeting she had been to following Bob's death, and she suspected that at least some of the members might view her return as rather premature. Several were on the conservative side and no doubt held very particular ideas regarding what constituted appropriate behaviour while mourning. Her decision to throw herself back into the WI so soon and with such enthusiasm – not even having the grace to take a back seat – would, she suspected, lead to some criticism.

Joyce, seated near the front, gave her an encouraging smile. Joyce could be a formidable opponent and Pat felt fortunate knowing she was on her side. A few rows behind, Gwen Talbot was scowling. Pat looked down at her notes.

'I think it's best if I get straight down to business,' she said. Then she stopped. She had intended on talking only about the project ahead of them, not mentioning her own situation, or making reference to Bob. And yet, she knew not everyone here was well disposed towards her. She took a deep breath. 'But before I do,' she said, 'I wanted to thank you all for the kindness you've shown me in these last difficult weeks.' She hesitated, seeking to take the temperature of the room. 'Without my friends in the WI, I wouldn't feel able to be here tonight.' She aimed a grateful nod at Joyce. 'The support and understanding each and every one of you has shown means a great deal to me, more than I'm able to put into words.' She looked at Gwen Talbot, whose scowl had been overtaken by a look of surprise. 'I wanted to let you know how extremely grateful I am.' Several of the women murmured their approval. Pat glanced at Frances, who nodded at her to continue, while Sarah mouthed, 'Well done.'

She knew that not everyone would approve of her, but she could only do what she felt to be right. There would always be people willing to find fault in the actions of others, no matter what. Having spent so many years trying and failing to win Bob's approval, she knew better than anyone that, sometimes, trusting in your instincts was all you could do. It felt right to be here tonight, making a contribution, rather than shutting herself away to mourn a man who had done all he could to rob her of any chance of happiness.

She took a deep breath and began outlining the plans for her sewing classes and the 'Fashion on the Ration' extravaganza.

Chapter 14

AFTER THE MEETING, ALISON walked home with Teresa and went inside for a cup of cocoa. 'How long have you known?' she asked, as Teresa warmed milk in a pan.

'A little while.' Three months, almost. 'I woke up one morning feeling horribly sick, thinking I must have eaten something that disagreed with me, and then it dawned on me I might actually be pregnant.' Teresa smiled. 'It was a bit of a shock, to tell the truth. We've always talked about wanting a family, but I suppose I hadn't imagined it would happen quite so soon.' Teresa hesitated. 'I'm not ready, Alison. I'm not sure I'll ever be.'

'You've time to get used to the idea. When's the baby due?'

'In the New Year.'

'Nick must be thrilled.'

Teresa laughed. 'You should see him. *Thrilled* is putting it mildly. He's utterly, completely overjoyed. He's counting down the days. It's all he talks about. We've already been discussing names, even though it's ages off.'

Alison nodded. 'Do you want a boy or a girl?'

Teresa smiled. 'A healthy child, that's all I care about. Boy or girl, I won't mind a bit.' The milk started to rise in the pan and she whipped it off the heat and poured it into cups. 'I'm still getting used to the idea, in all honesty. A *baby! Me!* I always thought that motherhood was out of reach, something that happened to other women.' She glanced at Alison. 'You know very well why I never thought of it as something I'd experience. Without you, steering me in a direction I'd otherwise never dreamed of taking, I suspect my life would have been very different. Less fulfilling, perhaps. I wouldn't be with Nick, married with a child on the way.'

'All I did was offer some encouragement.'

'You did so much more than that.'

They sat in silence for a moment. 'And Nick – he's still flying?' Alison asked.

'They need all the fighter pilots they can get, he tells me.'

'But haven't the bombing raids all but stopped now? Has that not made a difference?'

'I hoped it would. I prayed that things would go back to how they were before, with Nick on the ground co-ordinating things – but he's still going up. They all are – and pilots are still being lost. Don't ask me about the ops, Nick won't say. The Germans might have given up bombing our cities, but it doesn't seem to have got any better as far as I can make out.'

'This war,' Alison said sadly. 'We'll all of us come through it changed.'

'As long as we emerge intact.' Teresa sipped at her drink, deep in thought for a moment. 'That's my news, anyway. Now, tell me yours. How are things with John?'

Alison sighed, not sure where to begin. 'Well, he arrived the other day with a dog he'd found wandering the bomb sites in Liverpool. Half-starved little mite, lost-looking. Probably been through all sorts. He wants me to look after it.' She looked uncomfortable. 'I'm afraid I wasn't very gracious about it.'

'Why not? You *love* dogs. And I know how much you miss Boris.'

'I do, very much, but Boris was special. Don't forget we'd been together for years and rubbed along well. I always found him to be excellent company. Whereas this little one . . .' Alison frowned. 'It's as if she's in a world of her own. She behaves well enough – eats everything I put in front of her, walks to heel when I take her out, curls up on the chair in the evening. Beyond that, though, it's as if she'd rather keep her distance. A bit like a lodger who wants to have their landlady at arm's length.'

Teresa smiled. 'Perhaps she can sense that you're not keen on her being there. Animals can be incredibly astute.'

'I can't imagine . . .'

'What's she called?'

Alison looked away. 'I've not managed to come up with anything that suits her yet.' She had thought of calling her Milly after her first puppy, a boisterous Jack Russell, but it didn't seem quite right. Poppy, Betsy and

Dotty followed, only confirming that anything ending in a 'y' was just not going to work.

'There you are, then. It sounds to me that you've not yet made up your mind about her. If you were sure you wanted to keep her, the *first* thing you'd have done would be to come up with a name. The poor creature must have been horribly traumatised when John found her – imagine what she'd been through – and now she's probably waiting to be turned out again without notice and left to roam.'

'Perhaps you're right.'

After all, Teresa had a point. It was unfair to accuse the dog of being distant when Alison herself had made so little effort with it. Perhaps the reason she was behaving like a lodger was because Alison's coolness made it plain the arrangement between them was temporary. As Teresa had rightly said, dogs could be remarkably sensitive. Boris had certainly seemed able to read her moods. When she thought back, she had known right away she intended to call him after her favourite actor, Boris Karloff. They both had the same brooding eyes.

Truthfully, deep down, Alison *was* in two minds about becoming attached to this dog, and had considered suggesting to John that once it got its strength up he might return it to Liverpool. And do what with it, she now wondered? Leave it to fend for itself once more? What if the little stray had intuitively detected her half-heartedness and was guarding itself against rejection? She wondered how much of this John – also astute enough to work out what was going on in her mind – had guessed, and what he must think of her.

Teresa grinned. 'I must say, John does seem to have something of a knack for rescuing lost souls. Look at the way he scooped Noah up and brought him home.'

Alison would never forget that day. The overwhelming relief that Noah, hungry and cold, having run away from his hated boarding school, was safe. John's concern for the boy had shone through. How like him to feel sympathy for a stray rummaging about in the bomb ruins.

She wished she hadn't been so sharp with him for bringing the animal to her. It had been such a thoughtful gesture.

Part of the problem was that she simply didn't know where she stood with John. She wasn't even sure what she wanted from him. Simple, uncomplicated friendship? Something more? In which case, why did she always push him away? As for John, his very decency and sense of propriety made it nigh on impossible to know what his intentions might be. Was he content with an easy friendship? The occasional meal together, an innocent walk in the countryside? Was that sufficient to explain why he trekked to and from Liverpool to spend time in her company? Would he make such an effort if there was nothing more to it?

Perhaps he would. Alison had never had the courage to ask him.

'I think I may have been ... *oversensitive* about the whole thing,' Alison said. 'I was rather offhand, concerned that John might be taking me for granted. I hadn't asked for another dog, after all.' She saw Teresa's puzzled look. 'As I said earlier, I reacted rather badly.'

'Oh, Alison. John would never take advantage. He's far too decent, and you know it.'

'I'd hate to lose his friendship.'

'Then talk to him,' Teresa advised. '*Properly*. Ask for his help with the dog, for a start. Be honest. Say you can't seem to get through to her and you wondered if having him around more might make a difference. Go for long walks, the three of you. Take a picnic.'

'It's a long way for him to come to walk the dog,' Alison said, doubtful.

'Except that's not the only reason he'd have for coming, as we both know. From what I've seen, John's a perfect gentleman. He's the type of man to go out of his way to make sure he doesn't overstep the mark. He must feel he misjudged things by presenting you with a dog you hadn't asked for. He might want to keep his distance now, until things settle down between you again. So, it's up to you to let him know you want to see him. I don't suppose he has much of a life in Liverpool just now. The city's in a dreadful state, by all accounts. Didn't he lose his home in one of the bombing raids?'

Alison nodded. The entire street had gone. He now had a room in a hostel. She didn't even have an address for him.

'When are you expecting to see him again?'

'At the weekend.'

Provided he still felt like making the journey. And if he didn't, she only had herself to blame.

Chapter 15

MIRIAM WASN'T CONVINCED THEY'D done the right thing taking on the lease for the shop next door. David had been so determined, persuading his parents the 'once in a lifetime opportunity', as he put it, was too good to miss.

'If we wait someone else will come along and turn it into a roaring success,' he said, 'and then we'll be sorry.'

In the end, it had seemed impossible to deny him.

On the day they got the keys, the three of them inspected the new premises, David full of ideas to bring the place back to life, Miriam thinking only of how much work it would take. She had envisaged a bit of smartening up, a fresh coat of paint, not much more – but on closer inspection, the scale of the task ahead of them began to sink in. The old shop fittings had more than had their day. There were signs of damp in the storeroom. The floor was cracked and uneven, dangerously so in places, and would need to be replaced. They were practically going to have to gut the building and start again to bring the premises up to scratch.

Miriam thought back to when the Collinses were in business. Part of the charm of the old greengrocer's was its slightly shabby, old-fashioned atmosphere. A traditional, family-run establishment. Now, only a few weeks on, it seemed devoid of all appeal, as far as she could tell. Had it deteriorated in such a short time, or had she simply never noticed how run-down it had become?

David didn't share her concerns. 'It's *empty*, Ma,' he said, laughing. 'Of course it's not at its best. You have to think of how it's going to look when it's done up with all the stock in and a new awning. Something bright that catches the eye.'

'An awning?' Bryn repeated.

'We'll need an awning to shelter the produce we have out front,' David went on, as if it was the most obvious thing in the world. 'It's half the battle, getting the shop front right.'

Miriam stopped herself from asking how much it was all going to cost. Seeing David so fired up, brimming with enthusiasm, was something she couldn't put a price on.

'It's going to take a heck of a lot of work,' Bryn said, looking doubtful.

'And we'll get it done, you'll see,' David told him, striding across to the window and checking the frames. 'Solid,' he declared, and grinned.

The new shop wasn't the only reason for David having something of a spring in his step of late. Much of his cheerful demeanour was down to Jenny Marshall, the glamorous radio operator from Tabley Wood.

David had known Jenny all his life; they had been at school together. Not that they'd been friends then – she had always seemed vastly superior, confident, even somewhat intimidating. She was the kind of girl who got her own way. In the playground she had taken charge and bossed the other girls about, and they all seemed thrilled to be told what to do by their rather haughty classmate.

David had been slightly terrified of her.

Back then, she had never given him a second look. 'Boring Brindsley,' she called him on a number of occasions. Now, however, much to his amazement, things had changed. One day, when he was out walking, he ran into her on her way home from the air base. He was wearing the scruffy old trousers and shirt well past its best that he reserved for tramping about in the countryside, and Jenny was in her smart WAAF uniform, blonde hair pinned in neat waves, her face expertly made up. She was a beauty all right, if a little hard-edged with it. She had the look of the film star, Jean Harlow, about her. When she stopped in front of him, blocking his path, he felt at a distinct disadvantage. *Vastly superior*, he remembered.

'What are you up to?' she asked, eyeing the binoculars in his hand. As if she'd caught him doing something he shouldn't.

'Not much. A spot of birdwatching.'

'I just saw a kestrel,' she said, surprising him. 'On the base, next to the perimeter track, when I was coming off duty. It stopped dead in flight right in front of me and hung in the air, still as anything. I couldn't take my eyes off it. You wouldn't believe how long it was up there . . . *anchored*. They must be so strong to be able to hold fast like that when they're being buffeted about. It makes you wonder how they do it.'

'It's to do with how they fly into the wind and the speed of their flight,' David had said, and at once wished he'd kept quiet. It made him sound as if he was showing off.

'You seem to know a lot about it,' she had said, not taking her eyes off him.

'A bit.' Most of it was gleaned from *The Observer's Book of Birds* he'd received one Christmas. 'I've always liked watching birds. You never know what you're going to see. On the way up here I saw a pair of crows mobbing a much bigger bird. Working as a team, dive-bombing, chasing it off. It was a buzzard, I think. I couldn't get the bins on it quick enough to be sure.' He cringed. *Bins*. What was he thinking? It was impossible to read her expression. *Boring Brindsley*.

Only, it turned out Jenny Marshall didn't find him boring. Quite the opposite. She seemed genuinely interested in what he had to say, even suggesting he take her birdwatching with him one day. It was so like the fearless girl he remembered from school to put him on the spot like that, confident he would agree. She was used to getting her own way.

The idea of spending time alone with Jenny wasn't something David felt entirely comfortable with. She was vivacious, a head-turner, and he was . . . well, ordinary. He wondered what they'd find to talk about.

But, as it happened, he needn't have worried. The war had mellowed her. She'd seen things, she said. David didn't ask what; he could imagine only too easily what these 'things' might have been. He already knew she was on the radio the day the Spitfire crashed onto the village. He'd been in the Observation Post and watched the plane limp in, low in the sky, belching out a thick plume of sooty smoke.

'I was the one trying to talk to the pilot,' she told him. 'Saying the same things over and over, hearing nothing back, just an awful empty crackle that tells you something's gone badly wrong.' She had felt sick, she said, willing it to be a communications error, praying the plane would land and there'd be relieved faces all round. In her heart, though, she knew the pilot was dying or already dead. 'I could feel it in the pit of my stomach, an awful churning, cramping up,' she said. Dread, one of the other girls called it. It had been the worst moment of her life.

It wasn't anymore. Now she thought of it as the first of the worst moments. There had been many others since.

David had the feeling he'd underestimated Jenny. She was every bit as fearless and bossy as he'd always imagined, but she could be equally thoughtful and sensitive. He wondered if that other side of her had always been there and she'd chosen to keep it hidden, or if it was a product of the war. The latter, he expected. He knew well enough how it could change someone. When she asked about his ship going down he said little; just that he, too, had seen his fair share of 'things'.

* * *

The work on the new shop was keeping the Brindsley family busier than ever, with both Bryn and David working long hours. Both shops would eventually be combined so that shoppers could go straight from one to the other, and that meant alterations to both properties. Fortunately, they'd persuaded a builder with a first-rate reputation to come out of retirement to tackle the work – Old Mr Jenkins, they called him, although he wasn't all that old. Old Mr Jenkins drafted in a joiner, also retired, to handle the various cabinets and shop fittings required, and between them they came up with a schedule that minimised disruption to the butcher's. The plan was to get the empty premises ready and fitted out before breaking through the wall into next door. 'It won't be as bad as you think,' Old Mr Jenkins assured them.

It sounded to Bryn like a big job, far more involved and time-consuming – and pricey – than he'd anticipated. When he'd worked out the original costings with David, they'd expected to do the bulk of the work between them. 'I don't mind painting,' David said. 'And we'll be able to smarten up the display cabinets.'

But it turned out they couldn't. The wood was too flimsy and starting to go. Privately, Bryn wondered whether they'd taken too much on.

'What if it doesn't pay off?' he asked Miriam one night, when David was out with Jenny and it was just the two of them.

'You've been over the figures a hundred times. It adds up, doesn't it?'

At a pinch, Bryn thought. Fortunately, he'd had the sense to build in an amount they could draw on 'just in case'. At this rate it would all be gone by the time they'd finished. 'We'll manage as long as things go according to plan,' he told Miriam. 'The trouble is, it's not an exact science, shopkeeping, is it? And these are strange times. We don't know what's going to happen from one week to the next, what else they might decide to ration. We don't know anything for sure.'

'We've always managed before. Whatever's come our way, we've got through it.'

That at least was true.

'Are you worried we've done the wrong thing?' Miriam asked.

He thought about it. 'I don't know, Mim. Sometimes. Maybe I'm too old to take on something this big.'

She was silent for a moment. 'I don't think we had much choice,' she said at last. 'Once David made up his mind, we had to get behind him. And you can see what a difference it's made. He's been so much happier ever since.'

Bryn smiled. 'That may have more to do with Jenny than expanding the business.'

Miriam hadn't been sure about Jenny at first. She'd always found her a bit on the brash side – full of herself, sharp-tongued, not the kind of girl she'd want for her son. She had been worried that Jenny would toy with David's feelings, drop him at the first sight of someone better, perhaps one of those RAF boys. Not that there was any-one better than David, in Miriam's view. She just hoped he had the sense to keep his wits about him.

Then, one Sunday, David asked if he could bring Jenny for tea and Miriam promptly changed her mind. Either she'd been wrong about Jenny Marshall all along, or the girl had changed. *Haven't we all?* she thought. Jenny seemed altogether softer, sweeter. She was definitely sweet on David, too – anyone could see that from the way she looked at him.

'*Besotted*,' Bryn had said later.

'Jenny, you mean?' Miriam had asked.

'Both of them.'

'He was never going to be happy serving in the butcher's for ever,' Miriam said now. 'We both knew it wouldn't be enough. He needed something to get his teeth into, and it's not as if he's not thought it all through. Before he even ran it past us he'd done the groundwork. He's young, ambitious . . . looking to the future. And it's not just him we need to think about – there's Vivian, too. Everything we're doing now is about providing for our children. We want them to have the best chance, don't we?'

Bryn nodded.

'The best thing we can do is give him our support. Let him know we're in this together, that we believe in it.' She gave a shrug. 'We need to have faith.'

'You're good at this,' he told her.

'What?'

'Making me believe everything will work out just fine.'

'That's because it will.'

Bryn decided to spend an hour in the cold store before bed. 'Make a start butchering that pig. I was going to do it this afternoon before I got into a discussion with Old Mr Jenkins about shelving.' He suppressed a yawn. 'It'll be bedlam in the shop tomorrow if I don't get some bacon cut.'

'Don't be too long,' Miriam said. 'You look worn out. I'll make us a hot drink when you come in.'

She went upstairs and checked on Vivian, who was sleeping soundly, both arms raised above her head. Then Miriam sat down at the dressing table and unpinned her hair. She understood Bryn's concerns about the expansion; he was a man who liked order, certainty. Regarding the business, he had always been cautious, not given to taking risks.

When it got to ten o'clock and he still hadn't come up from the shop, she went looking for him. The door to the cold store was open a crack. 'Bryn Brindsley,' she called, 'you'll be fit for nothing if you don't call it a night. Whatever you're doing can surely wait until morning.'

There was no answer. 'Bryn?'

She pushed open the door and stepped into the cold store where the carcass of a pig was on the block. Her eyes went straight to the floor, where Bryn lay sprawled in the sawdust.

'Oh, God, no.'

Miriam dropped to her knees, panic washing over her. 'Bryn, *Bryn.*' She took hold of his hand and squeezed. His brow was clammy, his skin a strange colour.

'No, dear God,' she whispered. '*No!*'

Chapter 16

SARAH HAD TIME ON her hands. She was due at the 'Stitch in Time' class later but the morning was free. At home, left to her own devices, she knew she was likely to fret about Adam and imagine the worst, which would only leave her feeling even more anxious. What seemed to help more than anything, she had found, was spending time with other people – focusing on their concerns, rather than her own. Her recent conversation with Joyce had unexpectedly lifted her spirits and reminded her that there was another visit she had been meaning to make. She got ready and went to see Gwen Talbot.

She'd not been sure how she would be received, knowing how sharp Gwen could sometimes be, but she seemed pleased to see her, and showed her into the front room at once.

It was the first time Sarah had been inside the house, and she stood for a moment taking in her surroundings, aware of the steady ticking of the grandfather clock that occupied an alcove on one side of the tiled fireplace.

Opposite was a cabinet crammed with ornaments and a distinctive blue and white Wedgwood tea set. The mantelpiece was lined with photographs in ornate frames, one of a striking young girl with a wide smile and hair that tumbled in waves past her shoulders. Sarah was looking down at it when Gwen appeared, carrying a tea tray.

Gwen nodded at the picture. 'I looked a bit different when I was young, didn't I?'

Sarah's eyes widened. Gwen had been a beauty in her younger days.

'I was sixteen when that was taken,' Gwen told her. 'I'd just met Alan.'

'It's lovely,' Sarah said. 'You look so . . . *carefree*.'

Gwen smiled, a little wistful. 'When I look at some of the old pictures, I hardly recognise myself. Not a care in the world. Then life got hold of me and . . .' She fell silent.

Sarah waited a moment. 'It must have been very hard when you lost your husband.'

'Yes, it changed me. Changed the whole world, I suppose. I didn't feel the same anymore about anything. You get on with things, you have to, but when I buried my husband I lost a bit of myself too, if you can understand that.' She reached for a heavy silver frame and handed it to Sarah. 'That's us, on our wedding day. Alan was a good-looking man. He could have had his pick of the girls, but it was me he loved. We'd only been out twice when he asked me to marry him.' She smiled at the memory. 'Went down on one knee at the bus stop, daft thing.'

They ended up talking for hours, Gwen confiding in Sarah her worries about her son, Ronald, following his discharge from the army on medical grounds. He was still in bed today, she said, sounding embarrassed. 'I was so relieved to get him home,' she said. 'I thought, that's it, he's safe now, I'll look after him. But he's not right . . . in his mind, you know. That's what the war's done for him.' She was quiet for a moment. 'I keep thinking it'll be all right if I just give him time. Now I'm not so sure.'

'Is there anything that can be done – have you spoken to Dr Rosen?' Sarah asked.

'The trouble with my Ron is that he's stubborn, seems to think he doesn't need any help.' She frowned. 'He has this way of disappearing without a word. The back door slams shut and he's gone. Never says where he's been, what he's been doing. When I ask all I get is, "Thinking." Thinking about what? I suppose about what happened to him when he was away – but surely that won't help. Seems to me that thinking is sometimes the worst thing you can do. It sends you mad. I know all about that from when Alan died.' After a moment, she sighed and said, 'At least I've no worries about my youngest, Mary. She's in the WAAF at a station near Newark, and doing well for herself. Ronald, though . . .' Her brow was creased with concern.

'You can't sit here worrying,' Sarah told her. 'Do you think it might help if you had something to take your mind off everything? Why don't you think about coming to the WI sewing classes? There's one today, or I could call for you next week, if you like.'

Gwen shook her head. 'I can sew already,' she said. 'I don't need teaching.'

'In that case, you might be of help to Pat. She's also had a lot to contend with lately.'

Gwen's expression hardened. 'You'd never know, would you? Her husband isn't even cold in the ground and she's gadding about the village like the cat that's got the cream.'

'She's not exactly gadding about . . .'

'They say she's done very nicely out of it, come into a big pile of money.'

'We shouldn't forget she lost her husband in the most shocking circumstances,' Sarah said slowly. 'No amount of money can make up for that.'

Gwen pursed her lips. 'I went to Mr Simms' funeral, and I couldn't help noticing how Mrs Simms carried on. Up at that altar, not the least bit sorry. Never broke down, didn't shed a single tear. Some might call it *dignified*, but if you ask me it was downright callous. And now she's floating about the village like she owns the place, making speeches at the WI, running sewing classes. She has this big smile on her face whenever you see her.' She shook her head. 'How can you *smile* when you've just lost your husband? I couldn't.'

'I suppose we all deal with grief in different ways,' Sarah said, uncomfortable about the turn the conversation had taken. She suspected Gwen had already had plenty to say around the village on the subject of Pat and her inappropriate smiling. It must be hard, she supposed, for a woman whose own husband's death had affected her so much, to see how strong Pat remained, how well she coped.

'Makes you think,' Gwen said. 'Maybe she was glad to see the back of him.'

Frances was in the bedroom sorting through the contents of her wardrobe, Sarah watching her from the doorway. 'I'm actually feeling quite positive about this whole clothes rationing business,' Frances said.

'You must be the only one.' Sarah sighed. 'I've never heard so many people complain as much as they are about clothing coupons, although the thinking behind it all seems sound. The idea is to free up workers who'd be making civilian clothes so that they can take on war-related work.'

'It's certainly made me realise how much I have that I no longer need.' Frances removed a satin evening dress from its hanger and flung it onto the bed. 'This can go.'

Sarah retrieved it. 'Are you sure? It's exquisite.' She studied the label and let out a small gasp. 'You do know it's a Schiaparelli?'

Frances shrugged. 'I have one or two of hers. I remember wearing that one when Peter took me to London to celebrate my fortieth. We stayed at the Ritz. I shan't imagine I shall ever have cause to wear it again.'

'You can't get rid of it,' Sarah protested. 'At least think about having it altered, made into something more practical.'

Frances looked amused. 'Just give me a moment while I try to come up with an occasion when an impossibly glamorous evening gown might be *practical*.'

Sarah had already slid it back on a hanger and was putting it back in the wardrobe. 'Isn't that the purpose of the WI sewing initiative, to find clever ways of remodelling old clothes?'

Frances nodded. 'I'm not sure even Pat – who is an extremely clever dressmaker, by the way – could think of what to do with a slightly extravagant evening gown. However, if it will keep you happy, I shall hang onto it. For the time being.'

'How did yesterday's first "Stitch in Time" session go?' Sarah asked.

'A resounding success. Steph was on darning duty and took Teresa under her wing to show her the basics. Alison led a little group in the art of embroidery. Pat seemed completely in her element, advising on everything from simple repairs to quite challenging alterations. We had a wide range of abilities and something useful to offer everyone.'

Sarah was taken aback. 'Everyone? Don't tell me *you* were sewing. I don't think I've ever seen you with a needle in your hand.' When they were children, despite their mother's best efforts, Frances had never shown an interest, nor any patience, for needlework of any kind.

Frances gave her sister a withering look. 'I was there in my capacity as chair to ensure it all went smoothly, rather than as a participant.'

'What if Noah needs the hem of his trousers let down?' Sarah teased. 'How will you manage it?'

'Claire already fixes that sort of thing.' Frances pulled an embroidered blouse from the wardrobe and inspected it. 'Ah, there's a button missing on the cuff, which is probably why I stopped wearing this.'

'You could always take it to the next "Stitch in Time", and mend it yourself.'

Frances ignored the remark. 'I was expecting to see you there yesterday.'

'I had every intention of coming,' Sarah said, 'but I went to see Gwen Talbot and found I lost track of time.'

Frances raised her eyebrows. 'Gwen Talbot – whatever for?'

'I think she needs someone to talk to.'

'Goodness me. Well, we'll make a vicar's wife of you yet.'

Sarah smiled. Then, retrieving a blouse with puff sleeves and delicate pearl buttons from under a coat on the bed, she asked, 'Don't you want this?'

'I've not worn it for ages. I never really felt it suited me. It's the wrong shade of green.'

Sarah held it up and peered at her reflection in the mirror. 'It might do me.'

'The stitching on the collar needs looking at.'

Sarah inspected it. 'I'll soon put that right. I can do it at next week's sewing session. I have a shirt of Adam's that's frayed at the collar and I thought I'd ask Pat's advice on how best to repair it.'

It had also occurred to her to have a quiet word with Pat, let her know what Gwen, and no doubt the women Gwen counted as her friends, were saying about her.

Frances stopped what she was doing. 'Anything more from Adam?'

Sarah shook her head. 'Nothing. I don't know what to make of it. It's been weeks since his last letter. Why doesn't he write?'

'There could be all kinds of reasons. Perhaps he *is* writing and the letters aren't getting through.' Frances gave a helpless shrug. 'I'm afraid we can only guess at what's going on, and I'm not sure that's always constructive.'

'I can't help thinking about the camp, wondering what the conditions there are really like. I have so little to go on from his letters.'

'I expect there's only so much he can say and, of course, he doesn't want to worry you.'

The night before, unable to sleep, her mind refusing to switch off, Sarah had got up and gone into the kitchen where she sat for a while drinking tea, remembering the last night she and Adam had spent together, when they had made love and lain awake talking into the early hours.

'It's not knowing that's the hardest thing. If only I had a better sense of what he's dealing with – not to mention how long he'll be there – perhaps I might feel less anxious. I spend hours thinking about how he's living, what they're giving him to eat. I don't expect the Nazis are keeping him warm and well fed. Do you?'

'Try not to torment yourself,' Frances replied. 'In my experience, the worst thing you can do is give your imagination free rein. It can be an unruly beast, more likely to stoke up irrational fear than bring comfort. I understand, really I do, but you could tie yourself in knots thinking the worst. I can only begin to imagine how hard it is for you, this not knowing, but all you can do is trust that Adam is able to take care of himself, even in the most trying of circumstances. Nobody knows him better than you do, Sarah. You know his strengths, his capacity for dealing with whatever comes his way. If anyone can manage the privations of a POW camp, Adam can. And he'll be doing what he knows best, helping others get through the experience. He has his faith, remember, and I've no doubt it will serve him well in these testing times. All I'd say is try not to worry too much, however impossible that may seem. Keep yourself busy – sew! – and, above all, choose to think the best, not the worst.'

Chapter 17

MY DARLING MAREK,

You must think me mad, writing to you when I don't even know where you are and have no way of finding out. This is a letter I can never send. But it's been so long since I heard from you. Each day I wait for the post in the hope of something. Anything. A few words to say you're alive, that you haven't forgotten me, that you still love me. What I fear the most is that in the time we've been apart, your feelings might have changed. It's as if you've vanished and I have no idea where, or how, to begin searching for you.

She was no longer where Marek expected her to be either, she realised. Not that it made any difference. If he wrote, his letter would find her, wherever in Great Paxford she happened to be living.

How I hate this war for taking you from me. At times I feel I could lose my mind thinking about you, willing you to come back to me, and all the while hearing nothing.

The silence is terrible.

I take comfort from the memories I have. Our time together. Do you remember the day we met? I do, as clear as if it were yesterday.

If I close my eyes I can see it in a series of snapshots, some sharp, others not quite in focus. A clear sky, sun on my face as I walked home through the village. Up ahead, soldiers, a few of the local men drinking outside the Black Horse. Voices, an accent that was unfamiliar. A blur of uniforms, glasses filled with ale. Shapes, nothing distinct.

No hint of what was to come.

Nothing to say my life was about to change.

For once, I wasn't in a hurry. Bob was away, reporting on the war, and I had no one to answer to, no need to rush home as I usually did. No reason to feel anxious about being late, or for knots to form in my stomach at the thought of what Bob would say when I got in.

He was always so strict when it came to timekeeping. Mine, anyway. While he was free to come and go as he pleased, I was fettered. Whenever I left the house, I was conscious of the precise time I had to be back. No ifs or buts. Those were the rules. I understood what was required and the likely consequences if I defied them. And yet, there were so many times I rolled in late, infuriating him. He seemed to think I did it on purpose. I didn't. It was just impossible to live within the constraints he set and do all that I needed to. Innocent things, like the shifts I did at the telephone exchange. We needed the money and I enjoyed *the work, but Bob would never have approved and so I kept them secret. He caught me out, of course, and there was quite a scene.*

I was never able to keep things secret from him.

Sooner or later, he always caught me out.

Pat paused for a moment as she recalled the control Bob had exerted, how every aspect of her life had come under relentless scrutiny. Where she went, who she saw, how she spent every bit of housekeeping money; all of it subjected to examination and criticism. The pressure on her had been so great it was bound to rupture in the worst possible way at some point. Throughout their marriage, Bob had meted out punishment for her perceived wrongdoings. And yet still she felt guilty at the manner of his death. Surely the time had come to put it behind her once and for all. Otherwise was she not in danger of punishing herself in much the same way he had?

She began to write again.

And so, back to That Day. On the face of it, it was much the same as any other; a shift at the exchange, grocery shopping and home. I was relieved to be going back to an empty house, relaxed at the prospect of having time to myself to read or sew or simply do nothing. No one was regarding me with suspicion, demanding I account for my every move. My time my own, for once.

Already, even though I didn't know it, on that journey home, a countdown had begun to something new and momentous.

Five, four . . .

Some kind of commotion at the pub was spilling out into the road in front of me. I was too wrapped up in my own thoughts to see what was happening. A tangle of bodies. Breaking glass. Before I knew it, someone crashed into me and knocked me to the ground. I felt my bag skitter out of my hand.

Three, two . . .

I remember the shock of it. The feeling of fury and humiliation. A voice cutting through the chaos, English spoken with an accent.

One . . .

You. At my side. Apologising, offering to help, even though you were not to blame. Captain Marek Novotny. Doing the right thing, the honourable thing. That was what I was thinking, even as I gave you a piece of my mind, even as I told you exactly what I thought of drunken men misbehaving, making it impossible for a woman minding her own business to walk home in peace in broad daylight. I remember raising my voice: 'Watch what you're doing!' I hate to think the first words I spoke to you were in anger. I remember going on my way, thinking that at least someone (you!) had the good grace to come to my rescue.

That Day. Forever etched on my mind. The point at which my life changed forever.

The moment we met.

Pat stopped writing and put down her pen. She wasn't entirely sure what she was doing. Months had gone by with no word from Marek. Her hands were tied; she had no means of contacting him. He could be anywhere. Wounded, captured or worse. What if he was dead? What if he had changed his mind about her?

No, she refused to believe it. Not yet. She prayed their separation was temporary and that, in time, he would return and they would make a life together. He would find her.

Marek would always know how to find her.

Chapter 18

IT HAUNTED MIRIAM, THE thought of what might have happened had she not decided to go looking for Bryn that night. The image was stuck in her mind: him lying there, utterly still, her kneeling at his side, clutching his freezing hand, saying his name over and over. Begging him not to leave her.

Certain she had lost him.

'We have to take a collapse of this kind seriously,' Dr Rosen said. The peculiar dizziness Bryn had experienced before he blacked out, coupled with his high blood pressure, caused the doctor to suspect he had suffered a mild stroke. She ordered bed rest and, in the days that followed, called in regularly to check on Bryn's progress.

Gradually, he showed signs of improvement. He was sleeping less, looking better, a little colour back in his face – well enough to get up, Dr Rosen said.

'Treat it as a warning,' Dr Rosen told Bryn. 'A sign you've been pushing your body too hard. You're going to have to learn to slow down, which means no rushing or pushing yourself to the point of exhaustion. Moderation in all things.'

'Can I still work?' Bryn wanted to know.

'As long as you're sensible about it and not doing anything too strenuous,' the doctor said, replacing her stethoscope in its box and sliding it back inside her bag. 'I imagine a lot of what you do requires a fair amount of effort – handling carcasses, for instance.'

Bryn glanced at Miriam. 'I do all that. I'm used to it, and David can't help with that side of things now, with his injuries. But it's never been more than I can manage. All in a day's work, that's the way I look at it.'

'Not anymore, I'm afraid,' Dr Rosen said. 'I really can't emphasise how vital it is for you to take heed of what your body's telling you. This is an opportunity to reconsider how you do things.' She saw his look of disappointment. 'It needn't be a bad thing. Think about what you *can* manage rather than what you can't. I see no reason why you can't still be fully involved in the business – *provided* you stick to less challenging work. Lighter duties and fewer hours, I suggest. Follow my advice and there's every chance your body will continue to serve you well. Be glad it had the courtesy to warn you to make some changes – not everyone is as fortunate. The last thing any of us wants to see now is a return to the kind of behaviour that might put you at risk of another collapse.' She gave him a stern look. 'One which might prove more serious.'

'We need to listen to what the doctor says,' Miriam said. 'We'll do as we're told. I never want to go through that again, worrying sick I might lose you.'

'It was just a funny turn, Mim. I'm feeling fine now.'

'You felt fine before and look what happened.' Miriam sent an exasperated look at Dr Rosen. 'We *have* to take this seriously. Making sure you stay well is the priority now, whatever it takes.'

Bryn thought for a moment. 'We'll not manage if I take a step back,' he said, with a wince. 'There's no one else who can do my job. David can't take on the heavy work – you know he can't, not with his back the way it is. If I'm careful and take my time about things, like the doctor says, I don't see why I won't be able to keep doing my old job. Just at a slower pace.' He looked hopefully at Dr Rosen. 'We're busy expanding into next door. If ever there was a bad time to be taking things easy, this is it.'

Dr Rosen regarded him over the top of her horn-rimmed spectacles. 'Mr Brindsley,' she began, 'I appreciate this is a difficult time for you and your family, but it would be a dereliction of duty on my part if I allowed you to think you'll be able to carry on as before, albeit, as you say, at a slower pace. The *slower pace* is simply part of the picture. I hope I've made clear that the *nature* of the work you do will also have to change.' She frowned. 'I'm not telling you this to make life unpleasant for you but in order to keep you *alive*.'

Bryn stayed silent.

'We'll think of something,' Miriam said, her eyes on her husband.

Miriam was impressed by Myra Rosen. She'd only been in the village a short time, brought in by Erica Campbell when her husband, Will, was dying from lung cancer. Myra was relatively young – in her late twenties, Miriam guessed – which led some (Miriam included) to question how fitting a replacement she could possibly be for the highly regarded Dr Campbell. Some people in the village also doubted just how successful a female doctor could be. Yet in the space of a few months, she'd proved herself a force to be reckoned with. Dr Myra Rosen was self-assured, authoritative and straight to the point. What Miriam had once taken to be arrogance was, she now suspected, simply an expression of the young doctor's confidence. Although Myra could at times appear brusque and uncompromising in her attitude, Miriam had seen first-hand in her treatment of Bryn how dedicated and determined she was to do the absolute best for her patients. Miriam knew that Bryn's health was in good hands.

Myra snapped shut the bulky leather bag that accompanied her on home visits. There was something old-fashioned about her; few young women would have favoured the heavy tweeds she so often wore, or the glasses with their thick frames. Her hair was pinned back in a severe style, her face bare of make-up. The overall effect was that she cared little about her appearance. She was the kind of woman who demanded to be taken seriously.

'I'm off, then,' she said, doing up the buttons of her boxy jacket. 'If you're worried about anything, let me know, but I'm pleased to say you're on the mend, Mr Brindsley. Another week and you'll be feeling very much better.'

'What's the point if I can't pull my weight?' Bryn grumbled once Dr Rosen had left. 'I might as well give up.'

'I won't have that kind of talk,' Miriam told him. 'You're a husband and a father and your family needs you, so don't think for a moment I'll stand to see you feeling sorry for yourself. How's that going to help any of us? You heard what the doctor said – you're one of the lucky ones.'

Bryn looked perplexed. 'I'm not so sure about that.'

'Plenty of people don't get a second chance.' She sat on the bed and took hold of his hand. 'We're blessed, Bryn, can't you see it? Look at David, look at you. And our perfect little girl . . . pulled from the wreckage of a plane crash with not so much as a scratch on her. If that's not lucky, I don't know what is.'

He thought for a moment. 'You don't ever worry that we're only due to have so much luck?'

Miriam shook her head. 'Never. I trust things will work out for us because they always have. As long as we pull in the same direction, we can get through anything.' She squeezed his hand. 'I don't want you worrying about the shop, or the new business. It's all in hand. We'll manage, I promise. We'll find a way of coping.'

* * *

Bryn spent the afternoon in the living room playing with Vivian under Miriam's watchful gaze. At closing time, Miriam went into the shop to give David a hand clearing up, leaving Bryn in the kitchen warming through a pan of soup – the most she was prepared to allow him to do on his first day out of bed.

'The doctor made it clear your dad has to take it easy,' she told David as she wiped down the counter. 'No going back to how things were before. You know your dad – he'll think he's up to doing a lot more than he really is, so we'll need to keep an eye on him. I don't want him having another attack.'

David was quiet. 'Ma, you don't think . . .'

She turned to look at him. 'What?'

'It's just, I can't help thinking it's my fault what happened.'

'Why in heaven's name would you think such a thing?'

'Because it was me that pushed him to take on the new shop when we were doing fine as we were. I could see he wasn't sure, but I wouldn't let it drop. I kept going on about it, how we couldn't afford to stand still and we'd feel sick if someone else moved in next door and turned it into a goldmine. It was selfish of me, wanting things my own way. What if the only reason he agreed to go ahead was to keep me happy, and now . . .' He bit his lip, fighting tears. 'The night he collapsed, I wasn't even here. I was out enjoying myself, leaving you to cope on your own. I'm so sorry, Ma. I can't stop thinking about it, what it must have been like for you, finding him . . .' He looked away.

'Now, you listen to me,' Miriam said. 'For one thing, you didn't push him into doing anything he didn't want to. The two of us talked it all through, looked at the figures, and agreed it made absolute sense for us to take over next door's premises. You're right, we *do* want you to be happy, of course we do, and we'd already talked about whether the shop as it is now would be enough in the long term. So, yes, that was a factor – *but* we'd never have gone ahead unless we were sure it was the right thing to do for the business.' She took a breath. 'As for what happened to your dad that night, you can't stay home on the off-chance we might need you. More than anything, we want you to get out and live your life.'

The door to the shop opened and Jenny's blonde bob appeared. She was in her WAAF uniform, on her way home after a shift at Tabley Wood. 'All right to come in? I wanted to call and see how Mr Brindsley's doing.'

'That's kind of you, love,' Miriam said. 'He's up and about, keeping an eye on Vivian – or the other way round, it's hard to tell – and getting the tea ready. As long as he takes things steady he can come back to work in a day or two.'

'That's great news,' Jenny said. 'It'll be a relief once things are back to normal again.' She caught the concerned look that passed between Miriam and David. 'What it is?' she asked.

'The lifting side of things,' Miriam explained. 'Bryn's not going to be able to do any of it from now on. Doctor's orders. We just need to work something out.'

Jenny looked at David, knowing he was in no position to step in. 'What will you do? How will you get round it?'

Miriam managed an anxious smile. 'We've not got that far yet.'

Jenny thought for a moment. 'Have you got a spare apron?' she asked. 'I've had an idea.'

Chapter 19

ALISON AND JOHN WERE out walking, enjoying the countryside beyond the village, the little dog scampering about, stopping abruptly here and there to sniff at something interesting. John picked up a stick. 'Here, girl, fetch,' he called, hurling the stick. The dog looked up at him, tail wagging, making no move to go after it. 'Go on, get your stick,' John urged.

The dog pawed at his foot.

Alison burst out laughing. 'More sense than to go chasing sticks, that one.'

John was laughing too. 'I just need time to train her, teach her a few tricks.'

After a lengthy debate, they had decided to name the dog Elsa. John had come up with the idea of calling her after a character from a film starring Boris Karloff, the actor they both admired so much, and Alison suggested Elsa Lanchester from *The Bride of Frankenstein*. The name seemed to suit the little dog.

In recent weeks, John's visits from Liverpool had become more frequent, ostensibly to see how the dog was settling in. If the weather was fine, Alison packed a picnic and they took Elsa out, going deep into the Cheshire countryside, tramping for miles. The dog seemed delighted with its new surroundings, finding everything worthy of investigation.

'It's good for her to get out into the fresh air and have a run,' Alison said.

'Good for us too,' John said, gazing into the distance. They had found a spot for their picnic at Beeston Castle, high enough to see the range of hills in the distance. He tilted his hat lower over his eyes to shield them from the hot August sun. 'Looks like the rain's falling over there. We're in the right place.'

Alison followed his gaze. 'I think those are the Pennines, but don't take my word for it. I have a very poor sense of direction.' She poured tea from a flask and they sat for a moment in silence.

'Up here, you can almost forget the madness going on in the city,' John said.

'We're lucky – we've experienced nothing of the devastation Liverpool's seen. But you've lost your home, everything.'

He smiled. 'Not everything. I'm doing all right.' He looked away. The dog ran up and flopped at his feet, panting. He reached down and scratched her ear. 'Same as this one, eh, girl?'

'I owe you an apology,' Alison said, 'for being so off-hand about you bringing the dog. I'm sorry. I don't know why I was so opposed to the idea.'

John smiled. 'It doesn't matter now. It's all forgotten.'

After a moment, she asked, 'Do you mind living in the hostel?'

'I'm glad to have a roof over my head, and it's not so bad. A bit noisy at night. That's when you can get trouble among one or two of the fellas. Squabbles over things going missing, someone accusing one of his room-mates of stealing from him. Smokes, that kind of thing. After a drink or two, well, you know.' He shrugged.

Alison didn't know. She suspected he was making things sound less awful than they really were. When men were herded together in poor conditions there was bound to be trouble. Squabbles, John had said. More likely vicious fights. And it couldn't be easy, being the only black man in the place. If she asked, would he tell her?

It occurred to her that she was immune from many of the worst aspects of war. Her own home was comfortable and safe, her nights undisturbed. She had a shelter to go to should the siren sound. She had peace and privacy, no need to worry about strangers picking fights. She struggled to picture the hostel that was John's home. Rows of hard, narrow beds, she imagined, a single scratchy blanket, no privacy, nowhere to keep your belongings safe.

'Have you had any trouble?' she asked.

'Everyone has trouble.' He glanced at her. 'Nothing serious, though, not so far.'

'I don't know how you can stand it.'

'There are plenty worse off than me.'

Did he ever complain? she wondered. Whatever the difficulties he might encounter, John was one of those extraordinary individuals who always preferred to count their blessings. *Nothing serious.* It could have been his motto. When she thought back to the lack of tolerance among some of the villagers when he and the other trekkers began arriving in Great Paxford, she felt mortified. Members of the WI were among those opposed to the idea of offering assistance to people who were clearly in dire straits.

Alison glanced at John, propped up on an elbow, hat pushed back on his head; eyes closed, face tilted towards the sun. She was wearing a wide-brimmed straw hat to save her fair skin from burning. His skin was perfect, unblemished and unlined. It was almost impossible to tell by looking at him that he was fifty-three, just a few years older than her.

He opened his eyes and sat up. 'Out here you can almost believe the world's a peaceful place.'

Alison nodded. 'We have to hope it will be once more, when the fighting's over.'

He didn't answer.

'Be honest,' she said. 'Is it awful where you're living?'

John gave a slight smile. 'It's not forever.'

'That's not what I asked.'

'It depends what you call *awful.*'

She again considered her own surroundings, where she could sit undisturbed in the evenings in the front room, wireless on, Elsa curled up under the sideboard.

'I don't suppose you even have facilities to cook or make a cup of tea?'

'There's a place I can get something to eat, one of those workers' cafés not far from the docks. Most of the area's flattened but Hughes's is still standing. The woman who runs it does a bit of baking once or twice a week.' He grinned. 'Some of the pastries, I couldn't tell you what's in them, but they taste all right. Penny a piece.' He nodded at their picnic basket. 'Not as good as this.'

Alison smiled solemnly as she began to unpack their picnic: slices of corned beef and home-made pickle, hunks of fresh bread and tomatoes from the garden. Elsa sat up, suddenly alert. Alison handed her a carrot, which she took away and held between her front paws like a bone as she demolished it.

'She likes carrots?' John sounded surprised.

'I dropped one in the kitchen the other night and she pounced straight on it. Seems to enjoy them. It's the one thing we're not short of, so whenever she's after a treat that's what she gets.'

'Somehow, I can't picture Boris crunching on a carrot.'

'No – but he was thoroughly spoiled, always wanting some of whatever I had to eat. My own fault – I never could resist when he gave me one of his pleading looks.' Alison smiled. 'I'm trying to be a bit stricter with this one.'

John reached for the flask and poured more tea into their cups. 'Be nice to stay up here,' he said, looking out across the patchwork of fields, the pockets of woodland. 'Forget about the rest of the world for a bit.'

Alison glanced at him. 'I was thinking,' she said, slowly, 'why don't you come and live with me?'

Alison called on Teresa later that afternoon, and found her in an apron rolling out pastry. 'Jam tarts,' she announced, sounding pleased. 'This time last year I hadn't the faintest idea about baking, and now look at me. And I can stomach the smell now as well. Give me a minute and I'll get them in the oven.'

Alison watched her cutting the pastry into rounds. As casually as she could manage, she mentioned she had offered her spare room to John.

It was enough to stop Teresa – busy spooning jam into the pastry cases – in her tracks. 'John? Moving in with you?' She was wide-eyed. 'That's . . . wonderful news.'

'The same sort of arrangement we had,' Alison explained. 'Paying rent, all above board and perfectly proper, in case anyone wants to know. Where he's living now sounds dreadful. It's some kind of hostel, too many people, everyone piled in on top of each other. I don't even think it's safe. Fights, all kinds of trouble. He can't stay there, which is why I suggested he come to me. It seemed . . . the *right* thing to do.'

And yet she still wondered if it had been the wise thing to do and what the village gossips might say once word got out.

'There's no need to explain,' Teresa told her. 'Of course you're doing the right thing – the *best* thing – for *both* of you. Why would you sit back and do nothing when someone you care about is having a hard time of things and you're in a position to help? It crossed my mind a while ago that you might ask him.'

Alison was taken aback. 'Really?'

'It makes perfect sense. And you know what I think of him. He's a lovely man, thoroughly kind, and you get along so well. I can see how much he thinks of you – *likes* you.' She gave Alison a meaningful look. 'He definitely sees you as more than a "friend". If you ask me, you two are made for one another.'

'We've been spending a lot of time together,' Alison admitted. 'I asked him to help me with Elsa, as you suggested, and we've been out for long walks in the country. Taking picnics, going miles some days.'

'It sounds perfect.'

'It is, in many ways. I trust him. It's as if I can tell him anything.' When she told him about George, that they were never actually married, and that the only other person who knew was Teresa, John had merely nodded. *What happens between two people is their own business, no one else's,* he told her.

'I won't deny we've become close,' Alison said, 'although . . .' She hesitated.

'What?'

'I'm not sure what there is between us. Nothing's happened.' Less than nothing. No 'accidental' brushing against

162

one another in passing. Once or twice on their walks she had lost her footing and he had caught her elbow, steadying her before letting go again. That was all. John's behaviour had at all times been above reproach. It made it all the more confusing.

'We've had our chances,' Alison said. 'Once or twice when we've been in some lovely spot in perfect weather, enjoying the view, I've thought, perhaps . . .' She looked at Teresa and shook her head. 'And yet he's not even hinted he might like anything more than friendship. We couldn't get along any better than we do but I'm still not sure he *likes* me, as you put it. If he felt something more than friendship towards me, wouldn't he have said so before now?'

Teresa sighed. 'Not necessarily. Perhaps he's not sure of *your* feelings, and he's worried if he tries to take things further he might ruin the relationship you already have.'

'He must know I . . . *like* him.'

'Oh, Alison. It's not always obvious. People are complicated. Our feelings are rarely clear-cut and easy to read. We think we want something but we're too afraid to let it show in case we're rejected. We blow hot and cold, change our minds, lose our nerve. We say one thing and do another. It can be the hardest thing to know what's going on in someone else's head. You and I have both known loss, and I suspect John has too. It makes you wary. Once you've had your heart broken you're bound to be cautious about falling for someone again.' She gave Alison a long look. 'It can be a risky business, deciding to put your cards on the table when there's so much at stake. You could always find a way of letting him know that you're open to the idea of something more than friendship.' She caught Alison's expression. 'Discreetly, of course, without making things awkward between you.'

'I don't want us to be the subject of tittle-tattle, as much for John's sake as mine.' Alison sighed; she knew there was bound to be talk about him becoming her lodger. She would simply have to deal with it, and so would John. 'It's going to be difficult enough for him living in a small village where he's bound to stand out and draw comment.'

Teresa smiled. 'People will get used to him being here, you'll see. You've some good friends who'll make sure he knows he's welcome.' She took off her apron and draped it over the back of the kitchen chair. 'Shall we sit down for a minute?'

They went into the front room, where there were signs Teresa had been darning. She whipped one of Nick's socks off a chair and gestured at Alison to sit.

'Tell me,' Teresa said, flopping into the chair opposite, 'am I in danger of descending into drudgery? Be honest.'

Alison laughed. 'I doubt it. I've never seen a more glamorous "drudge".'

'I miss teaching, the challenges of the classroom. I miss being around the children.'

'You'll have a child of your own soon.'

'I know.' She rested a hand on her belly. 'The thought of it still terrifies me. Does it all simply fall into place, do you think, once the baby comes? Suddenly, by some miraculous process, you know what's required?'

'I'm afraid you're asking the wrong person.'

'Nick seems to think so.' Teresa thought for a moment. 'He's not in the least bit anxious about any of it. I can see him finding fatherhood completely natural. Nobody will have to tell him what to do. He'll know, instinctively.'

'And so will you,' Alison insisted. 'You'll work it out *together*.'

Chapter 20

F RANCES HEADED TO THE village butcher's, where
Miriam was now back behind the counter full time.
David was out of sight in the cold store, getting to grips
with the butchery work while Bryn was at home, resting,
minding Vivian.

'That's how things are, for the time being, anyway,'
Miriam explained to Frances. ''Course, Bryn sees no good
reason why he can't come back to work, but I'm not having
him rushing things. Not until I'm sure he's got his strength
back. He had such a fright – we all did. *I'm* still getting
over it, so I don't see how he can claim to be completely
better.' She sounded exasperated. 'With the best will in
the world, things can't go back to how they were before
just like that.'

'He'll make a full recovery, though?' Frances asked.

Miriam nodded. 'Provided he does as he's told. He's
been warned not to do anything strenuous. He's been
given strict instructions. Dr Rosen made it perfectly clear.
He might feel he's back to his old self, but after a collapse

like the one he had he's going to have to watch his step. No putting a strain on himself – doctor's orders.'

'Give him my best, won't you?' Frances said. 'Is there anything you need help with – someone to watch Vivian for a few hours, perhaps? You only need say.'

'It's kind of you,' Miriam said. 'We're managing somehow, although we've a lot on. The shop next door, for one thing. David's pressing on with it, determined to open on schedule no matter what, but it's going to be tight.' She sighed. 'Funny how you make plans, thinking you've taken into account every eventuality. When we talked about expanding and what might go wrong we were thinking more along the lines of how much it was all going to cost and if we could afford it . . . whether we'd find a reliable builder, that kind of thing. Not for a second did we imagine Bryn falling ill. If we had, we wouldn't have been in such a hurry to take on the extra responsibility.'

'I think it's a rather wonderful quality, our tendency to believe we can create an ordered future,' Frances said. 'We believe we can make plans and watch them unfold as we hoped, even in such challenging times as these.'

Miriam nodded. 'It's thrown us, no doubt about it.'

'Things will settle down again, I'm sure,' Frances said, 'and having David must be a godsend.'

'I'd be lost without him. Jenny, too.' Miriam explained how Jenny had arrived at the shop the night before, straight from a shift at the base, and rolled up her sleeves – literally – to lend a hand in the cold store. Afterwards, she helped David paint the storeroom in the new premises. It was gone midnight before they finished. 'She's been a huge help.'

Frances could not hide her surprise. 'You mean Jenny *Marshall*?'

Miriam nodded. 'What we're struggling with is the heavy work,' she explained. 'Bryn handled that side of things before – it's the one thing David can't manage. We weren't sure what we'd do, but then Jenny suggested she pitch in.' Miriam smiled. 'She's strong, that one. Between the two of us, we're making light work of it.'

Frances thought of the Jenny Marshall she knew: red lips, the sometimes cloying scent of lavender, an inclination to delight in stirring up trouble. She was not the kind of girl Frances would have expected to be much use in a crisis – and in a butcher's, of all places! She tried to imagine the Jenny she knew hefting animal carcasses, choosing to get her hands dirty when she could be at home curling her hair or doing her nails. It was a revelation. 'Well, well,' she said. 'People can be full of surprises, can't they?'

Frances was on her way to the post office when she saw Pat and waved to her. 'I've just heard the most extraordinary thing,' she said, and described how Jenny Marshall was helping the Brindsleys following Bryn's collapse.

Pat could not conceal her amusement. 'We *are* talking about the same Jenny I worked with at the telephone exchange?' she asked.

'The very same.'

Pat laughed. 'Perhaps she has a secret twin.'

'According to Miriam, she's proving an enormous help. I got the impression they wouldn't have managed without her.'

Pat was shaking her head. 'I don't care what you say, that's *not* the same girl. If the Jenny I remember so much as chipped a nail, you never heard the end of it.'

'Well, now she thinks nothing of lifting a side of beef. What on earth has happened to her?'

'David, I suspect,' Pat said. 'I saw them together when I was out walking, up by the castle. David had his binoculars – it looked to me as if they were birdwatching . . .'

This prompted more incredulity from Frances. 'Really? Well, good luck to them. David's a lovely young man and if he's interested in Jenny, there must clearly be more to her than meets the eye.'

A short distance away, on the opposite side of the street, Gwen Talbot observed this exchange. Pat was facing her, animated, *laughing*. Nothing to suggest a widow in mourning.

Earlier, Gwen had been at St Mark's, visiting the grave of her husband, something she did at least once a week, or more if it was a birthday or anniversary or she felt the need to share something with him. The one-sided conversations conducted as she ran a cloth over the headstone or arranged a bunch of fresh flowers were a source of great comfort. She'd been spending more time with Alan of late, telling him about Ronald and how worried she was, asking what she should do. If he'd been alive, he'd have been able to get through to their son. He'd never have put up with the door-slamming, the hours Ronald spent away from the house doing who-knew-what. 'I can see how angry he is,' she had whispered to the headstone, 'but he won't talk about it. Not to me. He won't listen to a thing I say. I wish you were here, love – you'd know what to do. I miss you. We all do.'

Afterwards, she went to look at the mound of earth that marked the grave of Bob Simms and was struck by its state of apparent neglect. There weren't any flowers. She wondered if Pat had even been back since the funeral. It certainly didn't look like it.

As far as Gwen could make out, Pat Simms wasn't in the slightest bit affected by her husband's death. True, at the funeral she had *looked* dreadful – pained, not a bit of colour in her face, great dark shadows under her eyes. But somehow, she had managed to speak about her husband without going to pieces. Gwen had never thought much of Bob Simms; he was too full of himself for her liking. Why he felt he was so much better than anyone else when all he did was sit at a typewriter, she couldn't fathom. What was so special about being a writer, anyway? It seemed pointless – a waste of time as far as she was concerned. Still, Gwen had attended the funeral in order to support Pat, a fellow WI member, and made a point of offering her condolences. She knew, after all, how it felt to lose your husband.

Apparently, Pat did not feel the same.

Gwen wasn't the only one to have noticed how happy Pat Simms seemed these days. She looked a good deal happier than when her husband was alive, in fact. Since she'd moved back into the village, she seemed utterly care-free. It was rumoured that she had come into money – a small fortune, more than enough to account for the smile on her face, according to Gwen's friend, Martha Dawson, whose husband ran the Black Horse and seemed able to find these things out. Perhaps, Martha had suggested, Pat was only too happy to see the back of the great writer. Gwen, remembering Pat's haunted look at the funeral, hadn't been so sure.

Now, though, she could not deny that Pat looked all too happy. She wondered about the accident Bob Simms was supposed to have had – tripping on a rug, apparently, falling down the stairs while Pat was out at a WI meeting. Very convenient, some might say.

So, when Gwen rounded the corner on the way home from the cemetery and saw Pat with Frances, the two of them highly amused by something, she felt outraged. She might not have liked Bob Simms, but all the same. Such behaviour was plain wrong – disrespectful. She watched the women go their separate ways, Pat in the direction of the house she could only afford thanks to the money left to her by her late husband, Frances coming towards her.

'Good morning, Mrs Talbot.' Frances still had a smile on her face. 'Such a lovely day.'

Gwen glared at her. 'I suppose so – if you've nothing better to do than indulge in high jinks in the street.'

Frances frowned. 'I'm sorry, I'm not with you.'

'Your *friend*.' An insult, spat out. 'Mrs Happy-Go-Lucky.'

'I don't quite follow . . .'

'She put on a good act at the funeral, I'll give her that.' Gwen Talbot's voice had risen. 'Managed to take me in, and plenty others. I had every sympathy. Poor woman, losing her husband. Tragic. Terrible. Only now I can't helping thinking she's been having us all on—'

'Mrs Talbot, if you don't mind—' Frances got no further.

'Oh, but I do. I *mind* being made to feel a fool. First thing this morning, I was in the cemetery, tending my husband's grave, something I do regularly, and I thought I'd pay my respects to Mr Simms.' Her lip curled in disgust. 'Looks to me as if no one's been near, certainly not his *grieving* widow.'

A voice interrupted. 'That's where you're quite mistaken, Mrs Talbot.' Joyce Cameron was walking towards them from Brindsley and Son, and Gwen Talbot seemed briefly thrown off-balance. 'I happened to be in the cemetery recently, taking flowers into the church, and Pat was at the grave,' Joyce said. 'She was deep in thought, so much so I hesitated to intrude on what was clearly a private moment. Before you go accusing anyone of anything, I'd suggest you take the time to establish the facts.'

Mrs Talbot chose to ignore this. 'All I know is whenever I've seen her, she's happy as you like. Just now – chatting away, laughing and joking. With respect, Mrs Cameron, you weren't here to see it.'

'Mrs Talbot, you're being quite unfair,' Frances said. 'What would you suggest – that Pat hides away and sees no one? What choice is there in the face of loss but to carry on with life as best we can? Isn't that a lesson we've all had to learn?'

'Mr Simms fell down the stairs, so we've been told.' Mrs Talbot aimed a challenging look first at Frances, then Joyce. 'An *accident*. Didn't the police look into it?'

Joyce gazed at her. 'I'd be very careful what you say.'

'And now she's rolling in money, *his* money, and not in the least bit sorry!' Mrs Talbot raised her voice. 'Not even sorry enough to put a few flowers on his grave until there's a headstone – *if* she's going to bother with one.'

'I thought you should know,' Joyce said softly. She had gone straight to see Pat following her rather bruising encounter with Gwen Talbot. 'I did my best on your behalf, my dear, but I'm afraid there was no getting through to her. Once Mrs Talbot has the bit between her teeth . . .'

Pat sat quietly. She had shown Joyce into the small front room, where a tray with tea and some of the plain biscuits that had come out of the oven earlier now rested on a side table. In the centre of the mantelpiece were the roses picked from the garden that morning, and in front of the fireplace was the rug that was a gift from the WI on the eve of Pat's move to the new house. The *old* house, as she now thought of it. The rug went well in the room, Pat thought, the rich burgundy a match for the hearth tiles. She saw it again sliding away from under Bob as he clawed at the air, seeking something to hold onto. Blinking, she stared into her teacup.

Joyce, in a crisp cotton dress belted at the waist and some kind of feather-adorned confection on her head, sat straight-backed on one side of the hearth, repeating, word for word it seemed to Pat, the conversation that had recently taken place with Mrs Talbot.

'And, of course, poor Mrs Barden was party to the whole thing,' Joyce said. 'She spoke up for you – we both did – but I was left with the distinct feeling that nothing we could say would make any difference.'

Pat managed to nod. She was not unduly surprised to learn that Gwen Talbot, whose reputation for gossip was well known, had something to say on the subject of Bob's death – and the subsequent behaviour of his widow. Pat had always known it would only be a matter of time before the village gossips got to work. Nothing got past Gwen Talbot, and Pat was not entirely innocent. She felt a sudden flutter of panic. Perhaps something in her expression, her bearing, gave her away. She swept the thought aside. Hadn't she been through all this already, and decided that to keep on punishing herself over Bob's death was futile?

Pat took a sip of tea, touched at the sense of outrage Joyce so clearly felt on her behalf. 'It's kind of you to try to put her straight,' she offered. 'I'm only sorry you became involved. It must have been quite unpleasant.'

'Of course, she's always been somewhat . . . *outspoken*, shall we say,' Joyce went on. 'Quick to judge, not the sort to hold back. If she has an opinion on something, she doesn't mind letting the world know.' She sighed. 'And, of course, she was changed by the death of her own husband. It was a very sad business. I've always been aware of what you might call her shortcomings, and it's not as if we've ever been *friends*, as such, but to some extent her forthright manner is something I've held a grudging respect for in the past. It can be refreshing to know what a person really thinks. Something of a rarity, I find.'

Pat wondered if it would have surprised Joyce to know that she once considered her to be overbearing and snobbish. Joyce had always struck her as being so grand, with her elegant clothes and fancy hats. All those feathers! She never thought they had much in common (well, they didn't). And then the Spitfire destroyed their home and Joyce took them in. Pat was grateful, of course – they'd lost almost everything – but moving in with Joyce would never have been her choice.

Bob, however, was cock-a-hoop. Straight away, he could see the benefits; not only a means of living cheaply but in the presence of an adoring fan. The arrangement could not have suited him better. Truthfully, seeing Joyce constantly heap praise on Bob turned Pat's stomach. *Mr Simms, this, Mr Simms that!* Joyce had always been reminding her how fortunate she was to have such a wonderful husband when nothing could have been further from the truth.

The one saving grace about the months Pat spent under Joyce's roof had been that Bob was forced to control his vicious temper. It wouldn't have done for his landlady to see the man he really was, although once or twice he'd come close to revealing his true nature. What would Joyce think if Pat told her the truth, that Bob had struck her across the face one evening moments before Joyce arrived home? Bob had entirely pulled the wool over Joyce's eyes, led her to believe he was so much better than he really was. And the worst of it all was, Pat had helped him.

Joyce looked uncomfortable. 'I'm not sure how to put this,' she began, 'but Mrs Talbot seems to think you have benefited from your husband's death – financially, I mean. It was as if she called into question the manner of his death.'

'What happened was an accident,' Pat said.

'The most appalling tragedy, terribly hard on you.'

Pat concentrated on her now-empty teacup. *If only you knew.* 'The truth is, I'm doing the best I can. I'm on my own, I have to get on with things, make the best of life. Isn't that all any of us can do? For those of us fortunate enough to be alive, isn't it our duty? If there's one thing the war has taught us, it's that life is short, flimsy, easily taken away. We only have to think of the young lives lost to know as much.' Pat thought of the pilot in the cockpit of the crashed Spitfire, no more than a boy. She had been first on the scene and the face of the pilot remained vivid in her mind. 'We can make all the plans we want, but none of us knows what the future holds. It's *now* that counts.'

Joyce nodded. 'I know, my dear. You're quite right.'

'Bob has gone – that's the reality. I could spend the rest of my days wearing black and being miserable, hiding away, but it wouldn't change a thing . . . other than what Mrs Talbot thinks of me.'

They sat in silence for a moment.

'He did leave me quite well off, you know,' Pat said. 'It turns out his books were selling in quite significant numbers.' She frowned. She knew that Gwen Talbot had nursed her husband through a long illness. She'd brought up her children alone, and there was always a look about her that suggested struggle. It was unlikely she'd been left well off. 'Perhaps I should talk to Mrs Talbot,' Pat said, 'and see if I can clear the air.'

Chapter 21

'How did you get on today?' Alison asked.

John looked up from what he was doing, patiently chopping vegetables.

'I went all about, asked if there was any work going, said I didn't mind what I did. Seems there's nothing.' He was making stew and dumplings for tea. Not the kind of dumplings Alison was used to – John's were light with a hint of nutmeg. The kind of food he ate every day as a boy, mostly with soup. He had learned how to cook by watching his mother, a woman who could turn a few simple ingredients into a pan of hearty food, he said. He resumed chopping, finely dicing an onion.

'What about the butcher's?' Alison asked. 'Bryn's still resting up and Miriam's back serving in the shop. They must be short-handed.'

'I spoke to the son. David, is it?'

Alison nodded.

'Nice young man. Told me he'd like nothing better than another pair of hands doing all the lifting and carrying, but their money's tied up getting the shop next door ready for opening. They can't afford to take on someone new.'

Alison frowned. 'I was sure they'd have something for you, even for a week or two until Bryn's back on his feet.'

'They seem to be managing all right without taking on any help.'

'What about the pub?'

'Got all the staff they need.'

From the village, he told her, he'd gone to the Farrow farm and spoken to Stan, but it was a similar story to Brindsley and Son. Stan couldn't afford to pay another wage, he said, even though he could have used an extra pair of hands.

'Don't be put off,' Alison said, risking a hand on his arm.

He kept on chopping for a second or two before freeing himself from her touch to drop a carrot into Elsa's bowl.

'There are other farms,' Alison said. 'Someone might have something.'

He gave her a long look. 'I'm glad I came here. I couldn't be happier with our arrangement. You know that.'

Arrangement. A simple transaction, Alison thought. That's all it is to him.

'I sense a "*but*" coming.'

'*But*,' John said, with an attempt at a smile, 'there might not be any work.' He shrugged. 'We're in hard times, everyone's struggling.'

'I'll have a word with Frances, see if she can suggest something. And maybe Teresa can ask Nick – there might be work of some kind going at the base.'

He turned to face her and placed his hands on her shoulders. Their faces were inches apart, and Alison held her breath. *This is it.*

'You're a good woman, Alison Scotlock,' he said. 'The best there is.'

He gave her shoulders a squeeze, before letting go and turning back to the chopping board.

John wasn't happy keeping things from Alison, but it wouldn't help to tell her everything he'd been through that day. She'd have been upset, maybe even wondered whether inviting him into her home was the best thing for either of them. Perhaps coming to a small community, knowing his presence would at the very least cause raised eyebrows, was rash. A solitary black face in a quaint little village. He was used enough to comments and hostility, having to go out of his way to show he was no different to anyone else. Except, of course, he *was*, in a way that some people, for reasons he couldn't understand, would always find offensive. It pained him to think that simply by his presence he might in some way tarnish the good name of Alison, a woman with the best heart of anyone he knew.

At the Black Horse, he had known better than to go into the bar, and had instead waited in the yard at the back until someone appeared. Almost an hour passed, but he knew to be patient. Eventually, a stooped man with thinning red hair, a half-smoked roll-up hanging from his lips, came out, and John had tipped his hat and introduced himself. He was looking for work, he said. Any work. He'd done all manner of jobs on the docks in Liverpool and was strong, capable of heavy labour. Lifting barrels, anything. The man – the landlord, apparently – dropped the cigarette and crushed it with his heel before spitting on the ground.

'See, this is what you call a respectable establishment. Got my good name to think of. My *rep-u-tation*.' Spelling it out, as if for an imbecile. 'Can't say it'd go down well with my regulars if I took on a darkie.'

At the Farrow farm, Steph invited him in and made him tea, before directing him to a neighbour who kept livestock. Sheep, pigs. A bigger set-up, she said; he might just be hiring. 'Bit of a funny bugger, Jim Morton,' she told him, 'but you never know.'

John felt uneasy at the second place. The farmhouse looked unkempt. Greying nets at the windows, paint peeling off the frames. He hadn't even got as far as knocking at the door when a man in overalls – Jim Morton, he assumed – appeared from a barn with a shotgun in his hand and threatened to run him off his land. John tried to say that Steph Farrow had sent him, but before he could get the words out the gun was being pointed at him.

He should have told Alison. She needed to know, in case people started taking out their prejudice on her. When he got home, though, her work was spread out across the table and he hadn't wanted to distract her. Instead, he sank into an armchair, feet aching from all the walking, as Elsa climbed onto his lap. He'd watched as Alison did calculations and added to columns of neat figures, the nib of her pen scratchy on the stiff paper of the ledger. Sun streamed in through the open front door and from the garden came a burst of sweet-sounding birdsong. Alison would have been able to identify the bird. She knew those sorts of things.

He decided to say nothing about the shotgun, or what the stooped old man at the pub had said to him.

As he made a start on their meal, it occurred to him how simple life would be if they could exist like this within their own peaceful little world, not bother with anyone else. He loved Alison. In an ideal world, a different world, they would be together. Not his landlady, his wife. He had almost kissed her. He'd wanted to, felt sure it was what she wanted, too. It was there in her eyes, the bluest eyes he'd ever seen.

But then he thought of her being subjected to the same kind of abuse and intolerance he lived with every day, and it just didn't seem fair.

Other people.

They were always the problem.

Alison left him cooking and took Elsa out, stomping away into the woods, sending pigeons scattering into the air. She had almost run from the house, her heart thundering, her mind in turmoil. She took cover among the ancient oaks and leaned against a thick trunk, waiting for her breathing to return to normal.

She had been so certain. *This is it.* That look of his when he had faced her. The feel of his hands on her shoulders. He *was* about to kiss her, she could feel it. And then . . . nothing. Something had changed his mind. Or was she simply seeing what she wanted to see, imagining feelings that weren't there?

It was the first time he had touched her. Since moving into the house, he had seemed more determined than ever to maintain a respectful distance at all times, to keep things proper and businesslike between them. He never so much as brushed against her when they were cooking or eating. On one occasion when they'd reached down at the same time to make a fuss of Elsa, he had sprung back.

But just then, in the kitchen, she had felt as if she couldn't breathe. For the briefest of moments, she'd had the oddest sensation that were John to take his hands from her shoulders she would simply float away. Surely, he had been able to tell just by looking at her what she felt for him? George had always claimed to know what she was thinking. 'I can read you like a book,' he used to say. And yet he used to say, too, that no one could read minds and that it was wrong of her to expect him to know what was inside her head. 'Tell me,' he'd say. 'Otherwise, how the devil am I supposed to know?' Perhaps John was the same. Was she being unfair, expecting him to gauge her feelings and act on them without her having said a word? Or, was he trying to let her know as gently as he could that he was not interested?

She kicked at the dry earth in frustration as Elsa snuffled about the clearing, following a trail that took her to the base of an enormous ash.

Perhaps he was waiting for her to make a move, to give him permission to take things further. Wasn't that what Teresa had said, that a man like John would be wary of overstepping the mark? She had invited him to move into her home as a paying guest, and made it clear from the start that this was to be a formal arrangement. He would never compromise her in any way or risk appearing to take advantage. If she was serious about him, if she really loved him, she was going to have to tell him.

She would have to find the courage to lay her feelings bare.

After dinner, they sat for a while with the wireless on low in the background, Alison busy unpicking a cardigan she hadn't worn for a while, working out how she could fashion it into something for Teresa's baby. John had offered to help, and had sat next to her while she looped yarn around his hands, creating a loose skein.

'I hope you're not sorry you decided to swap the big city for a quiet spot like this,' Alison said at last, breaking the silence.

John looked surprised. 'Not a bit. The city's not what it was. It's enough to break your heart the way it's been torn to pieces. I sometimes wonder if it's ever going to get back on its feet after what it's gone through.'

Alison nodded. 'All we can do is trust that things will recover, once the war is over. People are capable of great resilience. At least the bombing seems to have eased off.'

'It hasn't stopped, though, not yet. Some nights the Luftwaffe come over wanting to cause more destruction.'

Alison nodded and took the wool from him, tucking it into the wicker basket at her feet. She began unravelling a sleeve. 'As long as you have no regrets about leaving.'

'Why would I?'

'Coming to a village . . . spending your evenings winding wool.' She smiled at him. 'Hardly the most thrilling of pursuits.'

He chuckled. 'I'd say I've had just about enough excitement to last me a lifetime. There's a lot to be said for peace and quiet. Plenty folk would give their right hand to be able to move away. I count myself lucky to have a lovely home with good company. All thanks to you.'

They sat in silence for a while, Alison trying to keep her breathing in check, to muster up the courage to say what she wished to say.

John held up his hands. 'Do you want to carry on?'

Alison bit her lip. No, she did not want to carry on. What she wanted, more than anything, was to talk to him – to properly talk – to take his hands in hers and say what was really on her mind, to make a fool of herself, if need be. After all, what was the worst that could happen? John might say he didn't feel the same way, might apologise, even though his behaviour had been impeccable.

At least then she would know. At least she could stop tormenting herself.

She looked at the cardigan in her lap. *Talk to him.* But she only said, 'I'll leave it at that for now.'

'I think I might turn in.' John smiled. 'I'm tired after all that walking today. Must be the country air. Can I make you a drink before I go up?'

Tell him. She shook her head. 'No, I'm fine, thank you.'

She lay on her back in bed, hands folded across her middle, like the stone figure whose tomb lay inside St Mark's. Sleep would not come. Her mind was too busy, thoughts flying about, refusing to settle. A whiny voice she didn't recognise (her own? she wondered) demanded to know why she had such trouble speaking her mind.

She rolled onto her side and pulled the bedclothes over her head, but the voice showed no sign of quietening. She had missed an opportunity earlier. She knew exactly what she wanted to say, and yet when the moment came she had lost her nerve. She would never have believed she was capable of such cowardice. It wasn't as if she had to make a speech. All she had to say was that she had fallen in love with him. A few words, sufficient to express all that was in her heart.

She flung back the covers, and pulled herself out of bed. The house was silent, and Elsa would be sleeping under the sideboard as usual. She went softly to the window, glancing out into the night. A tawny owl was calling. Almost at once its mate answered.

Since she couldn't sleep, perhaps she should go downstairs and make a drink. She could open up a book, or unravel some more of that blasted cardigan. She went out onto the landing and stepped around the floorboard that creaked.

Then, at the top of the staircase, she hesitated, one hand on the banister. From downstairs came the sound of the clock ticking in the hall, and her eyes fell on the door of John's bedroom.

I'm not young, thought Alison, *but nor am I old. I still have time enough to do something more with my life. Provided I find the courage to act.*

She drew in a deep breath and made her way slowly along the landing. She paused outside the room, her breath caught, her heart hammering. Then she eased open the door.

John was lying there, sleepless as her, propped up against his pillows in the dark. When he saw her, his eyes widened.

'Alison?'

She said nothing, but she crossed the room, climbed into the bed, and pressed herself into his body, burying her face in his neck.

He wrapped his arms around her. 'Do you know how much I've wanted you to come to me?' he whispered. 'I prayed you would, every night.' He turned towards her, and his lips brushed hers. 'Alison, I've loved you for the longest time . . . I just needed to be sure you felt the same, that this was what you wanted.'

'I didn't know if you wanted anything more. I thought you might be content with the friendship we have,' she whispered. 'And I was too scared to say anything, thinking if I did and I'd got it wrong, I might just spoil everything.'

'Nothing's spoiled, it never could be between us.' He stroked her hair. 'As long as you're sure.'

She held onto him, feeling the beat of his heart, tears running down her face. She was utterly certain. None of the doubt that had once tormented her remained. 'It's what I want.' Her voice was a whisper. 'More than anything.'

Chapter 22

STEPH FARROW CALLED IN at Brindsley and Son to see how Bryn was doing.

'He's at home, taking things easy, like the doctor told him he had to,' Miriam said. 'Although, if you listen to Bryn, he's had nothing more than a "funny turn" and has no idea why he's having to spend so long resting up.'

Steph nodded. 'I think I know how he feels. I was the same after my heart attack, wanting to take on all my usual jobs around the farm. Being told I could barely lift a finger took some getting used to.'

'But you did get used to it?'

'It's taken a while. I felt bad at first, leaving everything to Stan and Little Stan, but between them they've got things running well. To be honest, it's been good for Little Stan having to take on more responsibility. And it's not as if I'm not busy. I seem to find plenty to do to keep me occupied.'

Miriam digested this. 'Why don't you pop round and have a word? See if you can talk some sense into him.'

Steph found Bryn in the garden. She could hear him as she rounded the corner. It was a warm September day, the yellowing leaves on the maple tree the only sign that summer was at an end.

'I reckon just a touch more onion and a pinch of sage makes them that bit tastier,' Bryn said. 'I grant you, it's not a huge change, but you do notice the difference. What do you think?'

Steph unlatched the gate, expecting to find Bryn in discussion with David. But there was no sign of David, just Vivian on her father's knee.

Bryn smiled, pleased to see her. 'Morning. I was just telling this one what we might do to improve our sausage recipe.'

Steph smiled. 'And what does she think?'

'Oh, she always agrees with her dad,' Bryn said, as Vivian beamed up at him. 'It's David I have to convince. He's all for change when it comes to certain areas of the business, but for some reason he seems to have dug his heels in over the Brindsley banger. We should stick with the tried-and-tested recipe, he reckons.'

'You could always keep the original and try something new alongside it, see how it goes.'

Bryn nodded. 'I'll suggest that.'

Steph sat down on the bench beside him. 'How are you?'

He sighed, exasperated. 'I'm fine – there's nothing wrong with me. I should be back at work by now, not sitting about in the sun.'

'I remember feeling like that after the business with my heart,' she said. 'But then I decided the doctors might just know what they were talking about, so I did as I was told.'

Bryn looked thoughtful. 'It's not easy, though, is it? Not when you're used to being busy and working hard. It's not in my nature to sit about doing nothing.'

'You're not doing nothing. You're spending time with your daughter ... and dreaming up ways of making a world-beating sausage.'

Bryn laughed. 'That's one way of looking at it.' He glanced at her. 'Have you found it tricky, you know, giving up the farm work?'

'At first I wondered what on earth I was going to do with myself, but I suppose I've learned to look at things differently. I've come to see how important it is to look after myself, for one thing, to make the most of having time on my hands.' She smiled. 'I certainly do a lot more baking now than I ever did.'

Bryn looked nonplussed. 'Baking,' he said. 'I'm not so sure about that.'

'I could always give you my recipe for carrot cake. After a bit of trial and error and a couple of disasters, I've got it just right. It's Stan's favourite. Imagine Miriam's reaction, coming in from the shop to find a cake cooling in the kitchen.'

'I wouldn't know where to start.'

'It's easy.'

'And I'm hoping to be back at work soon.'

Miriam might have something to say about that, Steph thought. She got to her feet. 'Right, I'd better be getting back or they'll want to know where their tea is.'

'I'll put Vivian in the pram and walk a little way with you,' Bryn said. 'That's one thing I can do, a bit of light exercise.'

They walked as far as the canal. Up ahead someone was on the bridge, hurling stones into the water. Steph frowned. 'What's he up to?' The swans and their cygnets glided out from under the bridge and a stone landed beside them, sending up a splash. Steph called out, 'Hey, what are you doing?'

Bryn immediately backed her up. 'That's enough of that.'

The figure glanced over at them. He was tall and strong-looking, a bit older than Little Stan, Steph thought. Nothing in his manner suggested he was in the least bit troubled by their admonishments. He had another stone in his hand, which he casually tossed into the air.

'Look, lad, you can see those birds have got their young,' Bryn said, adopting a conciliatory tone. 'So why not leave them in peace, eh?'

He didn't answer at first, eventually muttering something under his breath before turning to fling the stone in the opposite direction to the birds. Then he stomped off along the towpath.

Steph stared after him. 'Who was that?'

'Gwen Talbot's boy,' Bryn said. 'Ronald. I think we have to make allowances. The lad's a bit of a lost soul, from what I've heard.'

Chapter 23

To Teresa's amusement, Nick insisted on walking her to the WI meeting.

'There's no need,' she said, as she buttoned up her coat. 'It's not as if I can't manage to cover a few yards on my own.'

'I don't doubt it for a moment. You're one of the most capable women I know.' He caught hold of her and grinned. 'I simply want the pleasure of having my beautiful wife on my arm.'

Teresa smiled and kissed him. 'In that case, I'd be delighted to have the company of my dashing wing commander husband, even on such a brief outing.'

'Am I forgiven for agreeing to have dinner with Michael Buey and his dreadful wife before Christmas?'

Teresa made a face. 'I don't suppose it's easy to say no to an invitation from your group captain.'

'Not good form, I'm afraid.'

'I don't mind,' Teresa said. 'Or rather I *do* – but I'm willing to put up with it for you.'

Nick smiled. 'Thank you, darling. And in return I'll make a start on the spare room. Get it ready for the baby.'

'There's no rush. It's only September, we've got ages yet.' Another three months to go.

'I don't want to leave things to the last minute.'

Teresa looked serious for a moment. 'Do you ever wonder what it's going to be like, having a child, being parents?'

He laughed. 'All the time. It's almost all I think about.'

'You don't worry about . . .' She hesitated.

He frowned. 'What?'

'Well, knowing what to do. Getting it wrong.' She gave a small shrug. 'I sometimes panic about being the most hopeless mother, not having the first idea how to hold my baby, let alone change its nappy or bathe it . . .'

'We're beginners, my darling, but we're bright enough to work things out – *together*,' Nick told her. 'We just need to have a bit of faith. What's important is we've got each other. We'll muddle through somehow.'

'I hope so.'

'I *know* so.' He gave her a squeeze. 'And don't forget, there'll be no shortage of helpful advice available from your WI friends. There are plenty of experienced ladies there. Mrs Talbot, for instance.'

Teresa's eyes widened. '*Gwen?*'

He grinned. 'Erica, then. Miriam. Steph. I've no doubt everyone will rally round when the time comes – *if* we get stuck, which we won't, because I've every confidence we're both more than capable of getting the hang of looking after our own baby.' He pulled her close. 'Please, darling, trust me on this and stop worrying. I'll be here for you every step of the way, I promise.'

Teresa found a seat next to Alison near the back of the hall.

'Good turn-out,' Alison said. 'How are you feeling?'

'I'm fine, really well. Nick's being sweet, spoiling me. He even made our meal this evening – warmed up the soup I'd made earlier, at any rate.'

Alison laughed.

'And he insisted on walking me to the meeting.'

'The perfect husband, I'd say.'

Teresa smiled. 'I'm lucky to have him.'

'And he's lucky to have you.'

Teresa eased her coat off and folded it over her lap. 'How's it working out having John there?' she asked. 'Are the two of you getting along all right?'

Alison felt the colour rise in her cheeks. 'He's good company, easy to have around. A good cook as well, it turns out.'

'What about the other matter we discussed?'

'I decided to take your advice and be rather more . . . *forthright*,' Alison said.

'And?' Teresa persisted.

'It did the trick.' She lowered her voice. 'Since then, things have *moved on*.'

Teresa was smiling broadly. 'I'm *so* pleased to hear it – absolutely thrilled for both of you. You deserve to be happy.'

The rows of seats nearest the front were starting to fill up. Alison glanced at the women arriving, some deep in conversation. 'I wouldn't want it to be widely known,' she told Teresa quietly. 'Can you imagine what people would say? A respectable woman living in sin – and with a black man at that. It could hardly be worse.'

'It's no one else's business. Not that you have any reason to keep it hidden. Why should you? It's not as if you're doing anything wrong.'

'I'd still prefer to keep matters private, at least for now. People can be quite narrow-minded, as we both know. I sometimes think that the less people know, the better it is for all concerned – fewer opportunities to speculate and pass judgement.' She glanced at Teresa. 'You know only too well what I'm talking about.'

Teresa nodded slowly. She tried not to think about it now, but she had been driven from her teaching job in Liverpool when her affair with another woman came to light. Alison – and Annie – were the only people who knew this; she would never, could never, tell Nick.

Alison hesitated. 'I'm only sorry I failed to show more understanding of your . . . situation, at the time.'

'It doesn't matter now,' Teresa said. 'I put you in a difficult position, which wasn't fair. Scandal is never pleasant for anyone involved.'

'But easier to manage differences in a city, perhaps, where there's less chance of sticking out like a sore thumb. The problem with a village like ours is that anything out of the ordinary is bound to draw comment.' Alison sighed. 'I sometimes think John doesn't stand a chance.'

'Believe me, there are prejudices enough in cities,' Teresa said. 'People just need to get used to seeing John about the place.'

They fell silent as the seats around them were taken.

At the front of the hall, Frances got to her feet and the chatter in the hall died down as everyone stood for the usual uplifting rendition of 'Jerusalem'.

'Thank you so much for coming, ladies,' Frances began, as they once more took their seats. 'I must say, it's wonderful to see such a good turn-out, which I expect is as much to do with the popularity of our new sewing initiative as anything.' She aimed a smile at Pat. 'Do please keep supporting the "Stitch in Time" classes, where all manner of skills, from darning to dressmaking are on offer, and together we will beat the clothes coupon!'

Alison caught Sarah's eye and exchanged a knowing smile. Both knew that, despite her enthusiasm for the sewing project, Frances had so far declined to participate in the classes, opting instead to hover on the periphery of the various groups, offering encouragement to others.

'May I gently remind you all that we're still looking for donations for our "Fashion on the Ration" extravaganza,'

Frances went on. 'If any of you have any unwanted garments in good condition, please do consider letting us have them. Somebody will no doubt be able to make good use of them. Shoes, especially for children, are most welcome. Already, we have a most impressive collection of clothing, some of which looks to have barely been worn. For those of you who haven't yet gone through your wardrobes and removed the things you no longer want, can I recommend you do so? There's nothing quite like a good clear-out – it can be most exhilarating.' She turned to Pat. 'Was there anything else you wanted me to mention?'

Pat shook her head.

Steph Farrow, sitting at the front of the hall directly in front of Frances, rose to speak. 'There's something I wanted to mention, if it's all right.'

Frances nodded. 'Steph is our darning expert,' she explained, with a smile.

'It's not about the sewing,' Steph said, turning to face the women seated behind her. 'There's been some trouble on the next farm to ours. Jim Morton went to check on his animals the other morning and found some of his sheep dead. Their throats were cut.'

Several of the women gasped.

'Someone had been on his land and slaughtered his livestock for no reason whatsoever,' Steph went on. 'They have killed them for the sake of it – and not even cleanly, he says. They must have suffered greatly. He's had animals taken for food before, but this was different.'

Frances was first to speak. 'What have the police said? Some kind of vendetta?'

Steph shrugged her shoulders. 'We have no idea. We've said we'll keep an eye out, let him know if we see anything suspicious, if we spot any strangers on the land, that kind of thing. If we could all be vigilant, it might be a help.'

'Of course,' Frances said.

A voice came from the middle of the room. 'It was only a matter of time before something happened,' said Martha Dawson, a stout individual, with a solid helmet of grey hair. Her husband was landlord at the Black Horse. 'We had a darkie hanging round the pub the other day, one of them trekkers. Thought we'd seen the back of them. My husband had to chase him.' She looked round, indignant. 'Turns out he's living right here. In the village.'

'No one's accusing anybody,' Steph said.

Mrs Dawson pointed at Alison. 'She's only taken him in.'

Teresa placed a hand on Alison's arm.

'I'd seen a coloured hanging round the village. I didn't know he was *living* here.' The woman sitting next to Mrs Dawson sounded disgusted.

'It so happens the gentleman you're referring to is the one who found my son, Noah, after he ran away from school,' Frances said, seeking to calm the atmosphere. 'John Smith as good as saved his life, in fact. If you ask me, we need more people like him in our midst.'

Mrs Dawson snorted. 'It's no coincidence we've got someone butchering animals now there's a darkie living here. They think nothing of it where they come from.'

'Mrs Dawson!' Frances was incandescent. 'Allow me to remind you that we in the WI take pride in conducting ourselves in a civilised manner. We do *not* go about accusing people without evidence.'

'There's nothing *civilised* about the coloureds. Bunch of savages, the lot of them.'

Frances glared at her. 'Really, Mrs Dawson!'

Sarah was on her feet before anyone else had a chance to speak. 'Ladies, I understand emotions are running high. Not a single one of us wants to think that someone in our community is capable of killing livestock. But it does not help to go about making accusations, casting blame on someone whose skin colour is different to ours. I suggest we all remain calm and keep an open mind – be alert, as Mrs Farrow suggests, and leave it to the police to get to the bottom of things based on evidence rather than prejudice.'

'Absolutely,' Frances said.

Mrs Dawson turned to look at Alison. 'Maybe someone needs to tell the police that the first place they need to start looking is Mrs Scotlock's house.'

Several of the women were muttering, sending uneasy looks in Alison's direction. She felt her heart pounding as she stood up. 'Before everyone gets too carried away,' she said, trying to keep her voice calm, 'we don't know who's responsible for this spate of killings, but what I *can* tell you is that it was *not* my lodger.' She held Mrs Dawson's gaze. 'Only the most ignorant among us would assume a person to be guilty of a crime because of the colour of their skin.'

'I'm telling you, they're not like us,' Mrs Dawson retorted.

'*Us?*' Teresa leapt up, incensed. 'And what are *we* like? Intolerant? Small-minded? The kind of people to turn on someone because they *look* different? If that's the case, I want nothing to do with this.' She caught hold of Alison's elbow. 'Come on, let's go.'

Sarah caught up with them outside. 'Alison, wait, I'm so sorry. You know how Martha Dawson can be – she had no right to say those things.'

'She won't be the only one pointing the finger at John.' Alison was shaken. 'He's been all over the village trying to find work. I knew he'd asked at the pub but he didn't say a word about the landlord giving him short shrift. He tried some of the farms as well, probably got the same reception.' She shook her head solemnly. 'I don't know why I'm surprised.'

'It's only a handful of people who'll think like that,' Sarah said.

'Is it, though?' Teresa was shaking her head. 'It's not so long ago we had people coming into the village to escape the bombs being dropped on their homes, families from Liverpool, *my* hometown, looking for refuge, and I seem to remember there was no shortage of people ready to see them turned away – *especially* the ones with black skin.'

'We're living in strange times,' Sarah said, 'which only serves to fuel the kind of fear that would otherwise be seen as irrational. A few will always react badly to anything they think might threaten the status quo. An outsider in their midst – any outsider – makes them mistrustful. Once they get used to John being here, I'm sure things will change.'

'I wish I had your faith,' Alison said, 'but I have a feeling things will only get worse. You saw how the atmosphere changed in there, the way people were looking at me. They want a scapegoat, and who better than John? I'm afraid that until they find out who's really killing those sheep, he'll be blamed.' She was quiet a moment. 'It's my fault for asking him to come here. I should have guessed there'd be trouble – not that I ever imagined anything as bad as this. If they don't catch whoever's doing this soon, I can see things turning very ugly.'

In her heart, Alison had known there would be opposition to John living in the village. She had hoped it would only be a very few, however, and that in time, as Sarah suggested, he would be accepted. It had happened with the trekkers. Despite initial hostility, once the soup kitchen was up and running and accommodation was provided in the village hall, things settled down. She wondered now if it had been naïve of her, but she had assumed that having the trekkers in the village had led to a softening of attitudes, and that even those most vocal in their objections would now incline to a more open-minded approach. Surely, they had all grown used to seeing black faces and understood there was more to someone than the colour of their skin.

Well, perhaps not.

Teresa exchanged a worried look with Sarah.

'You did a good thing offering John a home,' Teresa said. 'The *right* thing. If it weren't for you, he'd be stuck in some grim hostel in a city that's been bombed to bits.'

'I *hoped* I was helping,' Alison said. 'I'm not so sure now.'

'We're all on your side,' Sarah told her. 'On *John's* side. Whoever's killing those sheep, it's not him, and we'll make sure everyone knows.'

Chapter 24

AFTER BREAKFAST, PAT SPENT an hour at the kitchen table, writing. Her letter to Marek now extended to dozens of pages. She wondered if she would ever finish it, this letter she would never send. When she began to write, she hadn't realised she would be unable to stop, that something would compel her to carry on. The more she wrote, the more it seemed as if the letter took on a life of its own, until it stopped being a letter and became something else. Something more. An expression of faith, perhaps – a means of giving voice to the hope she held onto that Marek, although absent, was not lost to her. Her words a sign that the connection between them was unbroken. The simple act of writing enough to keep their love alive. Everything she felt for him, she committed to paper. She had poured out every memory, no matter how small: a frayed collar, a snatched moment, flowers she had not been able to throw away that were now carefully pressed between the pages of a book. She would not allow him to become a ghost, a memory that gradually faded. *You see, I have not given up, my love. You are in my heart, always.*

He was real. As long as she kept on filling up blank sheets of paper with words, she could believe that Marek was still part of her life. Out there, somewhere.

At eleven on the dot she stopped, cleared away the papers and got ready to go into the village.

She had decided to pay Gwen Talbot a visit. It was time they had a chat.

Gwen came to the door clutching a tea towel and was unable to conceal her surprise at finding Pat facing her.

'I hope I've not picked a bad moment,' Pat said, with a smile. 'I've been meaning to have a word.' When Gwen didn't answer, Pat went on, 'A bit of WI business. I could do with another pair of hands. Of course, if you're in the middle of something I can come back later.'

Reluctantly, Gwen invited her in.

'I'd hoped to catch you after last week's WI meeting, but it was all a bit chaotic in the end and I didn't get a chance.'

Frances had managed to restore order, but even as the women were leaving the hall Martha Dawson could be heard complaining about the sheep killings, muttering loudly about 'savages' coming into the village.

Gwen nodded. 'Awful business what's happening on the Morton farm. I hear there was another animal killed, the night before last. Its throat was cut, same as the others, left to bleed to death.'

Pat shook her head. 'It makes no sense. Why would anyone do such a thing?'

'Plenty of folk think it's the black fella living at Mrs Scotlock's place.'

Pat frowned. 'John's an obvious target, a stranger who's never going to blend in no matter what. It's the easiest thing in the world to pick on someone because they don't look like us.' She gazed at Gwen. 'It's tempting, don't you find, to make all kinds of assumptions based on what we *think* we know when the truth is we're *guessing* most of the time? It's easy to allow our own prejudices to seep in and lead us to entirely the wrong conclusions.'

Gwen was watching her closely. 'I've always considered myself a good judge of character,' she said. 'And you can't deny the coloureds are different.'

'Are they, though? Have you actually spoken to Mr Smith – I mean, a proper conversation?'

Gwen didn't answer. She pursed her lips.

'I happen to think the only way to get to know a person and make an *informed* judgement about who they are is by sitting down and talking to them.' Pat smiled. 'A bit like we are now.'

Gwen looked away. 'Someone's killing those sheep, and you can't tell me it's one of the villagers.'

'I suppose we'll find out soon enough.'

Neither one spoke for a moment.

'I can be as guilty as the next person when it comes to making snap judgements,' Pat said. 'I make an effort not to, but sometimes without even thinking I've made up my mind about someone with almost nothing to go on beyond the clothes they're wearing or their accent. I can't tell you how many times I've been proved wrong. Mrs Cameron, for instance.'

Gwen looked surprised.

'I don't mind admitting I used to consider her snobbish. And then she took us in after we lost our home and I discovered there's so much more to her . . . generosity, a good heart. She's a surprisingly good listener, too, as I've discovered since Bob passed away.'

Gwen waited a moment. 'It must have been a shock, losing him the way you did,' she ventured. 'So suddenly.'

'I've always considered any loss, regardless of the circumstances, to be shocking.'

Gwen Talbot had nursed her husband through a long illness and seen the life fade from him, watched helplessly as the man she loved slipped away. She had been warned he would not get better, and yet she had never stopped hoping he might, that something no one had thought to consider might save him, that a miracle might happen. Having time to come to terms with what she was told was the inevitable outcome of his illness had not made things any easier for her. It had been no less shocking, no less dreadful.

When he took his final breath, without fuss, in his sleep, with Gwen at his side, the pain was unexpected, acute. It was as if she had been struck a physical blow. In the end, having notice of what lay ahead had been of no comfort. She was still plunged into a state of shock. Perhaps *knowing* wasn't the same as *accepting*. You could know a thing and not quite believe it, she thought. Even now, she had the peculiar sense of being pulled up short at the realisation that he was no longer there. Time was a great healer, they said, and yet some of the pain refused to go away. She glanced at Pat. It was not something she spoke about. Who else would understand?

'Do you ever wonder what other people think of you?' Pat asked.

Gwen seemed taken aback. 'I'm not sure I . . .'

'I do. I find it's impossible to know if the face you think you're presenting to the world is the one other people actually see. Do you know what I mean?'

Gwen looked perplexed. 'I'm not sure I do, no.'

'One day I was in the cemetery and someone – Joyce, I suspect – had put a few flowers on Bob's grave. They were larkspur, purple. They were lovely, although on their last legs when I saw them.' She smiled. 'Bob *hated* cut flowers. He wouldn't have them in the house – said he couldn't stand the sight of them slowly dying, rotting away. He always said it was the smell of decay. I happen to think flowers cheer the place up, but he found them depressing. He was always very particular – about that, about everything. It's why I would never put flowers on his grave.' She looked up at Gwen. 'I can't quite bring myself to say anything to Joyce.'

Gwen looked away, awkward. It had never occurred to her that Pat might have her reasons for leaving the grave bare. 'I admit I did wonder. I'm there every week with flowers for Alan. He loved roses. He planted the ones in the front.' There were glorious scented blooms filling the border, and a showy crimson climber next to the front door. They had lived, when he had not.

It was beginning to dawn on Gwen that she might have misjudged Pat. That business about the grave – she would never have guessed. Perhaps she should have a quiet word with Joyce Cameron, and put her in the picture.

'Bob never really had a chance to enjoy the success his writing brought,' Pat went on. 'He was only just starting to do well before the . . . accident.' She hesitated. 'Life can be cruel sometimes. Afterwards, I was left questioning what really matters – how we can be robbed of the things we take for granted without warning. It made me want to appreciate what I have – my friends, this village. It made me want to make the most of each day, and not to waste a moment.' She glanced at Gwen. 'Time is so precious. A gift from God, if you like. Those of us who are here have a duty to savour it. Don't you agree?'

Gwen had no option but to nod. When Alan first became ill, it was something they'd spoken about: time being short, making the most of things. And they had, for as long as they could. They'd gone on long walks, made time to gaze at the stars on clear nights. They'd talked, too, about everything. He wanted her to live her life to the full, he said, and she promised she would, wondering as she did how on earth she ever could if he wasn't there.

She had never quite managed to.

Someone was moving about upstairs, and Gwen glanced at the ceiling. 'My son, Ronald,' she said. 'Since he came home, he's been sleeping a lot, keeping odd hours.' Footsteps thundered across the landing, and Gwen stood up. 'I'll just see if he wants something to eat.'

'Of course.'

Pat went to the window and gazed into the garden while Gwen was upstairs. She looked out at the tea roses planted by Gwen's husband, then back around the room. According to the clock in the corner it was almost midday.

From upstairs came the sound of voices. Pat could make out only some of what was being said – Gwen offering to cook something or make a sandwich, whatever he wanted. Pat had not met Gwen's son, and was not even sure what was wrong with him. There must have been something serious for him to have been discharged. She heard a voice raised in anger – Ronald, saying something to his mother that Pat didn't catch. The tone he used was reminiscent of Bob, and Pat felt a prickle of concern at the back of her neck. Gwen was silent, Ronald doing all the talking now, using the same accusing tone Pat had become accustomed to.

Memories flooded back. A plate of food flying from the table. Crockery hurled against the wall. Bob's hand raised against her.

She should go and see what was happening.

But what if that only made things worse? For a moment she wrestled with her conscience, not knowing what to do for the best. Then footsteps crossed the hall and the back door banged shut.

Gwen appeared looking dazed, defeated. Pat wondered if her son was hitting her, and didn't dare ask.

'He's fed up,' Gwen explained, 'that's the problem. It's hard for him, stuck at home with only me for company. Poor lad needs something to do to take his mind off things.'

Pat struggled to think of what to say. 'Can he help you in the garden? A bit of weeding, maybe – or he could take charge of the vegetable plot. Not that it looks as if it needs much work – you've got everything neat. What about the hens?' She was gabbling, she knew, thinking about Bob. Hoping she was wrong about Ronald.

'It's hard to know what to do for the best.'

'His injuries . . . are they very bad?' Pat asked.

Gwen didn't answer at first. In the corner of the room, the clock began to chime. Twelve o'clock.

'The army sends lads home, some of them in a bad way, and expects the family to get on with it,' Gwen said. 'And I would if I knew what to do. I'd do anything for my boy. I don't know how to help him, that's the problem.'

'If there's anything I can do . . .' Pat began.

Gwen was quiet. The clock finished chiming. 'I seem to remember you came here wanting my help with something and, somehow, I've managed to turn the tables,' she said.

'It wasn't important.'

'Ask me, anyway. Take my mind off things.'

'"Fashion on the Ration",' Pat said. 'I could do with a hand. I still need to sort through all the clothing that's been donated and there's rather a lot. I'm beginning to wonder if I've taken on more than I can manage.'

Gwen frowned. 'I'm not sure why you think I can be of assistance. I know nothing about clothes.'

'It's not that side of things I'm concerned about,' Pat admitted. 'It's more organisational skills I'm after, and I remembered you've always done a good job with the annual flower show. You know how to bring order to chaos.' She gave her a pleading look. 'Even if you could spare a few hours, I'd be grateful. It would be a weight off my mind.'

Gwen thought for a moment, and then her face was lit by a slight smile. 'I'll see what I can do.'

On the way home, Pat bumped into Erica outside Brindsley's. 'You've heard there's been more trouble at the Morton farm?' Erica said. 'Dreadful business. It's the talk of the village.'

'I can well imagine,' Pat said. 'And I can guess who's getting the blame.'

'Sarah went to see Alison this morning to let her know that she and John have the support of the WI.'

'With the exception of Mrs Dawson and her crowd.' Pat wondered if anything she'd said earlier had given Gwen Talbot pause for thought.

'Frances is talking of suspending Mrs Dawson's membership, apparently.'

Pat was surprised. 'Can she do that?'

'Frances seems to think so. She's furious about what happened at the meeting, the unseemly language that was used. The constitution is clear about promoting ideals of tolerance and justice, she says, both of which were in short supply the other evening.'

'I can't imagine how Alison must be feeling.'

'It's awful. She told Sarah she feels responsible for asking John to come here in the first place.'

'It's all too easy for people to make him the scapegoat. I was just saying as much to Gwen Talbot.'

It was Erica's turn to look surprised. 'Gwen Talbot? I didn't know the two of you were friends.'

Pat gave a wry smile. 'Perhaps not friends, exactly. I've asked her to help out with "Fashion on the Ration".'

'I could give you a hand with that.'

'Thank you. The time will come when I'll be asking everyone to pitch in. We've had so many donations, I can't even begin to start sorting them on my own. I just felt . . . I wanted to make an effort with her.'

'Actually, she can be a lot nicer than you might think,' Erica said. 'When Will was unwell she arrived on the doorstep one night with a pie she'd made for us. To say it was unexpected would be an understatement. Will was good to her when her husband was ill, she said, and she wanted to do something for us in return.'

Pat nodded. 'I have my suspicions that beneath her rather stern exterior beats a good heart – she just doesn't want anyone to know.'

Chapter 25

DAVID WAS WALKING JENNY home, a journey they did their best to eke out in order to put off the moment when they would have to say goodnight and go their separate ways. Earlier, she had put on a white coat and helped Miriam haul a pig off a hook in the cold store and onto the block, where David had butchered it. There was something touching about the sight of Jenny in one of his father's white coats, the sleeves turned back, the hem almost skimming her ankles. To know that she was doing this for him was enough to melt his heart.

The more he got to know her, the more he came to realise she was not the girl he'd always thought her to be – that beneath the glossy veneer, she was kind and strong and capable of working hard without complaint.

He had, he realised, underestimated her.

Most nights after helping in the shop she stayed for something to eat, at Miriam's insistence. David knew how fond of Jenny his mother was; it was made plain by the way she fussed over her and paid her compliments, quizzing her about her skin and how she kept it looking so lovely. Jenny's 'secret' turned out to be Pond's Cold Cream, a layer to remove the day's 'muck and make-up' and another slathered on and left to sink in overnight. 'Flawless,' Miriam had said, impressed, making Jenny preen with pleasure. And how did she get her eyebrows so dark and dramatic-looking? Miriam wondered. Boot polish, it turned out. Bryn, the kind of man David would have expected to roll his eyes in amusement at such trivial matters, somehow managed to appear interested.

The truth was they were all slightly intoxicated by her, David most of all.

Bryn was back working in the shop, doing a few hours behind the counter on their busy days, which was as much as Miriam was prepared to sanction. The rest of the time, he seemed content looking after Vivian. His collapse had forced him to rethink his life and adopt a slower pace. David knew that his father had struggled with his new everyday life at first, but he was growing more accustomed to letting others do the work for him, and with Jenny helping out, they were getting by. He knew, too, that Bryn loved the extra time he got with Vivian. Occasionally, David would hear him discussing with Vivian what the plans were for the day ahead: 'You're stuck with me again today, sweet pea.' 'That clematis wants tidying up, but we'll not take the secateurs to it just yet, though, while it still has flowers. We want it to come back again next year, don't we?' 'Let me bring that washing in off the line, then we'll have a story.' On one occasion David overheard him telling Vivian a version of *Goldilocks*, in which the porridge belonging to the three bears had mysteriously been transformed into 'best pork chops'.

David and Jenny made their way across the village green, hand in hand. The moon seemed unusually bright tonight, giving the village a silvery cast. It was getting colder, and they both had jackets on, a sign that autumn had arrived. The tower of St Mark's loomed in front of them, bathed in light.

'You know, my house is the other way,' Jenny said, giving his hand a squeeze.

David kissed the top of her head. 'It's such a lovely night, I thought we'd have a stroll first. And I wanted you to myself a bit longer, if that's all right.'

Another squeeze. 'All right by me.'

They walked as far as the churchyard, everything lit up, the inscriptions on one or two of the headstones almost clear enough to read.

'We'd never have managed these last few weeks without you,' David said, turning to face Jenny. 'You're amazing.'

'I know,' she said, smiling.

'And not in the least bit big-headed about it . . .'

She laughed. 'You can't be annoyed if I'm agreeing with you.'

He looked serious all of a sudden. 'You'd say, wouldn't you, if you were getting fed up? I wouldn't blame you. I know it's not much fun working in a butcher's.'

He knew very well that she could be doing something more interesting with her time – going out with one of the pilots from Tabley Wood, for instance. He wasn't naïve enough to think she didn't get offers.

'Do you think I'd show up at your place night after night if I didn't want to?' Jenny said. 'Trust me, no one makes me do anything I don't want to do. I thought you knew me well enough by now to know that.'

'When you put it like that . . .'

'And I like being around your mum and dad. They're nice people.'

'They love you.'

She looked at him intently. 'And what about you? Do you love me?'

David blinked. In his wildest dreams he would not have expected a girl like Jenny to be interested in him, a girl so sure of herself, so perfect in every way. Not when he was . . . what? Damaged. *Im*perfect. She knew what he'd been through, the ship going down, that the injuries he was left with were severe enough for him to be sent home. She understood he could no longer do his job, not the way he had in the past, which was why they had to rely on her help in the shop. He had avoided going into detail when it came to the nature of his injuries, saying something vague about his back not being what it was. She didn't – couldn't – fully appreciate what the war had done to him, that it had left him feeling scarred and ugly. He knew he should have told her sooner, but every time he thought about it he ended up losing his nerve. He liked her too much to risk losing her – *loved* her too much. All the same, he should have told her; after all, what she had seen at Tabley Wood had opened her eyes.

She was watching him closely now, waiting for an answer. What if he admitted how he felt about her only for her to say she didn't feel the same?

'You know what I think about you,' he said.

She looked up at him, her expression solemn. 'Say it.'

His heart was pounding. Now was not the time to be half-hearted. 'I love you, Jenny Marshall.'

She put her arms round his neck. 'That's all right, then.'

He was almost home when he bumped into Alison and John, strolling along the deserted main street with Elsa.

'You're out late,' David said, surprised to see them.

'This one likes a walk last thing,' John said, nodding at Elsa, 'and it's such a nice night we thought we'd take our time.'

'Any luck finding work?' David asked.

'Not so far, but I keep looking,' John said, with an attempt at a smile. 'Let me know if you find you need an extra pair of hands.'

David nodded. 'I'm sorry we couldn't offer you anything.'

'That's all right. I know things are tight for everyone.'

'How's the new shop coming along?' Alison asked.

'We're nearly there,' David said, 'although it's taken a bit more work than we thought it would. Plastering, new floorboards . . . you name it.' He rolled his eyes.

'It'll be worth it,' Alison told him.

David looked across at the building, its windows still covered in whitewash. The striped awning he had argued was worth every bit of the not inconsiderable expense was now in the process of being made and due to be with them in another week or so, along with a set of blinds. It was important to get the front of the building smartened up, he felt – if only to stop the likes of Mrs Cameron continually referring to it as an eyesore.

'Any idea when you're opening up?' John asked.

'Soon.' That was, provided everything went to plan, which so far it hadn't. Only yesterday, when the builders knocked through from the new premises and opened up the storeroom so that it could be accessed from either side of the building, Old Mr Jenkins had told them that the wiring was all going to have to be ripped out and replaced. It was a death trap, he said, bound to be dangerous. It was lucky it hadn't gone up before now. Privately, David still had moments when he wondered if he'd been right about expanding the business, especially now that his father's health was no longer as robust as it had been. It meant having to step up, which was what he'd wanted. Now, though, he wondered if he was trying to do too much too soon.

'We've got a date in mind,' David said, 'but there's just one or two things to get finished first.'

As soon as David stepped inside the house, he knew something was wrong. There was a bitter taste on his tongue, something acrid in the air that made his eyes smart. For a moment he stood stock-still, rooted to the spot, his heart thundering.

Then he reached for the light switch and flicked it on. Nothing. Sweat prickled the back of his neck. There was enough light from the moon for him to pick out familiar shapes in the kitchen. Everything was as it was before he'd taken Jenny home: the table they'd sat at earlier, eating, making plans, his mother's best crockery arranged on the shelves of the dresser, his father's chair at the side of the hearth, a copy of *The Modern Grocer* propped open on one of the arms. Draped over the back of the settee was the blanket his mother had crocheted years earlier.

And there was something else, something he might not be able to see but that was familiar all the same.

Burning, coming from somewhere.

The moment he opened the door into the hallway he found his way barred by a dense, choking mass. Putting up his hands to shield himself, he pushed on through the wall of thick smoke. It stung his eyes and tore at the back of his throat.

Just like on the ship.

There was not enough air, not enough light. He couldn't work out where the fire was. At the back of the building somewhere.

His mind spun.

The wiring, of course. It must be something to do with the wiring.

David edged forward, feeling a sob rise in the back of his raw throat.

Keep going.

He dropped to his knees and crawled along the narrow passage, eyes shut, feeling his way, getting a mouthful of foul-tasting filth and soot. His hand found the banister at the foot of the staircase and he called out to his parents. They would be asleep upstairs, unaware of what was happening.

'*Ma! Pa!*' His voice was a hoarse, rasping sound.

Fighting for breath, he pulled himself up the stairs and onto the smoke-filled landing. His parents were in the room at the back, their door slightly ajar. David burst in and ran to the bed, grabbing his father, shaking him. 'You've got to get out!' he yelled. 'Now, Pa!'

Alison and John had got as far as the village hall when they heard the shouts. They ran back as David, doubled over, coughing and gasping for breath, stumbled into the street, pulling Miriam with him. Vivian was in her arms, her face pressed against her mother's body. Alison caught hold of Miriam and steered her away from the building, where smoke was now escaping through the open door.

'Oh my God!' Alison cried, frantic.

'My dad.' David heaved in great gulps of air. 'Where's my dad? He was following us.'

'You can't go back in there,' John told him. 'Wait here, I'll get help.'

'*No time!*'

David plunged back into the building, pushing along the smoke-filled corridor, faster this time, sure of what he needed to do. When he reached the stairs, he saw that the smoke had taken charge. It was all there was to breathe. He pulled the collar of his shirt over his nose and mouth. *No time.* He held his breath and raced back up the stairs, two at a time, losing his footing and banging his knee hard on the top step.

Bryn was in the bedroom, next to the open window. 'I lost you, son,' he said. 'I can't breathe, can't see where I'm going.'

For a fleeting moment David was tempted to shut the bedroom door and stay put, trust that someone else would arrive in time to save them. They wouldn't, though. If you wanted to be saved, you had to do it yourself. He knew all about that.

'Hang onto me, Pa,' he instructed, struggling to get the words out, feeling as if there were razor blades in his throat.

'I don't think I can.' Bryn took a step back. 'I'll never make it.'

David caught hold of him, pulling him onto the landing. 'Put a hand on the banister and count the steps going down. There's twelve. Keep hold of me. A minute, and we'll be out of here.'

He'd said the same as the ship was going down, not realising that some of those he did his best to save had already perished and couldn't hear him.

No time.

* * *

Alison settled a dazed Miriam on a bench at the edge of the village green, where she soothed Vivian. Then she ran with Elsa to the pub for help, hammering on the door until Trevor Dawson appeared, scowling, hair on end, his wife, in curlers and a threadbare dressing gown, peering over his shoulder. 'Fire!' Alison hurled the word like a missile, her voice rattling with fear. 'FIRE! Next door!' She was waving her arms, pointing at the butcher's, screaming at them to get help.

Mrs Dawson reached for the telephone as Alison hurried off down the lane to Erica Campbell's house. Minutes later, Dr Myra Rosen was pulling a coat over her night things and grabbing her medical bag, chasing after Alison, Erica a few paces behind.

The ship came back to him, the moment he knew he had to get out.

No time.

Sink or swim.

After all that he'd been through, he would not lose his family. He hauled Bryn behind him down the stairs, his father tripping on the bottom step, almost coming free from his son's grip.

But David held on tighter still, using every bit of strength he had to yank Bryn to his feet and plough on through the passage.

Seconds now.

He pushed his father from the house, Bryn managing a few steps on his own before toppling over. David sank to the ground, rolling onto his back.

He felt a cool cloth on his brow, a voice telling him he was safe.

John was nowhere to be seen. Alison ran up and down the road outside the shop, calling to him. She should never have left him. Surely, he hadn't gone into the building. He wouldn't. Would he? No. He knew better than to attempt anything foolish. She carried on, running, calling his name until she was hoarse.

Erica caught hold of her. 'He'll have gone to raise the alarm.'

Alison shook her head. 'What if he went in after David?'

When John saw David plunge back into the smoke-filled building, he almost chased after him, even though he knew it would be folly to do so. David knew the layout of the building. He knew where he was going, and might, just *might*, have a chance of getting out before being over-come. The odds were not good, but he just might manage it. John, on the other hand, would have been lost within seconds.

Instead he raced to the back of the building, where he clambered over the wall and into the yard. The window next to the door on the empty shop had blown out. Inside, flames leapt into the air.

He looked about him, seeing the tap on the wall. There had to be a hose, something to wash down the yard.

He flung open the door of an outhouse and found what he needed, attached the hose with trembling fingers to the tap and aimed a jet of water into the burning building.

He was still there, numb with the effort, when the fire brigade arrived.

Chapter 26

FRANCES HAD BEEN UP late reading, determined to finish the final few pages of *Rebecca*, when she heard the commotion. She went out into the street to investigate and saw the fire crew training hoses on the empty grocer's and the Brindsleys being helped into an ambulance by Dr Rosen and Erica. The door to the pub was open, and the Dawsons stood outside in their night things. On a bench nearby were Alison and John, looking utterly exhausted, their little dog at their feet. When they told her what had happened, Frances insisted on taking them home with her and giving them strong tea and brandy.

The three of them had sat in the kitchen talking until it started to get light. Alison paled as she described seeing David stagger from the house with Miriam and Vivian, and the look of desperation on his face when he realised that Bryn had somehow been left behind.

'We didn't want David going back inside,' she said, 'not the state he was in – but he wouldn't listen. He was gone before we could stop him.'

He had done the same on the ship as it sank, Frances thought. Gone back time and again, at great personal cost, it turned out, to bring others to safety. How hard it must have been, having already been caught in a fire, knowing all that it entailed, to face another one.

'I thought I could go with him and help,' John said, 'but I knew I wouldn't stand a chance. I just had to leave him to it. I was more use trying to put the fire out at the back of the shop.'

Alison shook her head. 'I couldn't see you. I thought you'd gone inside.'

He put a hand on hers. Frances pretended not to notice.

'That boy showed real courage,' John said. 'I only wish I could have done more.'

'You did as much as you could,' Alison insisted. 'If you'd gone in, you might never have come out. Pitch-black, choking on smoke, in a house you don't know. What chance would you have had?'

'Alison's right,' Frances said. 'Showing courage doesn't mean being reckless with your life or taking unneces-sary risks. You could very easily have ended up trapped, and then others might have had to go looking for you . . . putting more lives at risk. That wouldn't be brave – it would be foolish. You made absolutely the right decision, in my view, and I've no doubt David will say the same.'

John still had hold of Alison's hand, Frances saw.

'It seems to me that by your actions tonight, the two of you helped save lives,' Frances went on. 'Not everyone would have had the presence of mind to get the doctor there as quickly as you did, Alison. And John, were it not for you, the flames could easily have spread, putting the fire crew in greater peril.' She gazed at them. 'You both pitched in and showed great courage. If it hadn't been for the two of you, things would have been much worse, I'm sure. I have every hope the entire village will be grateful to both of you for your efforts.'

David woke, and for a moment wasn't sure where he was. Against his skin was cool, crisp cotton. At home, the sheets smelled of lavender – but these had a different scent, something he couldn't quite make out. He took a deep breath and felt a stinging in his nostrils. Opening his eyes, he stared up at an expanse of ceiling and a light suspended on a chain. The flimsy remains of a spider's web wafted from the glass lampshade.

'David, thank God.'

He turned his head to one side and saw Jenny peering at him, anxious, eyes swollen from crying.

She took his hand. 'You're all right,' she said, relief in her voice. 'They've said you'll be fine.' Tears ran down her face.

David reached over and brushed at them. 'The others . . .' His throat hurt.

She nodded. 'Everyone's safe, thanks to you.'

'Don't cry.'

Her face crumpled. 'You could have been killed,' she said.

He closed his eyes for a moment and squeezed the tips of her fingers, the awful choking smoke of the night before coming back to him. He remembered the look of terror in his mother's eyes when he said there was a fire and they had to get out. *Right away.* He remembered her lifting Vivian from her cot, his father obediently going with him only to stall on the landing at the sight of the smoke. A silent killer ready to swallow them.

David felt suddenly suffocated by the starched hospital sheet, tucked too tightly around him, as if he couldn't get enough air. He tugged at it and flung it back, easing himself up, panic squeezing his insides.

It wasn't as bad as the last time, he told himself, when he'd been out of it for days and come back to a spasm of agonising pain, half his body swathed in bandages. There had been no Jenny at his bedside then, no one he loved to take care of him. His family hadn't even known where he was, or if he was alive.

This was different.

Jenny plumped one of his pillows and propped it at his back. His lips were cracked, his throat dry and tender.

'I'm parched,' he told her and she poured a glass of water from the jug on the bedside table and helped him take his first few sips.

'Have you seen Ma, my dad?' he asked. 'Vivian?'

She shook her head. 'Not yet, but I'm told they're fine. Your mum's with Vivian, and your dad's on a special ward.' She caught his look. 'It's just a precaution, they said. His blood pressure was up, and after what happened before they wanted to keep a close eye on him.' She waited a moment. 'What happened?'

He told her about getting home and smelling smoke, opening the door into the hall and finding the place thick with it, getting his mother and Vivian out and then discovering his father wasn't with them.

Going back a second time.

She hung onto his hand. 'What if you hadn't made it? You should have waited for the fire crew.'

He shook his head.

No time.

He could not lose his family. He would not let fire hurt them, too.

Chapter 27

SARAH MOBILISED THE MEMBERS of the WI, who gathered outside the butcher's the day after the fire, armed with buckets and mops and cloths, ready to undertake the clean-up. It was hoped they'd be able to get things back to some semblance of normality before Miriam and the family came home from the hospital.

It looked like the fire had started in the storeroom at the back of the empty shop. An electrical fault, most likely, according to the fire chief, who'd carried out an inspection of the still-smouldering premises hours after the blaze had been extinguished. A stack of wood intended as new shelves and flooring, as well as other materials destined for the new shop, had gone up in flames. In a corner of the room a pile of old insulating material awaiting removal was identified as the most likely source of the choking smoke that had spread throughout the building. 'Lucky they got out when they did,' the fire chief said. 'That stuff's a killer.'

Most of the damage was to the new shop. Water from the fire hoses had gushed inside, streaking every surface with soot and filth, creating a foul-smelling sludge. Even the ceiling had not managed to escape. A sickly smell hung in the air.

Erica, who led the clean-up team for that section of the building, stood for a moment on the wet floor, surveying the damage.

'Right, ladies, let's get the windows open and the doors, back and front. Get some fresh air in. And mind your step, the floor's swimming with water.'

They began at the front of the shop, working methodically, wiping down the walls, mopping the floor. Erica found a set of steps and was able to reach the ceiling. 'We'll go over everything once, get the worst of it off, and then go back over it all again,' she said. 'Let's get to work!'

Soon, the scent of bleach and Vim filled the air.

At the back of the building, John was busy emptying what was left of the charred materials from the storeroom. Everything was a sodden, stinking mess. He shovelled it into a wheelbarrow and carried it away to the furthest corner of the yard. Earlier, he had checked the butcher's shop and found it largely unscathed, the cold store and its contents undamaged. There was a door into the butcher's from the corridor that now linked both premises but, thankfully, it had been shut. There was no reason he could see why they wouldn't be able to open up once the place had been given a thorough clean.

Sarah and Frances, meanwhile, were making a start on the house. 'It doesn't actually look too bad,' Sarah said, opening the windows in the front room. 'It's the smell more than anything. I'd say the best thing we can do is get it aired right through.'

'Thank goodness the fire didn't spread beyond the storeroom,' Frances said, 'although smoke can be just as deadly.'

Sarah started taking down the curtains. 'I'll sponge these and get them on the line,' she said, 'and the ones upstairs as well. There's fresh linen for the beds. Apart from that, if we clean everything as best we can, and wipe down the walls and the paintwork, at least it'll be habitable.'

Frances nodded. 'I wonder how they'll feel about coming back after such an ordeal – somewhat nervous, I imagine.'

'It doesn't bear thinking about what might have happened if David hadn't returned when he did,' Sarah said. 'He got here in the nick of time, by all accounts.'

Frances sighed. 'It must have brought it all back, what he went through on the ship.'

Sarah nodded grimly. 'I don't doubt it.'

Frances opened the door into the windowless hall. The corridor, she saw, led to a kind of lobby littered with obstacles: a coat stand at the rear, one for umbrellas nearby; a side table on which sat a rather lovely coloured vase. If you didn't know where you were going, what were the chances of reaching the stairs? she wondered. One wrong turn and you could miss the staircase altogether and end up crashing into the table. If that were to happen, you'd most likely blunder into the passage that now led to the new shop, going in entirely the wrong direction, plunging ever deeper into the smoke, edging closer to the source of the fire.

She closed her eyes and took a few tentative steps forward, aiming for the staircase, and was almost immediately disorientated, feeling she might lose her balance. She put her hands out in front of her and kept going, feeling her way, searching for the banister. When she opened her eyes she saw she had veered to the right and missed the stairs altogether, and was now only inches from the table. How much worse it would be in the dark, with your heart pounding, smoke filling your lungs. John had definitely made the right decision. She felt a sudden shiver, the hairs on her arms standing on end.

'What are you doing?' Sarah asked, coming up behind her.

'Thinking about John. He seemed to feel he could have done more when David went back in to get Bryn out.' She shook her head. 'I don't think he'd have stood a chance.'

'I just hope the people who've been so antagonistic towards him might now have a change of heart,' Sarah said. 'The Dawsons, for a start.'

'John's such a decent man,' Frances said. She remembered all too well the day that John had found Noah, after he'd run away from school, and brought him home safe. She would be grateful to him forever. She smiled, remembering his hand on Alison's the night before. 'And I think he's very fond of Alison.'

'They're certainly close.'

Closer than we might imagine, Frances thought.

'It makes you think about life, how fragile it is,' Sarah said. 'It brings everything into sharp focus, somehow, all that truly matters and how easily it can be snatched away.' She glanced at Frances. 'Sometimes, all that we hold most dear – what we most want to protect – can feel tantalisingly out of reach.'

Frances touched her arm. 'I know it must make you think about Adam. I take it there's no more news?'

Sarah shook her head. She'd had one more letter, and then nothing. 'I keep writing, but nothing comes back. It's been months.' She gave Frances an anguished look. 'All we seem to hear is bad news. The newspapers are full of how the Soviets are suffering now – hundreds of thousands dead, Leningrad under siege.' Germany's decision to launch Operation Barbarossa and invade Russia in the summer had caught Stalin out and was proving catastrophic. 'I was reading about the *Einsatzgruppen*, the so-called "special duty units" who kill any Jewish people they find as the Nazis push on into the Soviet Union.' She felt suddenly tearful and took a deep breath. 'It's all so terrible, and it makes me feel even more anxious. I can't help thinking something awful must have happened. Otherwise, why wouldn't Adam have been in touch – even just a few lines to let me know he's all right?'

'There could be any number of reasons. It may be something as simple as the post not getting through.'

Sarah was quiet for a moment. 'I was thinking earlier about what David did, risking his life to save his loved ones,' she said, 'preventing what might have been a terrible tragedy. It says so much about how we're set up, doesn't it? When it comes to those we love, our instinct is always to put them first. We don't stop to think, we simply *act*. We do what we can to protect the people we care most for – run into a burning building, sacrifice ourselves, if need be.' She sighed. 'One of the hardest things about all this is that I can do *nothing* for Adam. Whatever he's going through, whatever he might need, I'm utterly helpless. If it came to it, I'd happily run into a burning building to save him.' She smiled sadly. '*Happily* is the wrong word, perhaps. *Willingly*. What I mean is that I'd do anything for him, lay down my life without a second thought, just like David was prepared to for his family. But I can't. My hands are tied.' She frowned. 'Listen to me – do I sound completely mad?'

'Not to me you don't,' Frances said. 'Self-sacrifice, putting others first – it's what we do in the name of love. War takes no account of that, I'm afraid.'

'I just needed to get all that off my chest,' Sarah said.

'It'll be all right,' Frances told her.

Sarah shook her head. 'You can't possibly know that.'

'And *you* can't possibly know it won't.'

* * *

It was late by the time Sarah got home. Her shoulders and back ached from all the stretching and hard work they'd done. She was in no mood to start cooking, and rummaged half-heartedly in the pantry, looking for something that required almost no effort. She found a loaf of bread and cut a few slices, spreading them thickly with jam. She ate standing up, listening to the wireless.

More grim news. In Germany, the newsreader intoned, the Nazis were further singling out the country's Jewish community, who for several weeks now had been required, by law, to wear a yellow Star of David. During their time in Oxford, Sarah and Adam had been friendly with a Jewish family whose relatives had fled Berlin at the end of 1938 after *Kristallnacht*, when the windows of synagogues and stores owned by Jews were smashed. Homes were destroyed and tens of thousands of men arrested.

Sarah felt a chill go through her. The decision to make a Jewish badge compulsory felt so ominous, a precursor to something else, something worse. Why label people unless your intention was to make targets of them? It had already happened in Poland, where Jewish people had been made to wear armbands, thousands herded together in a ghetto. What would come next? she wondered. Surely nothing good.

She finished eating and switched off the wireless. These days, she could hardly bear to listen to the news. It put her on edge, and she already felt exhausted.

A bath and then bed. That was what she needed. At least tonight she was so tired she would sleep.

She put off the kitchen light and was almost at the top of the stairs when she heard a soft tapping at the front door. She could think of no one who would call so late, although one or two of the others were still busy in the new shop when she and Frances had called it a night. It would be Erica, perhaps, with something she felt couldn't wait until morning.

She went to the door, still in her oldest pinny, a few strands of hair escaping from the knotted headscarf she'd had on all day that was now beginning to work its way loose.

She stood on the top step and peered into the garden. There was no one there. The sky was full of thick cloud that obscured the moon, making it too dark to see much beyond the shapes of the trees. She waited a moment, the breeze gently shaking a branch of wisteria above her head. Perhaps that was what she had heard.

As she turned to go back inside, the sound of something crunching on the gravel made her freeze. She spun round to find a dishevelled figure facing her: long, straggly hair, a beard that had been allowed to grow wild, a tattered and dirty coat. The moment their eyes met Sarah knew him.

'Adam,' she whispered.

Chapter 28

Throughout the months that Adam had been gone, Sarah had never stopped dreaming about having him home again. Occasionally, she would while away several hours, an entire day sometimes, thinking about what it would be like when he came back.

In her mind's eye, she waited for him at the bus stop in the village wearing the yellow seersucker dress she kept for best. Her hair was left loose in waves and she had taken care over her make-up and dabbed rosewater behind her ears and at the back of her neck. The sun felt warm on her skin, the brilliant blue of the sky bringing to mind the topaz earrings she had worn on their wedding day. At the side of the road hollyhocks laden with pink and white flowers swayed in the breeze and the air was sweet with the scent of lilac. Somewhere, out of sight, a blackbird sang, a sweet, liquid call.

In her imagined version of events, it was the Adam of old who returned. He would be smiling, looking smart in his officer's uniform, stepping from the bus to take her in his arms. She imagined the two of them laughing as he lifted her into the air, kissing, not caring who saw them. She pictured the familiar sparkle in his eyes, the strength to sweep her off her feet.

That was how she chose to think it would be.

The night Adam came home was nothing like it.

She hadn't known him at first. He seemed a stranger hunched inside a shabby overcoat standing on the path in front of her, an old man with sagging shoulders. In the darkness, she couldn't see much beyond the unkempt hair poking out from under his hat and the sort of wild beard she associated with hermits; the tramp who wandered the countryside, arriving in Great Paxford each spring. For some reason a Rembrandt came to mind, a painting she had seen in the National Gallery with Adam.

Adam.

When the shambling figure looked at her, she had felt her legs threaten to give way.

There was none of the joy she had imagined. As she embraced him she felt how frail he was, as if he might fold like a paper bag. Inside, in the light, his ragged state became even more apparent. There was dirt in his hair and under his fingernails, and the wild beard was tangled and matted, his coat stiff with mud and stale sweat. She felt as if her heart would break as she sat him at the kitchen table, putting bread in front of him, along with the small scraping of butter she had, slices of tinned meat. She watched him devour every bit of food, and wondered when he had last eaten. When she filled a tumbler with whisky, he drank it straight down.

She ran a bath and gently soaped his skin and washed his hair. His body was nothing like the body she knew so well. He was thin, shoulder blades and ribs jutting out. At first, he told her almost nothing, only that he and two others had managed to escape from the camp. When she asked how they'd got away he gave a wry smile. 'A fluke,' he said, 'sheer luck.'

It seemed that was all he was prepared to say tonight. It was clear he was exhausted and she knew not to press him, even though her head was full of questions. The finer details could wait until he was ready. For now, what mattered was that he was back.

In bed they clung to one another, their lovemaking brief and frantic. Afterwards, Sarah laid her face against his chest, and felt his breathing change as he sank into a deep sleep.

The following morning, dressed in his own clothes and with the beard gone, he looked more like his old self. After breakfast, Sarah cut his hair.

'How are you feeling?' she asked.

'Strange,' he said, stroking his chin. 'I'd got used to all the hair, not having to shave. Even the rather ripe overcoat.'

Sarah wrinkled her nose. She had put it out first thing.

'When you look like a down-and-out, no one pays you the least bit of attention. I mean, they might *see* you in a vague fashion but they don't really *look* at you. It can be quite useful.'

Sarah smiled. 'When I opened the door last night, do you know what I thought?'

'What's that smelly old tramp doing on the doorstep?'

'I remembered our trip to the National Gallery, a painting I'd seen there.'

He gave her a quizzical look. 'Should I take that as a compliment?'

She laughed. 'Probably not. It wasn't the most flattering of portraits. Looking at you now, freshly scrubbed and clean-shaven, I'm hard pressed to see the resemblance.'

'I wasn't sure how you'd react, if you'd even recognise me.'

She reached for his hand. 'The village will be overjoyed to have you back,' she said. 'Everyone's been incredibly concerned about you, so kind. The entire congregation of St Mark's prays each Sunday for your safe return. It's become part of the service.' Sarah had begun attending church regularly; it was her way of expressing gratitude to those who had shown her such kindness. Despite her lack of faith, she found being with other people a comfort, and the services were starting to instil in her a sense of peace she had not expected. 'They'll be delighted to have their vicar back.'

Adam's smile disappeared. 'I don't want them to know, not yet. I've only just got home.'

Sarah was taken aback. 'We can hardly keep it a secret,' she said. 'Not when I'm stopped every time I go into the village by someone wanting to know if there's any news. How can I look people in the eye and pretend I've heard nothing when you're hidden away at home? It would feel wrong.'

'I don't want them knowing,' Adam insisted. 'I need time to settle in, to get a few things straight in my head. I can't just pick up where I left off.' He looked at her. 'After everything that's happened, I can think of nothing worse than people crowding in, making a fuss.'

'Aren't they entitled to make a fuss when you've been captured and held in a German POW camp and now, by some miracle, you're home? These are your *parishioners*, Adam, people who care about you.' Sarah gazed at him. 'You're their *vicar*. The one they look to for support of all kinds, spiritual guidance, someone to listen and show compassion and understanding. They've felt your absence keenly. I know, because they've told me. It seems only fair to let them know you're safe.'

Adam was quiet. 'I'm not their vicar, and I haven't been for some time.' He hesitated. 'I don't know if I have it in me anymore. Not after what I've seen . . .' He shook his head. 'All I'm asking for is time to catch my breath. I need to think, to be still.' He gave her a pleading look. 'And to be with you, just the two of us. I'm sure I'll be ready soon, but until then . . . Does that sound so unreasonable?'

'What if someone comes to the house?'

'I'll wait upstairs until they leave.'

She could see he was determined. 'I don't know how I can keep it from Frances.'

Adam thought for a moment. 'Frances, then, but no one else.'

They lapsed into silence.

'Do you want to talk about it, how you made it back?' Sarah asked at last.

'I will, I promise. Just – not yet. Give me a chance to do some thinking first.' He caught her look. 'It's still sinking in that I'm home, with you. Safe. At times, I wasn't sure it would ever happen. Now that it has, I need a moment to take it in, that's all.' He gave her a smile. 'You could always bring me up to date on what I've missed here . . .'

She told him about Bob Simms, about Teresa and Nick expecting a baby, Bryn's collapse, the fire at the new shop, David risking his life to save his family. There was so much he had missed.

'Not what you'd call uneventful, then,' Adam said wryly when she had finished.

'Which is why they'll all be so grateful to have you back.'

'All in good time.'

Chapter 29

GWEN WAS ABOUT TO put on her coat and go to the village hall when Ronald came downstairs, looking cheerful for once.

'Any chance of something to eat?' he said.

She put her coat back on the peg and went into the kitchen.

She cracked eggs into a pan with thick slices of bread in beef dripping, just how Ronald liked it. There was music on the wireless and he whistled along to the tune while the eggs sizzled. He'd always loved to whistle, and before he went away to fight the house was full of the sound. When he came back, though, the whistling had stopped.

Gwen smiled to herself, the whistling encouraging her to believe that everything would be all right after all.

She left him eating and went to check his room for dirty washing, picking up socks and a shirt lying on the floor. She wasn't even going to look under the bed, but something in the room was smelling, even though the window was open to let fresh air in. She knelt down and pulled trousers and an old vest from under the bed. Right at the back against the wall was a pair of overalls Ronald used to wear when he did the odd bit of labouring before he signed up.

It seemed strange that the overalls were under the bed. Gwen remembered washing and folding them while he was away and leaving them on a shelf in his wardrobe. As far as she knew, he'd not had them on since he'd been home, yet they were filthy and the smell rising from them was sickening. It was enough to turn your stomach. Like slurry, almost. They were damp, sticky to the touch. As she stared at them, she felt suddenly nauseous.

Downstairs, Ronald was tucking into his breakfast, looking happier than he had for weeks. 'Any chance of another egg?' he asked, grinning at her.

She held up the overalls. Her heart felt like a boulder. 'Ronald, what have you done?'

Pat arrived at the village hall early to begin sorting through the clothes that had been donated for the WI's 'Fashion on the Ration' extravaganza. She was grateful that both Sarah and Gwen Talbot had offered to lend a hand, as the request for unwanted clothes had produced far more than anyone had envisaged. Erica had also intended to help out, but her youngest daughter, Laura, now studying to be a doctor, was back from university for a brief stay and, understandably, Erica was keen to spend time with her. Pat gazed at the jumble of garments piled onto trestle tables at the far end of the hall, waiting to be put into some kind of order.

Fortunately, Frances had managed to secure the loan of several clothes rails from Browns in Chester, where over the years she had become a good customer. The store had also sent boxes filled with hangers.

Pat hung her coat over the back of a chair and prepared to make a start. She hoped to get as much done as she could over the next couple of days and work out how best to position everything so as to create the impression of a temporary shop rather than a jumble sale, ready for the event at the weekend. She'd already broken everything down into categories and made a comprehensive list: ladies' blouses, skirts, dresses (daywear and formal), jackets, suits, coats, knitwear, scarves, bags and belts. Similar lists existed for menswear and children's clothes. In a corner were boxes filled with shoes.

She made a start on the clothes, concentrating on womenswear and putting everything on hangers.

After a couple of hours, she had managed to pull every item of women's clothing from the pile. Now it was a case of getting it into some kind of order. She worked methodically, grouping styles and colours together. A few things were crumpled from being squashed under heavy coats, and Pat decided to wait and see whether the creases would fall out on their own over the next few days. If not, she would muster volunteers to run an iron over them.

Her own wedding outfit was on the formalwear rail, and next to it hung a full-length silk evening dress in almost the same shade of turquoise, that had come from Frances.

She had been generous with her donations, telling Pat it was the perfect opportunity to get rid of all the things she would never wear again that were simply cluttering up her wardrobe. The dress was Dior – Pat had seen from the label – in perfect condition, probably worn on only one or two occasions. How ironic that often the most beautiful clothes, the ones that cost the most – lavish evening dresses like this one from a Parisian fashion house – had only a few outings. The women who could afford the most extravagant garments made by top couturiers had no wish to be seen in them more than once or twice.

Pat studied the dress with its nipped-in waist and generous skirt. All that fabric. She could alter it, give it a shorter hemline, use some of the fabric left over to make sleeves. The skirt was lined with fine gossamer, the most delicate Pat had ever seen. She could work some of it into a panel to fill the deep V at the back. She set the dress to one side. Before it went into the sale she would offer to remodel it for Frances.

Then she stood back and surveyed her efforts, pleased with how much she had achieved in such a short space of time. Now that things were on racks rather than piled up willy-nilly, they looked altogether more appealing.

'Yoo-hoo!'

Pat looked up to see Steph making her way across the room towards her.

'The door was open and I thought I'd come to see how it's all going.'

'I'm getting there,' Pat told her.

'Isn't anyone helping?'

'I'm beginning to think I might have got my dates mixed up.' Sarah was usually reliable, and Gwen had promised to be there; it seemed odd that neither had been in touch to say they couldn't make it. She hoped Gwen hadn't decided against her after all. 'I've a flask of tea if you'd like to share it.'

'You look as if you're in your element,' Steph said five minutes later, sipping tea and admiring the rails of clothing that surrounded them. 'It's all very professional.'

'I'm enjoying it. It's been good for me having a sense of purpose.' Pat smiled. 'How's everything with you?'

'I've just had my regular check-up with Dr Rosen and she seems to think I'm doing well.'

'That's wonderful. And you're managing on the farm?'

She nodded. 'Stan's got everything under control.'

'What about this awful business with your neighbour's sheep?'

'Jim Morton's just about at the end of his tether. I'm worried he'll take matters into his own hands.' Steph hesitated. 'He's threatening to shoot anyone he sees on his land.'

'He's not still blaming John? I'd have thought, after what happened with the fire at the butcher's . . .'

Steph sighed. 'There's no talking to Jim Morton. Let's just hope they find the real culprit before things turn truly nasty.'

Before heading home for lunch, Pat decided to call on Gwen, hoping she might be free to help out for an hour or two in the afternoon. But as she turned into the lane, she saw the police car parked nearby. Gwen's front door was open, and the same young policeman who'd spoken to Pat after Bob's accident was on his way down the path. A second man, with sergeant's stripes on the shoulder of his uniform, emerged from the house, steering a burly young man towards the car.

It was Gwen's son, Ronald.

Gwen was last to appear, white-faced, as Ronald got into the car and was driven off. The elderly couple from the house on the other side of the road stood in the garden, all too obviously craning to see what was going on.

Pat hurried over. 'Gwen, what's happened?'

Gwen waited until the car disappeared out of sight at the end of the lane, her face pale with worry. 'I called them,' she told Pat. 'I had no choice.'

Gwen sat at the kitchen table, silent. Pat placed a cup of tea in front of her and stirred sugar into it. 'Have some of this,' she said. 'It'll make you feel better.'

Gwen stared at the wall opposite while the tea went cold, unable to meet Pat's eye.

'I'm not here to pry,' Pat said at last. 'I can just keep you company for a bit, if you like. You don't have to tell me anything if you don't want to.'

Gwen finally turned to look at her. 'Everyone's going to know soon enough.' She sounded on the verge of tears.

'Oh, Gwen, surely it can't be so bad.'

Gwen sighed. 'This morning, Ronald was up early for once,' she said. 'I thought he was looking better. Washed, hair combed, clean shirt. He was altogether much brighter, like a different lad. He was more like his old self, wanting to know what there was for breakfast, not snapping my head off.' She glanced at Pat. 'There's been no pleasing him – nothing's right. It doesn't matter what I do, it's not good enough. The strain of living with him, you've no idea what it's been like.'

Pat said nothing. All the years of suffering Bob's moods and outbursts meant she knew better than most what Gwen had been going through.

'I was hoping he was on the mend,' Gwen went on. 'I dared to think he might be turning a corner.' She squeezed her eyes shut. 'Not for a second did it cross my mind . . .' She shook her head, her voice close to cracking, and reached into the pocket of her pinny for a handkerchief.

'It's all right,' Pat said, 'take your time.'

She sighed. 'He's barely spoken these last few weeks, not a word about what he's been doing.' She went quiet and let her head sink into her hands. 'It's not as if I haven't asked. I've done my best.'

'He's not well,' Pat said.

'I'm his *mother*, I should have known.'

'Whatever it is, you can't go blaming yourself.'

Gwen waited a moment, biting her lip. 'It was Ronald,' she said. 'He's the one who's been killing the sheep.'

Chapter 30

ALISON AND JOHN WERE in the front room, Elsa snoozing on Boris's old chair. A jigsaw puzzle was taking form on the table before them, the outer edges complete. Alison stared at it in frustration. The piece she had in her hand, part of the chimney pot on a cottage, surely, refused to fit. She tried it all ways before conceding defeat and putting it back into the box. John smiled.

Alison had never been much good at jigsaws. The more complicated ones inevitably defeated her. Even as a child, she had found the idea of a jigsaw strange, questioning why anyone would cut a perfectly good picture into odd-shaped pieces in order to put them all back exactly the way they were in the first place. And yet, jigsaws were popular. Many people loved them. An aunt of hers always had at least one on the go, the more challenging the better, liking nothing more than an expanse of sea or sky.

Alison had not imagined John to be the type to take pleasure in poring over a jigsaw. And yet, seeing his look of concentration as he studied the pieces and slotted in one after another correctly, it was clear he had an aptitude. He had found the puzzle earlier when he was rearranging the contents of the cupboard under the stairs. ('Have to do something to keep myself busy,' he told her.) Alison felt sure the jigsaw wasn't hers and wondered if it belonged to Teresa and had been left behind.

'We should return it,' she said.

John smiled. '*After* we've done it.'

'There might be a piece missing,' she said, hoping to put him off.

'Only one way to find out,' he told her.

The picture on the box depicted a rural scene complete with thatched cottage, a pub called the White Lion and a cricket match in full swing. A couple in jodhpurs trotted past the pub on horseback. A dog that looked a bit like Elsa charged about. A family were enjoying a picnic next to the river. At the side of the road, a green sports car was having a wheel changed. It was meant to be an idyllic scene, Alison supposed, and yet the sense of peace was ruined by all the activity. It was not the kind of village that appealed much to her. As for the jigsaw, there was rather too much sky for her liking. It would have suited her aunt.

So, when she saw Pat coming up the path, she was grateful for the distraction.

Pat came straight to the point. Gwen Talbot's son had been arrested for killing Jim Morton's sheep.

John let out a sigh of relief. 'How did they catch him?' he asked.

'Gwen reported him.'

Alison's jaw dropped. '*Gwen* turned in her own son?'

Pat nodded. 'She'd no idea it was him until this morning, didn't suspect a thing. Then she went into his room and found an old pair of overalls covered in blood, and put two and two together. Once she was sure, she called the police.'

Pat didn't say that Ronald had threatened his mother with a bread knife when she told him what she'd done.

Alison was shaking her head. 'I don't know what to say.'

'I knew about Ronald coming home wounded, I just didn't know what had happened to him.' Pat sighed. 'Once or twice I saw him in passing and he seemed well enough, but you can't always tell. Look at David Brindsley – unless you were told, you'd never know how badly injured he was.'

Pat knew from Miriam that when David first arrived home, he had been full of rage and frustration, the bulk of which was directed at his parents. Miriam had feared for him at first, but gradually, he had recovered. Gwen must have hoped that, in time, Ronald would too.

'From what I understand, he had some kind of breakdown,' Pat went on. 'Gwen wasn't told in very much detail what prompted his discharge, and whenever she tried to find out from Ronald, he clammed up.' Gwen had told her more than that – that Ronald had shouted for her to mind her own business and stop going on at him, that he had stomped off out of the house in a fury, sometimes for hours at a time.

'Something like shell shock, you mean?' John asked.

Pat frowned. 'I'm not sure they call it that now. Whatever it is, Ronald's not the boy he was, and Gwen's been at her wits' end doing her best to cope. He hasn't been sleeping. Instead he's been prowling around the house at night, keeping her awake. When he has been able to sleep, there are nightmares ... Gwen is completely worn out. She's been trying her best to get him well, but just feels as if she's been getting nowhere. From what she's said, he needs proper help. Maybe now he'll get it.'

'She's kept it well hidden,' Alison said. 'I had no idea.'

'Makes you wonder how many people are coming home in no fit state,' John said, frowning. 'There are men who look no different on the outside, but are broken within. There were men at the hostel ...' He shook his head and broke off. 'When it's your mind and there's nothing to show there's anything wrong with you, I can't help thinking it's a harder thing to overcome.'

'You know we had the police here,' Alison said. 'They wanted to know where John had been on various dates. They searched the house, went through everything.'

There had been two uniformed officers, decent enough – just doing their job. When Alison asked why they were questioning John, the younger one had gone bright red, while his colleague, more senior, she guessed, said they were simply following a number of potential leads, talking to anyone whose name came up in the course of their enquiries.

'Is that a polite way of saying you've had reports of a savage moving into the village?' she asked, making the young one blush even harder.

'That's not the sort of language I'd choose to use,' the older one said.

'In that case, you're very much in a minority.' She had looked pointedly at John. 'Much the same as Mr Smith here.' She didn't expect the police had questioned Ronald Talbot 'in the course of their enquiries'.

'At least you don't have to worry about being blamed anymore,' Pat said now. Alison reached for John's hand and gave it a reassuring squeeze. Pat caught the look that passed between them, and tried to hide her surprise. She went on, 'Gwen's keen for people to know the truth. It's all going to come out anyway, and she'd rather it was sooner than later. An awful lot of people owe you an apology, John.'

Pat was rather looking forward to seeing Martha Dawson's face when she found out.

'Does anyone know *why* he did it?' John asked.

'I don't suppose even he knows,' Pat said. 'He's not well at all.'

'I can't help feeling for the boy,' John said, after Pat had gone. 'And for his mother, too. What a terrible thing to go through.'

Alison had rather less sympathy. Gwen Talbot had been among those ready to point the finger at John, despite an absence of evidence.

'They're not my concern,' she said firmly, 'you are. You were accused of something you didn't do because your skin's a different colour – that's the top and bottom of it. I wonder how many of the people who owe you an apology will actually bother to say sorry.'

She thought back to the WI meeting, Martha Dawson sneering, Gwen Talbot a couple of seats away, swivelling round in her chair. She remembered how the others had tutted, muttering about having to put up with savages. The news that someone was killing sheep provided the excuse they were looking for to complain about John being in the village.

Not one of us.

He took her hand. 'It's not as if it's the first time I've been blamed for something that was nothing to do with me.'

'Which only makes it worse. What gives anyone the right to accuse you? I'd love to know why it's often the most ignorant people who seem to think they know best. I've seen them all, looking down their noses at you, their minds full of nonsense.'

Martha Dawson and her husband, Trevor, came to mind. Jim Morton, casting aspersions where he had no right to. John was worth a hundred of their sort.

'You've never put a foot wrong, you're kind to everybody – and yet they turn on you at the first opportunity.

I hope they're ashamed. Maybe they'll have a bit more tolerance in future.'

'Oh, Alison, it won't make a scrap of difference. The next time something goes wrong, they'll do exactly the same. They'll look for a scapegoat – it's human nature.' He put up his hands, a gesture of surrender. 'And here I am.'

She was indignant. 'But hasn't this whole episode proved how wrong they were about you? They have no choice but to accept you're innocent. *They're* the guilty ones – guilty of making utterly baseless accusations. All the time they were spreading malicious gossip, convinced it had to be the outsider, it was one of their own. They'll be a lot more wary about what they say from now on.'

'I wouldn't count on it.'

Neither spoke for a moment. Elsa jumped off the chair and came to sit at John's feet. He reached down and scratched her head.

'So what can we do?' Alison asked. 'How do we persuade them to think differently?'

John looked thoughtful. 'We do what's right for us. We don't waste our time trying to change the minds of people stuck in their ways because it's a battle we'll never win.' He bent and kissed her hand. 'We count our blessings, thank God for what we've got. Each other.'

'But it's not fair,' Alison said. 'I hate to see people judging you for no reason.'

John looked round at her. 'They'll judge you, too, you know, for having me as your lodger. They'd judge you more, if they knew the truth.'

Alison shook her head. 'I don't care about any of that. Not one bit.'

John smiled. He turned to her and cupped her face in his hands. 'All this business in the village . . . it's nothing compared to what we've got. Great Paxford may not be perfect, but here, this house, you and me – this *is* perfect. You're one in a million, Alison, and I've got to be the luckiest man alive to have you. It makes me feel very blessed.' He gave her a tender kiss, then pulled back, looking at her seriously. 'I might not have much to offer you, and I know life might not be that easy for us. But I love you, Alison, I always will. You mean the world to me. There's nothing I wouldn't do for you. I want you to be my wife. I want a long and happy future with you. I've never wanted anything in this world more. What do you say – will you marry me?'

Chapter 31

SARAH FOUND FRANCES IN the dining room, surrounded by paperwork.

'Have I caught you in the middle of something?' Sarah asked.

'Nothing important,' Frances said, looking up. 'I'm just sorting through some old papers. Do you remember a talk we had at one of our WI meetings on the subject of beekeeping?'

Sarah nodded.

'I must have found it utterly fascinating because I took copious notes – and kept them all this time, for some reason!'

'You were considering getting some hives, I seem to remember.'

Frances frowned. 'Really? I have no recollection of that whatsoever.'

'It was short-lived.' Sarah smiled. 'One of your fads.'

'I don't have *fads*,' Frances protested.

'You were also considering goats at one point . . . prompted by a talk on cheesemaking.'

Frances laughed. 'Oh, I remember. Peter put paid to it – he said the goats would eat everything in sight and we'd end up with a scene of devastation where the garden used to be. I seem to remember Cookie putting her foot down, too.'

'I'd have enjoyed watching you trying to milk a goat.'

'That's what Peter said.' Frances smiled at the memory and began gathering up her papers. 'Anyway, I don't suppose you came over to discuss my various "fads", as you put it.'

Sarah hesitated. Then she noticed a series of sketches done in pencil – dress designs. 'Those are rather good,' she said, picking one up.

'Pat did them. She brought them round this morning,' Frances said. 'She suggested she might remodel the Dior evening gown I gave to the clothing sale to make it more practical – shortening it, using the net underskirt to create sleeves and panels, that kind of thing. She thinks there might even be enough fabric to make a jacket. Her drawings are really very good.'

Sarah studied them, impressed. 'They look like the work of a professional. What did you say?'

'I was persuaded by her enthusiasm. She's a clever dressmaker and I've no doubt she'll make a good job of it.'

'I had no idea she was so skilled.'

'I suspect there's a lot we don't know about Pat, mainly because Bob made sure she had no chance to express herself,' Frances sighed. 'She was so busy running round after him, I suppose she hadn't the time to pursue her own passions. I can well imagine Bob acting swiftly to crush any hint of creativity on her part. I find I'm only just beginning to appreciate her many talents. Did you know she's been writing?'

Sarah looked up in surprise. 'What kind of writing?'

'I'm not exactly sure, she was rather cagey on the subject matter, but she did say she recently submitted a piece to a magazine.'

'Good for her.'

'She also told me about Mrs Talbot's son.'

'Really? What about him?' Sarah had been avoiding people since Adam's return, and was out of touch with what was going on.

'You haven't heard? He's the one who's been killing sheep on Jim Morton's farm. It's the talk of the village.'

Sarah gasped. 'What happened? How did they find out?'

'Gwen found something in Ronald's room that convinced her it was him and called the police. I imagine that was not an easy call to make.'

Sarah took this in. 'He's not at all well, you know. He suffered a mental collapse of some sort, and I gather he's received very little in the way of help. Gwen has been doing her best, but I believe it has been very hard for her. From what she told me, he's a different boy to the one who went off to fight. She's had her work cut out coping since the army discharged him.'

Frances nodded. 'Terrible business. And now, this.'

Sarah remembered her visit to Gwen when the subject of the sheep killings had come up, how insistent Gwen had been that John was responsible. 'Does Alison know?' she asked.

Frances nodded. 'Pat went to see her. At least people will stop blaming John now. I just hope some of those most vocal in their accusations will have the grace to apologise – although I may be hoping for rather too much there.' She thought for a moment. 'Haven't you been spending time with Gwen? Now might be a good time to call on her.'

'I can't,' Sarah said, looking away. 'I've too much on.'

Frances frowned in surprise. 'You could spare an hour, surely?'

'Not at the moment, no.' Sarah took a breath. 'Listen, Frances. Something's happened and I want to keep it strictly between us for the time being. *Strictly*. I mean, no one can know.'

Frances gave her a quizzical look. 'What is it? Whatever's the matter?'

'Frances, this is a secret for now. You mustn't under any circumstances let it get out,' Sarah said. 'It's important. Promise me you won't breathe a word.'

'Of course, hand on heart, I won't say a thing.' Her face was creased into a frown. 'Just tell me, Sarah – you're starting to make me feel anxious.'

Sarah breathed in. 'Adam's home,' she said.

'*Adam?*'

'There was no warning. He appeared at the front door one night, late, as I was on my way up to bed . . .' Sarah gave a helpless shrug.

'But *how*?' Frances was incredulous. 'Where did he come from, how did he get here? Was he rescued? Is he all right?'

A few of the questions Sarah also wanted answers to. 'He escaped,' she said, and her sister's eyebrows shot up. 'I honestly don't know the details – he's not been home long enough to go into it all. I think it's been very hard for him, and I'm not sure he can bear to talk about it all yet. The main thing is he's back and he's all right.'

Was he, though? On the face of things, perhaps, but until she knew what he'd actually been through, she couldn't possibly be sure.

Frances was quiet for a moment, digesting what Sarah had told her. '*Escaped*, you say, from the POW camp?'

Sarah nodded. She knew as well as Frances that few succeeded in escaping the Nazis.

'But . . . how on earth did he *manage* it? How did he even get out of Germany? It's impossible, surely.'

Sarah was silent for a moment. 'All the time I was anxious, waiting to hear from him, he was on his way home. He's been in jeopardy every step of the way, suffering danger and deprivation for weeks, months.' She broke off, unable to continue. She was still not clear how long his journey had taken or what it had entailed, and the thought of what he might have gone through was sometimes too much for her. 'It must have been terrifying, requiring every scrap of courage he could muster, every bit of energy. I can only imagine what it must have cost him.'

Frances nodded slowly.

'I didn't recognise him,' Sarah admitted. 'I took him for a stranger.'

'You weren't expecting him, and I doubt very much he looked anything like the Adam you last set eyes on.'

Sarah shook her head, seeing once more the bent, bearded figure in the ragged overcoat. 'He's lost weight,' she said. A huge understatement. Adam, always slender, was now skin and bone. 'I want to know everything but I'm afraid of pushing him. Whenever I ask, he deflects me.'

Frances put a hand on her sister's arm. 'I don't doubt what he's been through was incredibly traumatic,' she said. 'It must have been testing in ways we can't even begin to imagine, pushing him to the very limits of his endurance, over and over, every second of every day. He can hardly have slept much, on such a journey – there won't have been a moment when he'll have felt able to let down his guard. It doesn't bear thinking about. To tell you what he's been through, he'll have to revisit it all and that's going to prove painful, bring it all to the surface again. Be patient, Sarah, give him the time he needs. There may be some things he will never be prepared to share.'

Sarah took a moment to consider what Frances had said. 'He's always felt so connected to his parishioners,' she said slowly, 'and yet when I mentioned how concerned everyone was for him and the prayers being offered up at St Mark's each week for his safe return, he . . . recoiled, I suppose. I thought he'd find it a comfort, but it seemed to have the opposite effect. He doesn't want anyone to know he's back. He said I might tell you, but otherwise no one is to know. It seems utterly at odds with the man he is.'

Or was, Sarah thought.

'I'm sure he has his reasons,' Frances said gently. 'For the moment, you need some time together, without interruption.'

That was what Adam had said.

Frances hesitated. 'He won't have to go back, will he?' she asked.

Sarah shook her head. 'There's no question of that, thank goodness.' She would not have been able to bear it. Following his debriefing, Adam had been discharged of his duties; the Army expected nothing more of him. Once the formalities were completed, he had chosen to make his way home on foot, alone, he told her, in the hope that a period of solitude might help clear his head. Sarah was not sure it had made very much difference. She bit her lip.

'Try not to expect too much from him,' Frances went on. 'He's been through an ordeal, after all, one that's bound to have changed him in ways even he might not yet understand.'

Chapter 32

H E WANTED TO SHARE it with her. Some of it; not all of it. There were terrors he had witnessed and wished never to think of or speak about ever again. At the same time, he knew that the very things he hoped to forget were the ones that would haunt him for the rest of his days.

After he'd been home a week, Adam sat Sarah down and poured a whisky for each of them. He said he'd tell her as much as he could. Enough, at least, for her to understand something of what he'd been through.

'We were being held in an *Oflag*, a camp for officers,' he began, 'in the north, somewhere near Hamburg.' He wasn't sure where exactly; he'd have to look at a map – if he could bring himself to. One day, perhaps. 'One of the chaps in the same hut as me was at Oxford a couple of years ahead of me and we hit it off right away.'

Edward Williams. Eddie. He was a linguist with a brilliant mind, clever enough to have found something safe to do from a bunker in Whitehall during the war, but instead he had chosen to fight. Adam had also got pally with a young medic, George Dixon. All three of them had been captured at Dunkirk. They talked constantly about escape – everyone did – in the knowledge the odds were against them. Escape was rare, and retribution swift.

But when an opportunity presented itself, they took it.

'They were moving us to another camp, marching us there, and the guards became . . . *distracted*.'

It wasn't the right word for what had occurred, but he had been at the rear of the column, too far away to see what was happening up ahead. There was some sort of eruption – shouts, shots fired – that sent the guards on either side running. A split second later, Eddie had grabbed his sleeve and yanked him from the road into the cover of the towering pine trees that flanked it, George scrambling along behind. Adam felt a surge of fear, and at the same time a rush of energy sufficient to propel him forward, even though he could barely get his breath and his heart seemed ready to burst.

They ran for what felt like hours, Eddie leading the way, as if he knew where he was going, Adam and George blindly following. All the while, Adam braced himself for a bullet in the back. He was convinced they wouldn't get far, that the Nazis were on their heels. There'd be no recapture – they'd be shot as they ran, left to rot in a forest in the middle of nowhere. What they were doing was madness. He kept thinking about how and when Sarah would find out – would he be missing for years, before she knew what had happened?

And yet no shot came. They kept on, following Eddie, pushing deeper into the forest, stopping only when the light started to go. Eddie, the only one who seemed to know instinctively which direction might ultimately lead them to safety, steered them north, into Denmark.

Without Eddie they'd have been lost.

Or killed.

'Isn't Denmark under Nazi occupation?' Sarah asked.

It was, Adam told her, but there was a resistance movement and they struck lucky. That was what Eddie kept saying, that luck was on their side. He refused to take credit for his own leadership skills and what seemed to Adam his uncanny sense of direction – not to mention an ability to speak a little Danish, enough to get by. Somehow, Eddie managed to lead them to a farm owned by an elderly couple who were sympathetic to their plight, providing food and shelter and clothes. They put them in touch with the Danish resistance, who spirited them as far as the coast and onto a fishing boat bound for Norway.

'Norway was our best chance,' Adam said, frowning into his whisky. That was what Eddie had told him. There were boats coming back and forth from the Shetlands, a fleet of fishing cutters known as the 'Shetland Bus'. The threat of attack from enemy aircraft and gunboats was constant as the volunteer crews undertook the treacherous North Sea crossing from Lunna to the Norwegian coast under cover of darkness, landing agents, arms and ammunition, then returning with refugees.

They just needed to get themselves onto one of these small boats.

Adam had no idea how far they walked. It must have been hundreds of miles. At times, their journey had seemed endless. He had truly understood what it meant to be 'dead on your feet' – a phrase he resolved never again to use lightly if he was lucky enough to make it home.

He stole a glance at Sarah, who looked anxious, and decided not to tell her that on more than one occasion he had been ready to give up, that as the days passed and they pressed on without sleep, cold and hungry, the fatigue became so extreme that he simply wanted to cease trudging and collapse, that nothing seemed worth the awful pain and exhaustion of carrying on, that he wanted to lie down and never get up again.

George was the same, but Eddie urged them on.

What kept him going, he wasn't sure. Partly – mostly – it was a sense of already having come so far, and a determination not to let down the others. The desire to keep going, to live, proved in the end more powerful than his deepest, darkest moments of despair. They were over the worst, he told himself. He said it again and again in his head. *Over the worst*. The words propelled him forward. The moment they had made their escape was surely the trickiest part, their trek through Germany a close second. Nothing else could be as bad.

He was wrong about that.

They had yet to see for themselves the worst of the Nazis' brutality. As they made their way onwards, they witnessed Jewish men, women and children rounded up and led into the forest to be slaughtered; they saw Soviet prisoners, weak from starvation, being worked to death in labour camps. What Adam had witnessed would never leave him.

And then there was Eddie, whose own luck ran out when the boat bringing them home came under German fire.

Adam swallowed down some of the whisky.

'For some of what I saw, there are no words.' Tears ran down his face. 'We think we know what the Nazis are capable of, the depths of their cruelty, but we know almost nothing. What's going on there, the killing of *innocents* – it's worse than anything you can imagine.'

Sarah knelt in front of him and took his hands in hers. 'It's all right,' she said softly.

'No, it's not,' Adam told her. 'It can never be all right.' He began to sob. 'Where's God in all this? What use is prayer in the face of all this death and destruction? The things I've seen, what men are capable of doing to one another ... the sheer inhumanity.' He covered his face with his hands. The sight of the Soviet prisoners, little more than skeletons, came back to him. *Dead on their feet.* Nazi soldiers, devoid of compassion, pushing their prisoners to the point of death, revelling in their suffering. Now Leningrad was under siege, its people facing starvation. 'I've asked myself countless times, how can He stand it?'

Sarah stroked his hair. 'Terrible things happen in war, atrocities beyond all our comprehension, unspeakable acts of brutality that most of us will never make sense of. I expect it's even harder to comprehend when you have faith. You question why God doesn't do something. How can He allow such suffering? You're not the first to ask such questions, and you won't be the last.'

She waited a moment, trying to steady her breathing. It must be hard, Adam knew, for her to see him like this.

'I know I'm shielded from the worst of it,' Sarah went on, 'that although I might *think* I know what war means, how bloody it all is – the truth is, I don't. But you, Adam, you've seen it, lived through some of the worst horrors. It's bound to leave you feeling raw in ways I can only begin to imagine.' She gazed at him. 'You're hurting, Adam. You're angry – with the Nazis, with God. Some of your deepest wounds are on the inside, and the process of healing is going to take time. All I'd say is, don't be in a rush to make any momentous decisions – about God, or anything else.'

Adam was quiet a moment. He felt lost, in a greater crisis than he had ever known. In the past he'd always found consolation in his faith, but it seemed to have deserted him. Or, perhaps, in his distress, he had shut it out – he wasn't sure which. 'It's as if every bit of certainty I once had is gone,' he said. 'It's as if my ministry has been about peddling lies, encouraging people to believe in a God who goes missing right at the point when you need Him most.'

He gave her an anguished look. 'I can't *hear* Him anymore, Sarah.'

'Tell me what I can do to help,' she said.

He shook his head. This was something he was going to have to work out for himself.

'There's an awful lot of competing noise inside your head just now,' Sarah said gently, folding her arms around him. 'And perhaps it's drowning out everything else – even God's voice. In time, the turbulence *may* just begin to settle. For now, try to be patient.'

Adam nodded. It was good advice. 'I'm just not sure I can pick up where I left off, and go back to my old life, as if nothing has happened.' He lowered his voice. 'And I don't know if I want to.'

Sarah held him tightly. 'Whatever you decide, I'm here.'

Chapter 33

ON THE DAY OF the WI 'Fashion on the Ration' extravaganza, Frances arrived early at the village hall. Pat was already there, checking the clothes rails and making sure every item was in its rightful place and clearly priced. Alison had helped her decide how much to charge, keeping everything affordable. The few relatively expensive items were confined to the formal and evening wear section from which Pat had retrieved Frances's Dior dress. It now hung in her spare room, awaiting alteration.

Frances stepped inside the hall, and was met by the colourful banner Pat had made from spare strips of fabric. Bunting hung from the walls, and the whole room looked bright. She stood for a moment, admiring Pat's efforts, aware that she'd been expecting help from Sarah, Erica and Gwen Talbot and that none of them in the end had been able to come.

'It looks absolutely marvellous,' Frances said. 'Nothing like the usual jumble sale.'

'Being able to put everything on rails is what's made the difference,' Pat told her. 'Once you put clothes on hangers, you lift them out of the realms of rummage right away.'

Frances wandered over to the womenswear section, where she was greeted by a mannequin in an elegant turquoise dress, a fur stole draped across its shoulders. Frances peered at it. 'Is the fur one of mine?' she asked.

'It is. And that's my old wedding dress.'

Frances took a closer look. 'It's lovely. Did you make it yourself?'

Pat nodded. 'The fabric cost a fortune, but I wanted to splash out. If you can't wear something nice on your wedding day, when can you?'

Frances turned back to her. 'I've been rather remiss, I'm afraid, leaving you to get on with all this, almost single-handed, expecting you to manage, assuming you're fine and that you've adjusted to an entirely new way of life. I didn't even stop to think you could do with a little support. Forgive me, Pat – I've not asked for quite some time how you are.'

Pat smiled. 'It's been six months since Bob died, and life has a way of going on. I hope this doesn't sound callous, but it's as if I'm coming into my own at last, becoming the person I was meant to be, if you can understand that.'

'I must say, I've noticed you growing in confidence, embracing the freedom you now have – dressmaking, *writing* – and it's a sight to behold,' Frances told her. 'And not before time, I'd say.'

'I heard back from the magazine,' Pat said. 'The one I submitted my story to. They're going to publish it.'

Frances beamed. 'That's wonderful news! Congratulations! A published writer, no less, what an achievement! Really, Pat, getting your work into print and at the first attempt . . . all I can say is you must have an outstanding ability. And I'm sure this is just the beginning, the first chapter, if you like. Are you able to tell me anything about the subject matter?'

'It's a love story, a couple who find each other against the odds, only to be separated by war.'

'I do hope you've given your couple a happy ever after,' Frances said. 'Isn't that what we all want, particularly in these trying times?'

Pat nodded. 'It's not quite so straightforward,' she said. 'In real life hope and longing, the dream of something better, is all too often unfulfilled. In the story, they lose touch and she's left waiting for news, wondering why he's fallen silent.'

'A story of our times,' Frances said.

Pat nodded. 'I found I didn't want to end on too final a note. The idea was to leave room for more of their story to unfold. And the magazine have already asked for a second instalment.'

'How clever,' Frances said. 'Get the readers hooked and then keep it running. It all sounds very intriguing. I will keep my fingers crossed that everything works out for your couple and that they get their happy ending after all.'

* * *

Once the sale opened for business, it soon became busy, and the rail of women's clothing was the first to be depleted. The children's section also proved popular. Pat, alongside Frances, was kept busy taking money at one end of the hall. Among the first items to sell was Pat's old wedding dress, to one of the women who'd been coming to the WI 'Stitch in Time' classes. Steph Farrow bought a couple of Bob's shirts and a suit of his that had hardly been worn.

In a rare moment of quiet, Joyce Cameron appeared, holding the fur stole donated by Frances. 'I spotted this as soon as I came through the door,' she said, pleased with her find. 'Extraordinary to think whoever this belonged to no longer wanted it.'

Frances avoided looking her in the eye as she took payment for the fur. 'We're not actually sure where it came from,' she said. 'I can definitely see you wearing it, though.'

Joyce tucked the stole into the Browns' bag she'd brought with her. 'Actually, Frances, I wonder while you're not too busy if I might have a word?'

'Of course.'

'I must confess I feared this might end up a glorified jumble sale,' Joyce said, steering Frances to a quiet corner. 'You've really worked wonders.'

'All credit belongs to Pat,' Frances said. 'She has worked tirelessly, almost entirely on her own, to make it happen.'

'I understand she was hoping that Mrs Talbot would lend a hand and then, unfortunately . . .' She left the sentence unfinished. 'And if I'm not very much mistaken, didn't Mrs Collingborne have every intention of helping out too?' Joyce gave Frances a penetrating look.

Frances frowned. 'I really couldn't say.'

'I must say, I'm surprised to see she's not here today.' Joyce's beady eyes scanned the room. 'I'd have thought she'd want to show her support.'

'I expect she's busy.'

'No doubt. I'm sure she must be fully occupied at home.'

Frances gave nothing away. 'Most likely. I'm really not sure what she's doing.'

Joyce kept her eyes on Frances. 'I was walking past her house the other day and glimpsed someone in the garden. A man. When I called out a greeting, he shot inside the house.' She paused. 'It was as if he didn't want to be seen. It really was most peculiar.'

'Sarah did say that Stan Farrow was going to take a look at pollarding the pear tree,' Frances said. It was a poor lie, but, having been put on the spot, it was all she could think of. She wondered if 'pollard' was the correct term for cutting back a pear tree, and if so, whether November would be the right time to do it. She felt herself starting to wilt under Joyce's scrutiny.

'It was most definitely *not* Mr Farrow,' Joyce said, not taking her eyes off Frances.

Frances gave what she hoped was a nonchalant shrug. 'In that case, I don't think I can help.'

'Although I caught only the briefest glimpse, something about the gentleman was familiar,' Joyce went on. 'In fact,

I could have sworn it was . . . the Reverend Collingborne.'
She waited a moment before saying, 'I wonder, do you
happen to know if he's back from the war?'

Frances gave her a stern look. 'My dear Mrs Cameron,
this is exactly how rumours start.'

Joyce hesitated. 'As you're aware, I'm not one to gossip, and I have no wish to pry into private matters – but I
would like to know if our vicar has returned. It would be
a boost to the village, a source of great joy to those of us
who have kept him in our prayers in recent months.'

'Of course, I understand, but I'm afraid you're very
much mistaken.'

Joyce arched an eyebrow. Frances wished she would
stop looking at her in such an accusing manner. 'Am I?'
Joyce said. 'I happened to call at your sister's this morning
on my way here in the hope of speaking to her about this
very matter, but I got no answer. It's not the first time of
late that I've felt there was something . . . not quite right
about the house. More than once I've noticed the curtains
have been left closed until lunchtime.'

'I'll call on her myself once we're finished,' Frances
offered. *And warn her that word about Adam's return will
soon be all over the village.*

'Frances, I'm not seeking to make mischief. I assume
there's a very good reason why the vicar hasn't yet made his
presence felt. There are villagers, however, in need of comfort
and spiritual counsel. Mrs Talbot, for one. Perhaps if you find
your sister at home, you might be so kind as to let her know.'

'I have something to tell you,' Alison said.

She was with Teresa, examining the rack of baby clothes, looking through knitted jackets and all-in-ones, dresses in pale pastel colours. Teresa held up a fussy pink confection with an embroidered hem and ruched bodice. 'If I knew I was having a girl, I'd buy this,' she said, grinning at Alison. Then she folded the dress and put it down. 'Right, I'm all yours – this "something" is to do with John, I'm guessing.'

Alison's cheeks were pink. She checked to make sure no one was within earshot. 'We're getting married,' she said, her voice a whisper.

Teresa let out a joyful whoop that caused several women to turn and stare at them.

Alison shushed her. 'Nobody knows yet, and we're only telling a few close friends, so a little less of the jumping for joy, if you don't mind! Especially in your condition.'

'But I'm *so* happy for you,' Teresa said, giving her a hug. 'I've always felt the two of you were well-suited – long before you were prepared to admit to it, in fact.'

'I know, and you were right. The idea of falling in love was so unexpected, the last thing I'd ever have imagined happening. It took me by surprise, you know. So much so, it was a while before I was willing to acknowledge my feelings. But I can see now how fortunate I am.'

'And so is John,' Teresa reminded her. 'Have you decided on a date, made any plans?' Her eyes widened. 'What about a dress?'

'We're busy working all that out. I'm not sure what I'll wear, I was hoping I might see something today.' She glanced in the direction of the formalwear rail. 'Nothing's quite right, though.'

'Have you anything you could alter?'

'I'm not sure.' She had a satin frock she'd worn to a friend's wedding some years earlier. It still fitted, but Alison wasn't sure that it looked sufficiently special. It was her *wedding day*, after all, and whatever the rest of the village might think, she had never been married before. She wanted to make the most of it, look the part. She might have a word with Frances, and see if she had something she could borrow.

'Our wedding won't be anything like on the scale of yours,' Alison went on. 'We only intend to have a few guests. You and Nick, of course, will come?'

'I can't wait.'

Alison frowned. 'I do wonder . . . how people will react to the news.' She knew their marriage would cause quite a stir in the village and that, inevitably, some would find the idea of a 'mixed marriage' beyond shocking. 'It'll give them something to talk about, I suppose,' she said, making an effort to sound less concerned than she really was.

'The usual small-minded individuals will have an opinion, no doubt,' Teresa said. 'Not that it's anyone's business but yours. Most people, certainly the ones who matter, will be overjoyed for both of you.'

Alison nodded. 'If only there wasn't such *hostility* towards John.' She still felt raw over the business of the sheep killings and how quick certain individuals had been to blame him. Gwen Talbot, to her credit, had come to the house to speak to them and say how sorry she was that John had been accused, how ashamed she felt for having been among those to assume his guilt.

Even so, Alison struggled with the notion that John would ever be truly accepted here.

'It's one of the drawbacks of a small village, as we both know,' Teresa said. 'I'm not saying cities are much better – you find ignorant people everywhere – but at least there's a degree of anonymity in larger places, and that can be of some comfort when you find you're out of step with the majority.'

Like you, Alison thought, thinking once more about Teresa's clandestine relationship with another woman. Somehow, with Alison's encouragement, Teresa had succeeded in adapting to a way of life those around her found acceptable. She had married, was about to have a child. She would be a wife and mother. By submitting to convention, she had been afforded respectability.

In order to conform, however, she had to keep a part of who she was concealed. Not just now, but always; not just from the wider world, but from her husband too. Alison had been so concerned with safeguarding Teresa's reputation – and her own, as the young woman's landlady – that she had not properly considered the degree of heartache involved in her decision to jettison the very essence of her true self. It was only now, when she knew what judgement society might cast on her relationship with John, that she was struck by the enormity of the sacrifice Teresa had made.

'You don't have any regrets?' Alison asked quietly. 'About all you gave up in order to make a life with Nick?'

Teresa shook her head. 'I'll admit I've had my moments when I've questioned the decisions I made, but isn't that something we all do from time to time? I never thought I could be happy with a man, but Nick is a true companion, and always good to me. Sometimes, to be sure, I do wonder if things might have been a different way, especially on a bad day, when things aren't going as planned.' She smiled. 'In the early days of marriage, I remember despairing, thinking I'd never even master the basics of being a housewife, just putting an edible meal on the table . . .' She laughed. 'Thanks to the recipes you loaned me, I managed to overcome that particular obstacle.'

She could not bring herself to tell Alison about what she now thought of as her moment of lunacy with Annie. That she had gone behind Nick's back while he risked his life, betraying him with a woman he considered to be a trusted friend. Annie had meant more to her than she could bear to think, but she had made her choice; she had chosen a life with Nick, and she had to be true to him.

'You're happy, though?' Alison persisted.

'I couldn't wish for a better man than Nick,' Teresa said. 'Sometimes I wonder what I did right to deserve someone as special. Like you, I consider myself extremely fortunate.'

As the extravaganza began to wind down, they left the village hall together.

'I'll walk you home,' Alison said.

'There's no need – it's the opposite direction for you.'

'I'd like to make sure you get back safely.'

Teresa laughed. 'You're as bad as Nick – he'd have me wrapped in cotton wool if he could. I know the baby's due soon, but I am still perfectly capable.'

Alison only smiled.

'I love this time of year,' she said, linking her arm through Teresa's as they walked. 'Even on a day like today when it's grey and there's no sun to be seen, autumn bursts with colour.' She bent and picked up a leaf that was a rich shade of reddish brown. 'Do you know, I collected leaves when I was a child, kept them in a bowl on the windowsill in my bedroom.'

'It was conkers with me,' Teresa said, laughing. 'There was an enormous horse chestnut not far from us. I always had one in my pocket, a bit like a talisman. If I felt anxious I'd reach for it and say a quick prayer.' She smiled as they stopped briefly outside the butcher's. The awning had gone up outside the new shop now. 'You can't even tell there was a fire,' said Teresa. 'When I was in the other day, Miriam told me they're still on course to open in time for Christmas.'

'They had a lucky escape,' Alison said. 'I always get the impression Miriam thinks they're shielded by Providence in some way.'

'She must have something better than a conker in her pocket,' Teresa joked.

They were nearing Teresa's home now, and Alison frowned. 'Is that car stopping outside your house?'

Teresa watched as a young man in uniform stepped from the driver's seat and went round to open the rear passenger door. 'Oh, no,' she said, watching as a man stepped out. 'It's Nick's group captain. Michael Buey. Awful man. He's a bore and a snob with a wife to match. We had them round for dinner and now they want to return the favour.' She sighed. 'I suppose I'd better speak to him.'

Alison watched Group Captain Buey knock at the door while his driver waited at the side of the car. Something didn't feel right. 'I'll come with you,' she said, feeling a sudden tightness in her stomach.

'I warn you, he's a crashing bore,' Teresa said. She turned up the path to the house. 'Group Captain,' she said, 'this is unexpected.'

He turned to face her, removing his cap. 'Mrs Lucas.'

The tone of his voice was grave, and at once the purpose of his visit became apparent. Teresa's smile slid away, cold fear on the back of her neck. She had an urge to run and shut herself inside the house before Michael Buey was able to say the words she could not stand to hear, the words that would end her life as she knew it.

Panic rose inside her and she began to shake. *I just need to get inside. Get away before he has a chance to speak.* But Michael Buey was in the way, barring her escape. She felt an urge to strike him, knock him off his feet.

'I'm so very sorry . . .' he began.

'No. *No.*' Alison's grip on her arm tightened as Teresa backed away, her hands over her ears. 'Don't – don't.' She felt light-headed, felt her legs give way beneath her.

Alison had hold of her with both hands now and struggled to support her. When Teresa collapsed Alison went with her, the two of them on their knees on the cold ground.

Chapter 34

'I<small>T WAS A TRAINING FLIGHT</small>,' Frances said. 'There was some kind of problem as they were coming back in to land – they don't yet know what. Nick was thrown clear. He was dead by the time they got to him.'

'I just don't understand.' Sarah's voice shook. 'He was an excellent pilot, one of the best.'

Frances sighed. She had arrived with the news earlier, aware of how fond Sarah and Adam had been of Nick, keen to bring them up to date. The three of them were in the living room now, a tray of tea untouched on the table in front of them.

'He wasn't actually flying. It was another pilot, a much younger man,' Frances explained. She'd gone with Alison, on Teresa's behalf, to the RAF station at Tabley Wood, and spoken to Group Captain Buey, in the hope he might be able to furnish them with more details – but in the end they'd been able to ascertain little. Until its final moments, Nick's flight had gone according to plan. It was simply an exercise, the sort of thing that took place every day, in itself nothing out of the ordinary. What went wrong had yet to be determined. It was probably mechanical failure, engine trouble, something mundane and awful. The plane had hit the ground with considerable force and burst into flames, the young man trapped inside the cockpit consumed by the fire. There wasn't much left of him, Buey told them, looking grim. If it was of any consolation, Nick, at least, was still able to be recognised.

'He *lived* with us.' Sarah was tearful. 'We *knew* him. This war . . . it seems intent on taking our best people.'

Adam bowed his head, thinking not only of Nick but of Eddie. Eddie, who'd kept him going in Norway in his darkest moments, who'd come within striking distance of safety only to lose his life when the escape craft carrying them across the North Sea came under German fire. Without Eddie, Adam would never have made it home. He wouldn't be here now with Sarah, hearing about yet another tragedy. One more senseless loss. Eddie first, and now Nick.

Our best people.

'How's Teresa?' Adam said.

Frances shook her head. 'Alison's with her a lot of the time and Dr Rosen's going in every day. Erica's been a tower of strength.' Erica knew all too well what it was to have an RAF officer at the door, bringing the kind of news no one wanted to receive. Her daughter, Kate, had lost her husband, Jack, within weeks of them being married. He was another pilot killed during what was meant to be a routine training flight.

Sarah was thinking about the baby Teresa was soon to have, a child who would now be born into a world that had suddenly and irrevocably changed. Its father was gone, its mother grieving. Teresa was due to give birth early in the New Year, just a few weeks away. Was it long enough, Sarah wondered, for Teresa to begin to emerge from the darkness now enveloping her and be ready to embrace motherhood?

'What about the baby?' she asked Frances.

'She spent a night in hospital and was thoroughly checked over,' Frances said. 'And Dr Rosen's keeping a close eye. But, for now, everything's as it should be.'

No, it's not, thought Sarah solemnly. *Nothing is as it should be.* Sarah was deep in thought, her mind whirling. The idea that Nick was dead seemed inconceivable. Nick, so bright and upbeat and *alive*. Nick, about to be a father. It made no sense. *Why is it that some die and others are spared? Who decides? How can it be fair?* She was asking herself questions she knew to be absurd. *No one decides. Such things happen.* In her heart she understood the random nature of life and death. And yet—

She reached across the table for Adam's hand. It seemed even more impossible, even more of a miracle, that Adam could be home, alive, after what he had been through, when Nick had died on a training flight.

It was one thing to be shot down by the enemy, another to die because the plane had suffered a 'mechanical failure' during what should have been an uneventful exercise. The explanation seemed flimsy, Nick's death abhorrent. It was a waste of a good life – a good man.

She glanced at Adam and at Frances, both lost in their own thoughts, and stopped short of saying what she was thinking. Perhaps she was wrong to rail at the circumstances. All that mattered was that Nick was dead.

Another casualty of war.

'What happens now?' Sarah asked.

'He'll be buried in the Midlands, where his family is,' Frances said. 'He's from a village by the name of Kibworth Beauchamp. There's a family plot in the churchyard there. Teresa leaves in the morning.'

'I'd like to see her before she goes,' Sarah said.

'I'll come with you,' Adam said. 'Nick was a friend, I'd like to pay my respects.'

Sarah threw him an anxious look. In a short space of time, he was looking much better. Sleep and food were doing their work. Already, he had gained a little weight – but he was still in the early stages of recovery, and quite how well his mind was healing was less easy to determine. The last thing Sarah wanted to do was risk the progress he had made so far. Her instinct was to spare him from anything that might bring his own recent trauma to the surface once more.

'There's no need for both of us to go,' she said gently. 'Teresa doesn't even know you're here, she won't be expecting to see you. And anyway, I can't help but worry . . .' Adam waited for her to go on, and she looked away. 'It might set you back.'

'I can't spend the rest of my life avoiding anything that might upset me,' Adam said, with a sad smile.

'It just feels . . . too soon. Once people know you're here, they're going to want to see you.' She gave him a meaningful look. 'At the house. In church. As their *vicar*. Are you sure that's what you want? Are you ready to have the needs of the village laid in front of you? Because that's what will happen.'

'In all honesty, I'm not sure how much longer you'll manage to keep your presence a secret,' Frances said. 'It's obvious Joyce knows, and I very much doubt the rest of the village will be far behind her. It's too small a place to keep anything secret for long. It would be better to make an appearance, perhaps, than let things reach the point where people know you're here and question why you're choosing to avoid them. The reasons for your seclusion could be misinterpreted and result in hurt feelings.'

'I was thinking the same thing,' Adam said. 'This feels to me like the right moment to get back into the community and do some good if I can, albeit in a small way. Teresa's in a dark place, and I'd like her at least to know she's in my prayers.'

Sarah looked at him, surprised. There'd been no mention of prayer since the conversation they'd had in which Adam admitted to being in the grip of a catastrophic crisis of faith.

'I'm sure she'll appreciate it,' Frances said. 'She's in shock, as you'd expect. Alison's hardly been able to get a word out of her.'

Adam took Sarah's hand. 'We'll go together,' he said. 'In all conscience, I can't just sit here and do nothing.'

Chapter 35

ALISON THOUGHT THE BEST thing to do was postpone her marriage to John. She couldn't imagine making arrangements for a wedding when Teresa was about to bury her husband. It felt wrong, disrespectful somehow. John was a little disappointed, she could tell, but he understood. They would wait, he said, if that was what she wanted.

At the same time, he did not think that Teresa would want them to put their happiness on hold. Nick's death had served as yet another stark reminder of the fleeting, sometimes heartless nature of life. It was made worse, too, that the news had arrived at the cruellest moment, just as Nick and Teresa looked forward to having their first child. They had been planning for a future that would now never come.

'Might not the best way of honouring Nick be to make the most of whatever time we have?' John suggested gently. 'To cherish each and every second and take nothing for granted?'

Frances, who had shown not a flicker of surprise when Alison told her that she and John intended to be married, said much the same thing. 'You're closer to Teresa than anyone. I honestly think the last thing she'd want is for you to abandon your wedding plans. I can see why you'd want to but, sadly, it won't change anything.'

Frances told Alison she thought she might have a dress that could be made into a suitable wedding outfit. She was thinking of the oyster-pink Schiaparelli evening gown she had intended to donate to the extravaganza. 'Sarah persuaded me not to give it away,' she said, 'even though it's something I'll never have occasion to wear again. She must have had an inkling it would one day be of some use to one of my dear friends.'

Alison was taken aback when she saw the dress. 'It's so beautiful,' she said, 'but I couldn't possibly take it.'

'Nonsense.' Frances held the gown up in front of Alison and gave her an appraising look. 'The colour suits you very well, and I shall never wear it again. I'd much rather it found a use than spent the rest of its days out of sight at the back of my wardrobe.'

Pat agreed to alter the dress and produced a sketch for Alison. It showed a hemline that ended just below the knee, a belt, perhaps with a bow detail. From the swathes of spare fabric in the skirt she proposed to create an entirely new bodice with a sweetheart neckline and puff sleeves. The back of the dress, which was fastened with a row of pretty pearl buttons, would stay as it was.

'Can you really do all that?' Alison asked, impressed.

'It's actually more straightforward than you might think,' Pat told her.

Alison struggled to see how. They were in Pat's spare room, now filled with sewing paraphernalia, and Alison was in the process of trying on the dress for the first time.

'I'm nervous at the thought of taking the scissors to such a beautiful garment,' Alison said, as Pat did up the fiddly little buttons at the back. 'It must have cost a fortune, more than I dare imagine. It seems, I don't know, *sacrilege*, to cut it up.'

Pat smiled. 'Let me worry about that. Just remember, if it weren't for you, this fabulous dress would be left to languish in the back of a wardrobe, probably never worn again. Surely *that* would be sacrilege.' She stood back for a moment and gazed at Alison. 'It suits you, you know. You could easily carry it off exactly as it is.'

Alison laughed. 'If I was attending a glamorous ball rather than a modest wedding at my local registry office, I might consider it.'

'Well, I'm very happy for you,' Pat said. 'For both of you.'

'We've been so careful about keeping things private, and yet none of my friends has seemed in the least bit surprised to hear that we're getting married.'

'I must admit, I had an idea you were . . . *close*,' Pat said. 'The day I came round to tell you about Gwen Talbot's son, I saw the way you were with each other, how concerned you felt for John. There was a tenderness about it, rather more than I'd have expected a landlady to have for her lodger.'

Alison's eyes shone. 'I think I sensed something between us from the first moment we met. I don't mean romantically, exactly, more a feeling that here was someone I had something in common with. As if we were already *familiar* on some level when, in fact, I knew almost nothing about him. Does that sound ludicrous?'

Pat shook her head. She understood exactly what Alison meant, had felt the same about Marek – as if she knew it was safe to trust him right from the off. He was a man of his word.

'I always felt *something* for John,' Alison went on, 'although for a long time I was afraid to admit it, even to myself.'

'You were seeking to protect yourself, perhaps,' Pat told her. Her thoughts had strayed to Teresa and Nick. 'Once we allow ourselves to love, we open ourselves up to the possibility of loss. The two go hand in hand.'

Alison nodded. She seemed to know what was in Pat's mind. After a moment she said, 'Sometimes, I just don't know what to say to help Teresa. It's as if she's retreated behind a wall and I can't find a way of reaching her. She seems utterly numb.' She sighed. 'I feel worse than useless.'

'Without warning, everything has changed for her in the worst way imaginable,' Pat said. 'The life she had before is over. The future she imagined is gone. I doubt she can even think straight. But in time, she'll find a way of getting through this, and you'll be there to help her.'

'When George was killed in the last war I remember thinking I'd never recover. The idea of life without him was beyond imagining. I wasn't sure I'd survive, or even if I wanted to. I think I expected to gradually fade away and cease to exist. It seems incredible now to think there were moments when I didn't want to live.' She gestured at the gown she was wearing. 'Look at me now – about to be married, *happy*. I'd never have believed it.'

'We find a way of moving on,' Pat said. 'We decide against squandering our lives because we understand the value of being here. It's how we honour our loved ones.'

She was thinking of Marek again. She was almost certain now that he must have been lost to the war. If he was, she might never know. No one would come to her door with news of any kind. All she could do was accept there was no longer any possibility of what Frances called their 'happy ever after' and get on with her life.

It tore at her heart, and yet she had not a single regret. Marek had taught her what it meant to love and be loved, created lasting memories that were safe inside her heart for all time. He had shown her that a relationship did not have to be all anger and cruelty, as Bob and hers had been, that there was a potential for happiness, for respect, for real love, in her life. While she mourned his loss, she also felt his presence at her side, on the walks they had once taken together, in her writing each time she put pen to paper. The letter she had begun so long ago had, over time, become a powerful testament to their love; to love itself. Soon, all that they felt for one another would be immortalised in print. He was part of her in all she did, now and always. It was almost enough.

'We go into love never knowing how things will turn out,' Pat said. 'We hope for the best, trusting our hearts won't be broken and at the same time knowing there are no guarantees. And still we take a leap of faith. I suppose we know it's worthwhile.'

Alison looked suddenly serious. 'It just feels so selfish of me to be planning my wedding when Teresa's so utterly bereft.'

Pat took her hand and squeezed it. 'I don't think so, and I doubt Teresa will either. She's your greatest friend – of course she wants you to be happy. If it were the other way round, how would you feel? Would you want her to go ahead?'

Alison nodded.

'Well then. Marry John and be happy. Give all of us something to feel glad about.'

Chapter 36

DAVID COULDN'T HELP THINKING that the fire at the shop was his fault. If only he'd left things as they were, been in less of a hurry to push his parents into expanding what was already a perfectly good business. If only he'd had the sense to see his father's collapse as a sign to ease up rather than assume even more responsibility.

If, if, if.

He'd been blinkered, so determined to press on with his plans it had almost cost him his family.

The damage caused by the fire took weeks to repair. Every bit of electrical wiring throughout the new shop had to be replaced, and the plasterwork redone. To be on the safe side, the butcher's was rewired too, at considerable inconvenience, not to mention expense. It seemed there were hitches and hold-ups at every turn. Before work could resume on the new shop, the building, left sodden by the water from the fire hoses, had first to be thoroughly dried out. That alone seemed to take forever. The pressure was on to complete the work and open in time for Christmas, and

David felt it most keenly, wanting to make up for what he saw as the mistakes he'd made so far. Once they were up and running, he told himself, the shop would do a roaring trade, and the problems of the past would be forgotten.

On the day they opened, towards the end of November, Joyce Cameron was first through the door. Bryn and David, wearing the smart white coats favoured by grocers, greeted her warmly as Joyce processed regally throughout the store, conducting a thorough inspection, pausing to pick up various items which she examined before putting them down again.

'This is a brand I'm not familiar with,' she said, studying a tin of processed meat. 'Oh, I see you've managed to get hold of Turkish Delight.' The jars of sweets behind the counter caught her eye. 'Lemon sherbets, an absolute favourite of mine,' she declared, moving towards them. Bryn took the jar from the shelf and hovered next to the scales with it while Joyce dithered. 'Pear drops!' she exclaimed. Bryn put the lemon sherbets back.

'Two ounces of pear drops, then?' he suggested, keen to make his first sale.

Joyce continued to waver, drifting off to examine the festive biscuit selection, the tempting boxes of Cadbury's Milk Tray and, next to them, cans of instant coffee. 'Coffee? Is it popular?' she mused. 'I suppose time will tell.'

Bryn and David exchanged a look.

'I must congratulate you on a thoroughly splendid job,' she said. 'You have transformed the place. What a wonderful asset to the village after all those months of having an *eyesore* in our midst.'

'Thank you, Mrs Cameron,' David said. 'I hope we can count on your custom.'

'Absolutely,' she replied, and took her leave without having bought anything.

David rolled his eyes as the door shut behind her. 'Couldn't resist the eyesore dig, could she? She had no intention of shopping – she just wanted to have a good old nose about the place. She didn't even bring a shopping bag with her – that's how serious she was about making a purchase!'

'Don't worry, son,' Bryn said. 'Once people get used to the new set-up, things will pick up.'

By the end of the first week, however, business remained slow. Plenty of customers arrived, curious to see what the Brindsleys had done to the shop, but few seemed in the mood to spend. Bryn, left to hold the fort alone after the first few days, began to wonder if it had been a mistake to think a shiny new 'emporium' would go down well in a traditional village. Not that he said so – whenever David bemoaned the lack of custom, Bryn assured him it was entirely normal for a new business to take time to find its feet.

'But it's nearly Christmas,' David said. 'If we can't do well now, I'm not sure we ever will.'

Miriam refused to admit defeat. 'We need to hold our nerve and trust that things will come good,' she said. 'Think of how much we've come through as a family, all of us pulling together. We're *meant* to succeed and we will, you mark my words.'

Bryn, who knew better than to argue, simply nodded. 'Let's hope you're right, Mim,' he said.

'I am.' She sounded defiant. 'We just need to believe we're on the right track. We survived the fire, didn't we?'

Bryn frowned, wondering where she was going with this. 'Well . . .'

'And I won't believe it was for nothing. We're closer than ever, a family nothing can break. The shop *will* pick up, you'll see. If this war has taught us anything it's that we never know what's round the corner.'

'Usually something bad,' Bryn countered.

'Not always. David came home, didn't he?' She gave Bryn a steely look. 'So we'll have less of that gloomy talk, if you don't mind!'

'What if we can't make a success of it?' David asked Jenny. 'It'll be my fault.' He was walking her home after a late finish at Tabley Wood. 'They were perfectly happy with the butcher's until I persuaded them to expand and take on a business we know nothing about. The first week's takings were pitiful. If that's a sign of things to come, we might as well give up now.'

Jenny nodded slowly, but didn't answer.

'I can't even talk to Ma because she just goes on about God having a plan for us and how we must have faith and . . .' He sighed, exasperated. 'Never mind that we've sunk almost every spare bit of cash we've got into a shop that everyone agrees looks wonderful and no one seems to want to spend money in! It's all my fault, Jenny. If one more person says how smart the awning is, I swear I'll scream.'

David stopped and turned to face Jenny. 'I'm so sorry. There's me going on, not even asking how you are. It must be difficult at the base just now after what happened.'

'It was the funeral today, in the village where Nick grew up,' Jenny said, sounding close to tears. She had been on duty the day that his plane crashed. 'All the top brass went, so the base was deserted. I can't stop thinking about Mrs Lucas, expecting a baby, her husband going out to work and never coming home. It's unbearable. Why, when they had everything in front of them?'

David pulled her close. 'I don't know, it doesn't make sense.'

His mother held an unshakeable belief in Providence, but in his experience, there was no such thing. Weren't good people lost when his ship went down? He had lost friends. He remembered one, Johnny, who carried a tiny crucifix with him, a talisman given to him by his mother. He had perished. As far as David saw it, in war, and in life, there were no special dispensations. Whether you lived or died was completely random.

'Try not to think about it too much,' David said. 'Sometimes it doesn't help to dwell on things, to wonder why. There is no *why*. Bad things just happen, and we can't always find a way of explaining them.' He kissed the top of her head. 'It's why we need to count our lucky stars and be glad for the good things. We just need to work out what's important and hold onto it.'

Her arms tightened round his waist. 'We'll be all right, won't we?' she said, her voice muffled against his chest.

''Course we will. I promise,' David told her, aware that he was in no position to know.

He sounded like his mother.

Chapter 37

WHILE TERESA WAS AWAY for the funeral, Alison kept an eye on the house, going in every day to open the curtains and let a little fresh air in. Each day brought more letters of condolence in the post. She put them on the sideboard in the front room, ready for Teresa's return. It was likely she'd be away at least a week, she told Alison, staying with Nick's parents.

In anticipation of her return, Alison put bread and milk in the pantry. She didn't want Teresa to have to think about such things, not at a moment like this. The chrysanthemums and asters in the front garden were flowering and she cut a few and placed them in a vase on the kitchen windowsill.

The following morning, when she arrived at the house and let herself in, the atmosphere felt changed. Teresa must be home. Alison called out a cautious 'hello', and when there was no answer, she assumed Teresa must still be sleeping.

She went quietly along the hall into the kitchen, where she found the curtains already drawn back, the kettle warm and cups and plates in the sink. As she waited for Teresa to appear, she filled a bowl with water and did the washing up.

She was putting the last of the dishes away when a woman appeared in the doorway. She was slender, with tousled blonde hair past her shoulders, still in her night things, with a dressing gown too big for her. She was familiar, although at first Alison couldn't place her. Then it came to her – Nick's pilot friend, the one who flew for the Air Transport Auxiliary. Annie. The previous year she'd been seriously injured in a crash and spent some of her time recuperating with Teresa and Nick. She seemed unperturbed to find Alison there, greeting her with a sleepy smile.

'You must be Alison. You've been keeping an eye on things for us.' She raked a hand through her hair. 'You must excuse my rather sloppy appearance, I'm afraid we got back late and I've not been awake long.' She yawned. 'I'm Annie – I think we might already have met.'

Alison nodded. She wondered if the dressing gown was Nick's. 'Yes, I seem to recall you were in a wheelchair the last time I saw you.'

Annie pulled a face. 'I was a bit smashed up for a while, but I'm pleased to report I'm good as new again.'

'You were at the funeral?'

Annie nodded. 'Nick was a very good friend. We'd known each other for years.' She winced. 'I always had the sense he was charmed, that he would come through the war unscathed. I suppose it was what I hoped, as if thinking it would make it true.' She looked away, her face solemn. 'You want the best for the people closest to you.'

Alison found herself wondering how close they'd been, if Nick and Annie were once more than friends. Or, perhaps, Annie and Teresa. She dismissed the thought. 'How's Teresa?' she asked.

Annie went to fill the kettle. 'Bearing up. She's been making an effort to create the impression she's coping. Hoping to persuade everyone, Nick's family included, that they've no need to worry about her. Probably trying to persuade herself, too.' She put the kettle on the stove and lit the gas. 'I'm not convinced. Beneath that brave exterior, I think she's in pieces. Her situation is about the hardest it could be. Enough to break your heart.'

Alison was quiet.

Annie rummaged in a cupboard for cups and decanted milk into a jug. 'Will you stay for tea?' she said.

'Of course. I'd like to make sure Teresa has everything she needs.'

'Oh, no need to worry,' Annie said, with a slight smile. 'I'm here now – I can take care of that.'

When Teresa appeared, Annie was attentive, bringing a cushion to put at the back of her chair. She made toast – 'burnt to a crisp, just the way you like it' – and smothered it in jam, instructing her to eat.

'There's no need to fuss,' Teresa told her.

'There's *every* need,' Annie countered. 'When I was under your care I seem to recall doing as I was told.'

Teresa gave her a weak smile. 'Really? I recall no such thing,' she said.

'Well, it's my turn to look after you now,' Annie went on, placing a hand on Teresa's shoulder. 'I'm at your beck and call. Anything you need, just say the word.'

Teresa took her hand and held it for a moment.

'Now, eat your black toast,' Annie said, wrinkling her nose, 'before it gets cold.'

'I'd forgotten how bossy you can be,' Teresa said.

Annie made an innocent face. 'We need to keep your strength up.'

We.

Alison watched, struck by their closeness, the unmistakable signs of intimacy that passed between them. As Teresa ate, Annie hovered at her side. She tucked a stray strand of hair behind her ear and topped up her tea.

Alison's suspicion that Annie and Nick might once have been more than friends was definitely misplaced.

It was Teresa she must have been involved with.

'How long are you intending to stay?' Alison asked, rather more sharply than she meant to.

Annie raised an eyebrow. 'Oh, I'm here for the duration,' she said.

Alison stared at her. It was impossible, surely. Nick had just died, barely weeks ago, and for Annie to be here, perhaps taking advantage of Teresa's fragile situation . . . She glanced between the two of them. 'I suppose they'll be expecting you back at the ATA before too long,' she said to Annie.

'I've left the ATA,' Annie said.

Alison looked surprised.

'I was busy thinking about what I might do next when . . .' She glanced at Teresa. 'So here I am. As I say, *for the duration.*'

Teresa gave her a grateful look. 'It means I'm not on my own,' she said.

Alison gazed at her. *You were never going to be.*

'I know you and all my friends here would have rallied round and done as much as you could, but you've got your own lives, and I can't expect to be handled with care in the coming weeks and months. Besides, there's no substitute for having someone in the house with me. If I go into labour in the middle of the night, Annie will be on hand, and once the baby comes we can muddle through between us.'

'That's quite a commitment,' Alison said, looking at Annie. 'Won't you be missed at home?'

'I rather think this is home now,' Annie said, with a smile.

Alison made a point of calling on Teresa every morning, hoping for a private word, just the two of them – but Annie was always there.

After a week or so, Alison arrived at the house and finally found Teresa alone. 'Annie's popped out,' Teresa said. 'She won't be long.'

In that case, I'd better be quick. Alison declined tea and they went into the front room.

'How are you?' she asked.

'Sleeping better, and Annie makes sure I eat.' Teresa smiled. 'You've seen what she's like, how strict she can be.'

Alison swallowed hard. 'I just wonder, are you sure it's such a good idea . . . Annie being here?'

Teresa frowned. 'Given my situation, having a friend to keep me company makes complete sense. I'd be lost without her.'

'Oh, Teresa, I'm not blind. I can see what's going on. It's obvious Annie is more than a friend. I've seen how she is with you, all the cosseting and fussing . . .'

Teresa flushed. 'And you disapprove – is that it?'

'It's not a case of disapproving, Teresa. I'm concerned for you, that's all. You've only just lost Nick—'

'I hardly need reminding.'

'—you're grieving, in no position to make decisions about anything, let alone launch into a relationship with one of Nick's friends, someone you haven't even known all that long.'

Teresa took a breath. 'Alison, I know you mean well, but how I choose to live my life is really no concern of yours. Not anymore. I'm not your lodger. I don't need advice on how to behave.'

'I'm not trying to tell you what to do – I just want what's best for you and the baby.'

'Then respect my decisions.' Teresa gave her a defiant look. 'As it happens, I know Annie rather better than you might think, and she's *exactly* what I need in my life now. She's strong and confident and . . . comfortable with who she is. Which is something I've always struggled with, as you know only too well.'

'I thought things changed when you met Nick.'

Teresa gazed at her. 'I became the person I was expected to be – not who I truly am inside. The *real* me never disappeared, Alison, it just – I made myself hide it. Annie's good for me. Somehow she's able to, I don't know, breathe life back into me . . . make me believe that things will, eventually, feel less hopeless than they do right now.' She was close to tears. 'Having her here in no way diminishes how I feel about Nick.'

'Is that how other people will see it?' Alison persisted. 'At some point, they'll work out what's going on – and have something to say about it. You'll be the subject of gossip. At least think about it, please.'

'I already have, Alison. It's my life. Nick would want me to be happy. He loved Annie, you know, held her in the highest regard. Whatever you might think, she's a good person, and she's good for me.' She held Alison's gaze. 'I'm sorry, I'm quite worn out with all this talking, so if you wouldn't mind . . .'

Alison waited a couple of days before calling again, allowing time for the dust to settle. She felt bad about how she'd left things and confided in John, swearing him to secrecy about Teresa, knowing there was no one else in the world she ever could have told. John urged her to make up with Teresa – and take a step back.

'The woman knows her own heart,' he said, 'and, whatever you might think about the rights or wrongs of what she's doing, having someone there day and night has got to be a good thing. Annie must really care about her or she wouldn't be here. Surely that's what's important.'

Privately, Alison worried about Annie taking charge, pushing Teresa into an arrangement she might not otherwise have chosen. Teresa was vulnerable, grieving, in no position to think clearly about the wisdom of changing the entire course of her life. And she'd only just lost Nick – it was too soon.

Teresa had been the subject of rumours before, and Alison understood how corrosive gossip could be.

'People can be cruel,' she told John. 'We both know that.'

'And we both also know you can't dictate to someone how to live their life,' he replied. 'She's got to work it out for herself, mistakes and all.'

All the same, Alison was not so sure.

'You look tired,' Annie said.

Teresa yawned. 'I'm always tired these days.' She rested a hand on her bump. 'I have you to thank for that,' she told the bump.

They were relaxing in the sitting room before bed. One of Annie's records was on the gramophone. Annie placed a stool on the rug and gently eased Teresa's feet onto it. 'It's good to put your feet up,' she said. 'Something to do with circulation.'

'Thank you, Doctor.' Teresa smiled. Annie knelt beside her and began rubbing her feet. 'That feels nice. Do you think my ankles will ever look anything like they did before?' Teresa wondered.

'You're lucky, they're barely swollen at all. You just need to make sure you get plenty of rest and keep your feet up.'

Teresa yawned again. Since losing Nick, she had felt exhausted all the time. At Annie's insistence she had been taking an afternoon nap, sleeping soundly for an hour before being woken with a cup of tea. Often she emerged from sleep disorientated and deeply distressed. It was as if her grief was at its most raw in those moments when she was not quite awake. Somehow Annie knew what to do, holding her and soothing her until her tears subsided. It wasn't easy for her, Teresa supposed, dealing with so much heartache when she too was grieving for Nick.

'Thank you,' Teresa said.

'What for?'

'Everything. For being here and for being so under-standing. Especially after . . . before.' She looked away. Months earlier, after they had slept together, Annie had been keen to keep things going between them. *I don't want to deny the feelings between us* was how she had put it. As long as they were careful, she had said, no one need get hurt. Nick would never find out. Teresa could not take the chance, and had wondered if their friendship would survive.

'I wasn't sure I'd see you again,' Teresa said quietly, 'or that you'd want anything to do with me after what happened.'

'I never blamed you. If anything, I was cross with myself for thinking we could conduct any kind of secret relationship. I wasn't being fair, to you or to Nick.'

'We're all right now, though, aren't we?'

'I think so.'

Teresa closed her eyes. 'I'm glad you're here. I'd be scared on my own, even more than I am already.'

Annie gave her ankle a squeeze. 'What is it you're most afraid of?'

Teresa looked at her and sighed. 'It might sound ridiculous, but even now I can't quite imagine having a baby.'

'You've still time to get used to the idea.' Annie smiled. 'Not much, mind you.'

'But seriously, I can't help thinking – what's it going to be like when the moment comes? Will I know when I'm in labour? What if I can't tell the difference between a touch of indigestion, which I seem to suffer from rather a lot these days, and an actual contraction?'

Annie gave a wry smile. 'I think you'll be able to tell.'

'And then I worry that when the moment comes, I won't be able to manage it.' The idea of giving birth was alarming. It was something she had mentioned to Dr Rosen, who simply said in that calm way of hers that she had no doubt Teresa would manage perfectly well. She gestured at her bump. 'Look at the size of me, Annie. I'm huge.'

'Try not to worry. When the time comes I've every confidence your body will know what to do even if you don't. And you'll be in very good hands.'

Teresa nodded. 'Thank goodness one of us is calm.'

'It's easy for me,' Annie said. 'I'm not the one who actually has to do it.' She looked serious. 'I'll be with you every step of the way, I promise – holding your hand if you want me to.'

Teresa nodded sleepily. 'That really does make me feel better.'

Annie came to the door. She explained that it wasn't a good time, that Teresa was resting.

'I don't mind waiting, or coming back a bit later,' Alison offered.

Annie hesitated. 'I hope you won't mind me being frank, but the last time you were here, you managed to upset her.'

Alison frowned. 'That certainly wasn't my intention.'

'I know, but—' Annie folded her arms, giving the impression she was ready to do battle on Teresa's behalf. 'She shouldn't be upset in her condition.'

'Will you let her know I called? She could always come to me when she's feeling up to it.' She hesitated. 'You'd both be welcome, of course.'

Annie nodded. 'Oh, she did say one thing – she asked if you wouldn't mind leaving your key. We could do with a spare.'

Alison felt inside her handbag and brought out the key on its leather fob. As she gave it to Annie, she felt suddenly sad. Teresa was slipping from her, further than ever. She knew she couldn't leave things like this. John had urged her to make things right and be there for Teresa – for Annie too, if need be.

'Annie,' she began, 'I've a feeling we got off on the wrong foot.' She looked awkward. 'Or rather, *I* did. I can be a little . . . overprotective of Teresa at times.' She remembered what John had said about trusting Teresa to know her own heart. 'I can see how well the two of you get along, and I'm glad she has someone who cares so much for her, I really am.' She took a breath. 'I'd like to think you and I can be friends.'

Annie seemed a little unsure but finally she nodded, relieved. 'She'll be awake in an hour. Why don't you come back then?'

Chapter 38

'THE LAST TIME YOU came to see me, I seem to recall feeling embarrassed at the poor state of the china cup I was forced to serve your tea in,' Joyce said.

'I remember,' Adam said, smiling. 'I didn't mind in the least.'

'You must have thought me rather foolish to have been concerned about something so trivial when I was about to move house and had far more important matters to think about.'

'Not at all. Sometimes it's easier to focus on the small things as a way of not thinking too much about the more challenging aspects of life. We all do it.'

It was certainly something he had done increasingly of late, when trying to make sense of what he now knew was a deep crisis of faith. He felt lost, no longer sure who he was or what he stood for. There were so many questions to do with what (or indeed if) he believed, and whether or not he and God were even on speaking terms. It was all proving extremely vexing, this search for answers he seemed unable to find. Overwhelmed at times, he would push such difficult thoughts aside and instead simply recite the Lord's Prayer.

It seemed to help.

'I wanted to come and see you,' he told Joyce, 'because I think you deserve to know why I shut myself away for a time when I got back to the village.'

Joyce shook her head. 'I've no doubt there was a very good reason.'

He hesitated. 'The truth is, I really wasn't myself.' He frowned, thinking back. 'I arrived on the doorstep late one night in a bad way. From the look on Sarah's face, I'm not sure she even knew me.'

'Oh, but surely . . .'

'It was quite a journey getting here.' He sighed. 'I'm not even sure I knew myself by the time I got home.'

Joyce was quiet, taking this in. 'Once I heard you were back I was overjoyed,' she said at last. 'It was an enormous relief to know you were safe and that our prayers had been answered. And yet *how* you got here and what you might have experienced on the way is something I know nothing about. I imagine it took quite a toll, both physically and mentally.'

He kept his head bowed. 'I thought I understood about suffering. Christ on the cross. And yet . . . there was a child, a boy, he couldn't have been any older than Noah.' Adam could see the boy again, a slight figure in a cap and overcoat, knee-length socks, among a group of Jewish families being driven deep into the forest. 'The Nazis were rounding up Jews and taking them to remote spots,' he said. Adam had watched from a distance with Eddie and George as the ragged procession made its way to a clearing and came to a stop. The boy who had caught Adam's eye was among the first to be shot. He winced at the memory, so vivid. 'They killed them all, even the children, and left them where they fell.' He looked up. Joyce's eyes were bright with tears. 'We could hear the soldiers laughing.'

She searched in a pocket for a hanky. It was a while before she was able to speak. 'It must make you wonder how God can allow such things,' she said quietly.

'It does, I'm afraid. I've been left with so many questions.' And, as yet, very few answers.

Adam studied the drab mounds on the plate Sarah had placed in front of him. He was not entirely sure what they were meant to be.

'Carrot biscuits,' she informed him. 'Try one.'

The biscuit fell to pieces as soon as he picked it up, sending a shower of crumbs across the table. Sarah frowned. 'The texture's not quite right. It's only my first attempt.'

Adam scooped up a few of the crumbs. The taste reminded him of shortbread. 'Do I detect the hand of Lord Woolton?' he said.

'Actually, Gwen Talbot gave me the recipe.' It was a Ministry of Food invention, Gwen said, crediting Marguerite

Patten. Sarah had been impressed with the uniform round shapes Gwen had managed to produce; they were sweet and light, proper home-made biscuits. At Sarah's request, Gwen had copied out the recipe.

Nothing to it, she said. Sarah begged to differ.

Her own batch had cracked in the oven and emerged looking like ... what? Meringues gone wrong, she decided. She couldn't understand it. The recipe was straightforward enough, just four items, and she had followed it to the letter. At the very first stage, however, as she creamed together margarine and sugar, she sensed she was in trouble. The mixture was supposed to be 'fluffy' but hers looked more like a paste. There seemed too little grated carrot, too much flour and, despite her best efforts, it refused to bind. Taking great care, she had patted the dry mixture into rounds and hoped for the best. After twenty minutes in the oven on a brisk heat, the result was beige, misshapen lumps.

'They're not bad.' Adam had resorted to a teaspoon to scrape up what was left of the crumb mixture on his plate. 'Definitely an improvement on that "chocolate" cake you made – which, if I remember rightly, didn't actually have any chocolate in it.'

Sarah pulled a face. She had used beetroot. It was not her finest effort.

'I went to see Gwen the other day and she produced a rather impressive cake,' Adam said. 'Couldn't tell you what was in it, but it was delicious.'

'Carrots, I expect. She's got more than she knows what to do with.' After a moment, Sarah said, 'What did you think – does she seem to be managing?'

'Better than I expected, if I'm honest. It's a weight off her shoulders knowing Ronald's finally getting the help he needs.'

Ronald had appeared before magistrates and received a suspended sentence for the sheep killings. A sum was agreed in compensation to Jim Morton for the loss of his livestock. Dr Rosen told the court that Ronald had suffered traumatic injuries while serving his country, sufficient to be medically discharged from his unit, and would greatly benefit from specialist treatment.

'But the asylum,' Sarah said. 'It seems so . . . extreme. Some people go in and never come out again.'

'Almost always when that happens you'll find the patient has been abandoned by their family, and that's not going to happen in Ronald's case. Despite everything, Gwen is utterly devoted to him.' Adam paused. 'I've said I'll go with her to see him, if she'd like me to.'

Sarah was surprised. 'Is it wise to become so involved when you're still not sure you even want to resume your role as vicar of St Mark's?'

'I've been giving it a good deal of thought. I've been . . . asking for guidance.' He smiled. 'From a God I thought I no longer believed in, which tells you something.'

He'd spent hours closeted away in his study, reading and thinking, doing his best to unravel the scramble of thoughts that pulled him in different directions, certain at times that he had lost his faith entirely. Sometimes as he prayed he lost the thread of what it was he was trying to say. On other occasions, it was almost as if God was so close he could feel His presence, a powerful force that was both uplifting and transformational. Following such periods of quiet contemplation, he would emerge feeling as if he had the beginnings of clarity, an idea about which path to take. Filled with optimism, the following day he would attempt to pray once more and be met with . . . silence. Unwilling to bow to disappointment, he determined to press on, finding comfort in ritual, forming the habit of lighting a candle before kneeling at his *prie-dieu* and asking for God's guidance. Gradually, he began seeing his parishioners and was touched to find that everyone had missed him, even those who rarely attended the services at St Mark's.

At every turn, he was overwhelmed by the warmth with which the villagers greeted him. Miriam Brindsley had wept when she saw him.

It made him think that perhaps he was still capable of doing some good.

'When I first got back, I couldn't even see myself in church, let alone at the altar leading a congregation in prayer,' he said. 'I'd have felt a fraud, pulling the wool over everyone's eyes.'

'And now?' Sarah asked.

'I realise I'm starting to miss it, that there are useful things I might do by focusing my attention on the needs of others rather than allowing my thoughts to turn constantly inwards. Too much introspection can be defeating. All the wondering why, the asking of questions no one can answer. It feels as if I've done enough of that of late, and that it might now be doing more harm than good.'

Sarah took his hand. Only the slightest trace of the troubled expression he had worn when he first arrived home now remained. 'You know I'll support you in any way I can,' she said.

'I feel as if I need to *do* something,' Adam said. 'I can't see this war ending any time soon.'

Across Europe, Jewish people were being massacred. A campaign was under way by the Nazis and their allies to crush the Soviets. In Odessa, in late October, as Adam was on the final stage of his journey home, tens of thousands of Jews had been executed, some burned alive. The following month the RAF sent bombers to pound Berlin, Cologne and the Ruhr, suffering heavy losses in the process.

'There's a sense of things escalating, especially now, after Pearl Harbor,' he said, frowning.

A week earlier, on 7 December, Japanese aircraft had launched an attack on the American fleet in Hawaii, killing thousands, sinking the USS *Arizona* with the loss of more than eleven hundred lives. Within hours, both Britain and America had declared war on Japan. In the days that followed, Germany declared itself to be at war with the US.

'It's a good thing, surely, now the Americans have entered the war,' Sarah said.

'I struggle to find much "good" in any of it.' Adam sighed. 'But I feel ready to serve the parish again, properly. At least I should make a start, do what I can.' He smiled. 'I've decided to take the service on Christmas Day.'

Sarah called on Frances and found her in the dining room immersed, as she so often was, in WI business. From outside came the sound of hammering.

'Are you having some building work done?' Sarah asked.

'Not exactly.' Frances smiled. 'John has taken on the challenge of building a treehouse for Noah.'

They went to the window. At the bottom of the garden at the back of the house John, in his usual trilby hat and a pair of Spencer's overalls, was driving nails into planks of wood. Noah stood close by, watching his every move.

Sarah smiled. 'How did that come about?'

'I was in the village the other day with Noah and I bumped into John walking Elsa. As you know, Noah's extremely fond of John and always makes a fuss when he sees him. Before I knew it he was saying something about a treehouse, and John happened to show a degree of enthusiasm. Noah seemed to take this to mean they would get on and build one together.' Frances gave an amused shrug. 'John said he'd be only too happy to give it a go, so I suggested he take a look in the garage and see what materials there might be and . . . *voila!* I'm told we should have a treehouse by the weekend. I offered to pay him for his help, but he refused.'

Sarah smiled. 'Noah's completely absorbed, look at his face.' The hammering stopped and he helped John rummage among the pile of offcuts for another suitable plank of wood.

'They kept going all through lunch, Claire took them sandwiches,' Frances said. 'I thought I'd take the opportunity while Noah's occupied to turn my mind to WI matters. I was wondering whether we might consider starting a choir. We have some rather good voices among our ranks, and it seems a waste to confine them to a rendition of "Jerusalem" once a month. What do you think?'

'What sort of music had you in mind?' Sarah asked.

'I hadn't got as far as that. Something choral, perhaps. "Messiah". The "Hallelujah Chorus".' She caught Sarah's look. 'I realise that might be somewhat ambitious, but the right kind of music can provide a great deal of succour.'

Sarah nodded. 'Can I suggest you look to the wireless for inspiration . . . *Music While You Work*? It's hugely popular, and not just with factory workers. Apparently lots of people tune in at home and claim it does wonders for morale. Why don't you consider borrowing from their repertoire?'

'That's not a bad idea.' Frances nodded slowly. 'We could tackle it together.'

Sarah hesitated. 'I don't really want to take on any commitments, not just as Adam's about to get busy.' She told Frances about his decision to resume his duties as vicar of St Mark's, starting with the Christmas Day service.

'I think it's a marvellous idea,' Frances said. 'A sign he's finding his way.'

Sarah nodded. 'I think so.' That was as long as he wasn't taking on too much too soon. She knew how busy the parish was, the scale of the work involved. Once he took back the reins, he would have little time to himself. But then, perhaps that was exactly what he needed – something that would occupy so much of his time it left little space for the things that were so depleting to him. 'He's so much better now that he's made a decision,' Sarah went on. 'Before, he seemed . . . adrift. Unsure. Now he has a sense of purpose he's more *alive* somehow.'

'I can see why. Adam's always had a clear sense of who he is and how he fits into the world. His vocation was central to everything he did. I can only imagine how perturbed he must have been to think it might have deserted him.' Frances looked hard at Sarah. 'I'm relieved for him, and for you. I don't doubt there were moments when you questioned whether the old Adam was gone for good.'

Sarah smiled. 'Of course, the experience of war has changed him, but the core of who he is, what drives him, remains much as it ever was.' The differences she had detected in him were ones she could live with; Adam had his secrets now concerning some of what he'd been through. There were things he was not willing to share – not with Sarah, not with anyone. At times, it was as if he disappeared into another world, one to which she had no access. She would watch him absorbed by something on the wireless, or poring over the newspaper, his face etched in pain. If she asked what was on his mind, he simply shook his head. Whatever he was thinking was private.

She understood. She too harboured thoughts and feelings that were for her alone.

We all have our secrets.

'I suppose we're all changed by war to an extent,' Frances said softly, 'but we're here, at least. Unlike so many others.'

Nick.

For a time Sarah had almost fallen in love with him. *Almost.*

They were quiet a moment, each lost in their own thoughts.

'I bumped into Alison on the way here,' Sarah said, breaking the silence. 'She was coming from Pat's after a fitting of her wedding dress.'

Frances smiled. 'I can't wait to see what Pat's done with it. We probably won't recognise it.'

'Alison's face lit up when I asked how it was coming along – not that she'd tell me a thing about it, only that Pat's proposing to embroider the date of the wedding into the hem of the underskirt in blue thread.'

'That's her "something blue" then, and the dress qualifies as "something old". I've got the mother-of-pearl earrings I wore with it, a birthday gift from Peter.' Frances smiled. 'He always had good taste in jewellery. Perhaps they could be her "something borrowed". Did she say whether they've decided on a date yet?'

'21st January, a Wednesday. It'll be at the registry office in Chester, followed by lunch at the Grosvenor. She's keeping it intimate, just a few close friends: you and I, Pat, Erica and Teresa. Alison doesn't want word getting round until after they've tied the knot.'

'I'd like things to work out for them,' Frances said.

Sarah nodded. 'So would I.'

'As we've already seen, people can be narrow-minded. I do wonder if John will ever truly be accepted here, if he'll be able to find suitable work, be in a position to stroll through the village with Alison without turning heads for all the wrong reasons.'

Sarah sighed and said, 'We must hope so, for their sake.'

'Surely some good will come from this war. I like to think we'll all emerge more tolerant, altogether kinder – less likely to object to a person because they happen to be a different colour.'

'We can only hope,' Sarah said.

Chapter 39

Early on Christmas morning, Sarah woke to find that Adam wasn't in bed.

She discovered him downstairs in the front room, sitting in the dark. He was thinking, he said, too full of anticipation to sleep.

'You know Father Christmas won't be able to come with you here,' Sarah said, making them both laugh.

'There's always the chimney in the dining room.'

She smiled. 'Do you feel like some company?'

He patted the sofa. She sat down next to him and rested her head against his shoulder.

'Am I doing the right thing?' he asked.

'You and your questions,' she said, taking his hand. 'That's one only you can answer. For what it's worth, I think you've been happier since you made up your mind ... lighter, almost. And I can't go into the village without someone stopping me to say how thrilled they are that you're back. So, I'd say it's the right decision. Are you having second thoughts?'

'Only about having less time to spend with you.'

'We'll find a way of managing.' She squeezed his hand. 'I can't help thinking how little I've contributed in terms of your ministry in the past, that I've managed to absolve myself of responsibility on the grounds that I have no faith. I've hardly been the finest example of a vicar's wife.'

'You never made a secret of the fact you don't share my beliefs,' Adam told her, 'and it was never an issue between us. You've been the best wife I could have wanted.'

'I've left you to it, though, haven't I? Someone more . . . *traditional* would have been far more involved with the parish than I've been.'

'I didn't want someone more "traditional". I wanted you.'

'Do you know, while you were away, I got more involved in the village – not out of duty, because I wanted to. It made me realise there's more I can do to support you. From now on, I want us to be a team, Adam, in *every* respect.' She paused. 'Saying that, I'm still not sure I could successfully host a tea party at the vicarage. I'd need Frances to give me one or two pointers there.'

Adam laughed. 'I promise I will never ask you to host a tea party.'

The church was filling up. Sarah and Frances had taken seats at the very front, Noah at their side. He was clutching the model aeroplane Spencer had helped him put together from bits of balsa wood before breakfast, waving it excitedly at anyone who passed.

Joyce Cameron touched Sarah on the sleeve and wished her Happy Christmas before taking a seat in the pew behind.

Frances whispered to Sarah, 'She's wearing my stole from the "Fashion on the Ration" sale.'

Sarah glanced over her shoulder. Joyce, the fur stole draped stylishly over a camel coat she kept for best, was deep in conversation with Pat.

'It actually looks very good on her,' she told Frances.

'Better than it ever did on me.' Frances looked around her. 'It looks as if the whole village has turned out.'

Sarah felt a jolt of anxiety as the pews filled up. Opposite, Erica and her girls, Kate and Laura, were filing in. Dr Rosen was at the far end of the pew. Nearby, Miriam gently rocked Vivian on her lap, flanked by Bryn and David. Jenny, glamorous in a double-breasted red coat and matching lipstick, was nearby accompanied by her mother. Alison and John squeezed in next to Pat. Spencer and Claire arrived next. Near the back of the church, Sarah spotted Gwen Talbot on her own and tried to catch her eye. Late arrivals Steph and Stan Farrow with Little Stan slid into the pew beside her, shuffling along to make space for the man who farmed the land next to theirs and rarely attended St Mark's, Jim Morton.

The organ came to life in a burst of triumphant notes and the congregation rose for the opening hymn, 'Hark! The Herald Angels Sing'. Sarah watched Adam take his place at the altar. The moment he caught her eye and smiled she felt her fears melt away. *Glory to the new-born King!*

'Thank you for coming this morning to celebrate the birth of Our Saviour,' Adam began. 'A baby wrapped in swaddling clothes lying in a manger. A God-given miracle. Christmas is a time to give thanks, to rejoice, to remind ourselves that in darkness, at moments of despair, Jesus is light everlasting, His love for us constant.

'I give thanks to God for having been safely delivered from a war that continues to be the cause of enormous suffering within our community and beyond. I feel truly fortunate that my life was spared and for the warmth and love you have all extended to me on my return.' He found Sarah again, and their eyes met. 'We are now witnessing sacrifice on an unimaginable scale. So many lives have been lost, and many of those who left to fight return home having sustained terrible injuries. Let us not forget the wounds we cannot see and are yet a source of enormous pain and distress.' He gazed at the faces looking up at him. Gwen Talbot's head was bowed. 'If there was ever a time to show compassion and understanding to our friends and neighbours, this is surely it. Be kind, and ask God to bring His love and light into the lives of those now in difficulty.' He paused, allowing his words to sink in. 'Now, let us consider those who are less fortunate than ourselves.'

Teresa had intended to go to church on Christmas Day. When Sarah said it was to be Adam's first service since coming home, she was keen to lend her support, even though the baby was due very soon now, and she was beginning to feel as if everything, even simple every-day tasks, required a supreme effort. She and Annie had stayed up late on Christmas Eve and exchanged gifts on the stroke of midnight. Her gift to Annie was a book of Wordsworth's poetry bound in scarlet and embossed in gold that Teresa had chanced upon in a bookshop in Liverpool years ago. Annie had given her a pair of gold and aquamarine earrings inherited from her grandmother, still in their Garrard box. Afterwards, in bed, Teresa wept silently, thinking of Nick and the Christmas they'd been looking forward to. *Just the three of us*, he'd said.

As she sat at the dressing table on Christmas morning dabbing rouge onto her cheeks, Teresa blinked back more tears. It was pointless to give in to her grief. Nick was gone. Their future life together was gone. There was nothing she could do. Crying only made her feel worse, not better.

Annie, already dressed, was in the kitchen making a start on lunch. 'We'll need to get going if we want a seat,' Teresa told her. 'There's bound to be a good turn-out.'

Annie looked up from peeling potatoes. 'Let me put these in water first.'

Teresa went into the hall to put her coat on. As she reached for it, she felt a strange sensation deep inside – not a kick, she had become accustomed to those. She opened her eyes wide. Something was running down her legs. Her waters had broken.

Panicking, she called to Annie, who rushed from the kitchen.

'What is it? You look as if you've seen a ghost.'

Teresa struggled to stay calm. She longed for Nick.

'It's started,' she said. 'The baby.'

The service at St Mark's was well under way – as were her contractions – by the time the ambulance arrived for Teresa. She was taken to nearby Seaton Hall, a grand country house now being used as a temporary maternity hospital.

'You're lucky,' the chirpy young woman driving the ambulance told her. 'It's a lot closer than the main hospital.'

Teresa, bracing herself for another contraction, didn't feel lucky. 'The baby's not due for another ten days,' she said.

'Oh, I wouldn't worry about that,' came the woman's cheerful reply. 'As far as I can tell, they tend to come when they're good and ready.'

Annie squeezed Teresa's hand as the ambulance rattled along the narrow country roads. 'Deep breaths,' she instructed. 'Think happy thoughts.'

Teresa waited until her contraction subsided before saying, 'Is that official medical advice?'

Annie grinned. 'Let's put it this way – it won't do you any harm.'

The ambulance swung onto the drive of Seaton Hall and pulled up at the front door where a nurse was waiting with a wheelchair, ready to whisk Teresa inside.

'We'll soon get you comfortable,' she told her, steering her with impressive speed along a corridor and onto a ward with only four beds, none currently occupied. Another painful contraction struck and she gasped.

'All right,' the nurse said, 'let's get you into bed and take a look. Looks as if you're having a Christmas baby.'

She turned to Annie. 'You'll have to wait outside, I'm afraid.'

As Alison and John were leaving St Mark's, Martha Dawson came out of the Black Horse and hurried over to them. She had seen an ambulance arrive at Teresa's earlier, she said.

'I know you're friends,' she told Alison, 'and I thought you'd want to know.'

Alison glanced at John, her eyes wide. The baby must be on its way. 'Thank you,' she said.

Mrs Dawson nodded. 'And a Happy Christmas to both of you,' she added awkwardly, glancing between Alison and John.

John smiled graciously. 'And to you.'

After the service, once everyone had left, Adam and Sarah sat quietly for a few moments in the front pew. He reached for her hand.

'Thank you,' he said.

'For what?'

'Everything. For being my wife. For being *you*.' He bent and kissed her hand.

'I'm only me because of you,' she said.

Adam smiled. He gazed at the plinth where the final advent candle, lit that morning, was burning, the Christ candle, a symbol of light. Swathes of gleaming holly and heavy clusters of ruby berries held together with ornate ties adorned the front of the altar. 'It almost looks as if Mrs Cameron has taken a cloth to the greenery and given it a polish,' he said.

'I wouldn't be surprised,' Sarah said. 'She wanted everything to be perfect. I did offer to lend a hand with the decorations, but she was quite insistent that she needed her most experienced flower arrangers. There's rather more to it than meets the eye, apparently.'

Adam nodded. 'The same can be said of most things.'

Alison arrived at the hospital to find Annie pacing up and down in the visitors' room.

'How is she?' she asked.

Annie looked a little frantic. 'She's about to have the baby. *Now.*' She kept walking. 'They wouldn't allow me to stay with her.'

'I'm sure she's in good hands,' Alison said, steering her towards a chair. 'Now, sit down before you wear a hole in the linoleum.'

Annie shook her head. 'But I promised I'd be with her, and I can't do a thing.'

'There'll be plenty for you to do soon enough.'

They sat in silence for a moment. Annie was jittery, barely able to stay in her seat. She glanced sideways at Alison.

'I never wanted to push you out, you know,' she said eventually. 'And I would never take advantage of Teresa or anything like that. She knows her own mind and she's stronger than you might imagine, even now.' She hesitated. 'We make a good team. I know her, better than most, and I care very deeply for her. I can see how devastated she is about Nick – so am I – and at the same time I see the colossal effort Teresa's making to keep going. She's about to have a child, she can't just give up. I want to do everything I can to help, Alison – to prop her up when she needs it and help her to mend. What Teresa felt for Nick, what she *still* feels, will never change, whatever happens in the future. My being here makes no difference to the love she has for him. I just want to be at her side through all this. I want to be there for the baby, too. Nick was a great friend to me, and it will mean a lot to be there for the child of two of the people I love most in all the world.' She glanced at Alison. 'And I know you want to be there for Teresa, too. I can see how fond Teresa is of you. Not everyone would have been so understanding about . . . everything.'

Alison nodded, grateful. She felt bad for being so wary of Annie initially, for fearing that Teresa was too fragile to plunge into another relationship so soon after losing Nick. But she could see, too, how much Annie cared for her, and that what Teresa felt for Annie was something strong. She knew from her own experience that it was possible to love the living and be true to the dead; her feelings for John did not make the bond she and George shared any less strong. And who was she to judge Teresa's decisions when she loathed the idea of coming under scrutiny for having fallen in love with John? Whatever happened, she did not want to lose Teresa. She valued her too much for that.

'I do want her to be happy, you know,' Alison said. 'And I can see how close the two of you are. Just – take care of her, won't you?'

Annie looked solemn. 'Of course, I will.'

Teresa had taken on board all that Dr Rosen had told her about childbirth being a natural process. She knew it was painful – she'd heard enough stories – but nothing had prepared her for how excruciating it truly was. Teresa had derived comfort from what the doctor said about her being fit and relatively young, and had persuaded herself she would cope well with the actual birth. When Dr Rosen assured her there was no reason to be unduly concerned, Teresa had believed her.

But that was before she'd lost Nick, of course, when she'd been introduced to an entirely new level of pain. It had been a knife through her heart. She had not believed she would survive.

And yet, here she was, having their child.

Hands balled into fists, teeth clenched, each agonising contraction made her scream. She sounded wild, like an animal. Sweat ran off her and drenched the bedsheet. If she had somehow survived losing Nick, she could surely cope with anything. But *this*. Never before had she experienced anything like it.

The nurse attending her was joined by a doctor, a man with silver hair and spectacles, who examined her and said she was doing well, nothing to worry about.

Teresa gritted her teeth. *What did he know about it!*

'The pain,' she told him.

He nodded. 'Nearly there,' he said, sounding infuriatingly unconcerned.

The nurse smiled in encouragement. 'Not long now,' she told Teresa, echoing the doctor.

Teresa glared at them. What was wrong with these people, grinning like idiots? Were they all on drugs? *Drugs.* Of course! 'Can't you give me something?' she begged. 'For the pain.'

They didn't seem to hear her. 'Nice big push,' the doctor urged. 'Well done. Deep breaths.'

And think happy thoughts.

She shut her eyes.

Annie's arms around her. Alison's smile. Walking down the aisle on her wedding day. Nick, handsome in his uniform, looking at her as if he couldn't believe his luck.

She had been the lucky one.

She strained and pushed and screamed so hard her throat hurt.

'Congratulations, Mrs Lucas, you have a baby boy.'

Teresa watched in a daze as the nurse gave her a tiny infant with a shock of dark hair. *Like Nick.*

Teresa cradled him, tears streaming down her face. 'Hello,' she said, 'my beautiful boy. The best Christmas present I could have wished for.'

'Have you thought of a name?' the nurse asked.

'Nicholas,' Teresa said. 'After his father.'

Alison hung back when the nurse showed them in to see Teresa. Annie seemed on the brink of tears as she gazed at the infant lying so peacefully in his mother's arms. 'He's utterly perfect.'

Teresa's eyes shone with happiness. She planted a tender kiss on his cheek. 'Look who's here, Nicholas. My best friends in all the world.' She looked up at Alison. 'Would you like to hold him?' she asked softly.

Alison glanced at Annie, who beckoned her forward. She carefully took the baby from Teresa. 'Hello little one,' Alison said, suddenly overcome. 'Aren't you the most adorable boy?' Tears ran down her face, and she found herself laughing. 'I'm only crying because I'm so happy!'

'He seems to have that effect,' Teresa said, beaming up at a tearful Annie.

'Nicholas,' Alison said. 'A Christmas baby, what could be better?'

'It's the most perfect timing,' Teresa said. 'Although that wasn't what went through my mind as I was about to go to church this morning and realised he was on the way . . .' She hesitated. 'Alison, I wanted to ask . . . would you be his godmother?'

For a moment Alison was lost for words. 'Are you quite sure?' She felt honoured, deeply touched.

Teresa nodded. She looked up at Annie, who gave her hand a squeeze. 'Of course, Alison. Of course.'

Chapter 40

JOHN WOKE AS SOON as Elsa started barking. He got up and pulled on some clothes, hurrying towards the door.

'What's going on?' Alison asked, sitting up.

'Just going to see what's set her off,' John said. 'You stay here.'

He hurried down the stairs and shushed the little dog. Elsa was at the front door, sniffing excitedly. 'What's up, girl?' he said, keeping hold of her collar as he unlocked the door.

On the step was a box tied with string. A message, he guessed, like the ones he'd had left for him from time to time in Liverpool. Entrails. A sheep's head. Dog mess. *Go home, darkie.*

He shut Elsa inside and stepped onto the path, a flash of movement at the end of the garden drawing his eye.

'Hey!'

In the grey half-light of morning, John couldn't make out the figure that stopped then turned and came towards him. He heard the door open behind him and Alison calling his name.

'Go inside,' he told her, not taking his eyes off the figure that had stopped a few paces away.

John peered at him. *Jim Morton*. He felt a rush of anger, as the farmer took off his cap.

'I brought you something,' he said, looking up, glancing in the direction of the box.

'I see that,' John said.

'What I thought about you – I was wrong.' He picked at the frayed edge of the cap. 'I don't suppose that's an excuse for being so . . . *abrupt* the day you came looking for work.'

John stayed silent. *Abrupt*.

'Losing the sheep put me in a bad way. I swear, I thought you'd done it. Getting your own back after I chased you off the farm. Didn't think it could be anyone else.' He looked John in the eye. 'I regret that, I really do.' He cleared his throat. 'I want you to know I'm sorry for the trouble you've had.'

John gave a stiff nod. 'I appreciate you coming.'

Jim Morton seemed to have run out of things to say. He stood a while longer, twisting the cap in his hands. 'So . . .'

'The box?' John asked.

'Something for you and Mrs Scotlock.' He put his cap back on, a sign the conversation was over. 'I'll leave you good people be, then.'

Alison had put a coat on over her night things and was standing behind John in her slippers. They watched Jim Morton turn and stride away along the path at the edge of the woods.

Inside the house, Elsa was still barking. John carried the box in, put it on the kitchen table and undid the string. It contained a plump chicken, a dozen eggs, honey and a slab of butter – and a scrap of paper with a single scribbled line: *Sorry for the trouble*.

'Well, well,' Alison said.

John was shaking his head. 'I wasn't expecting that.' Elsa pawed at his leg. 'No wonder this one was so worked up, fresh chicken meat on the doorstep.' He bent and stroked her head. 'Easy, girl.'

'It makes me wonder ... if Jim Morton's changed his tune, perhaps it's a sign people are finally getting used to having you here,' Alison said hopefully. 'It must surely have dawned by now how mistaken they've been in their view of you.'

John shrugged. 'You might be right.' He looked thoughtful. 'And then again, they might just change their minds back again once I'm your husband. I can see at least some finding the idea of us living together as man and wife unacceptable.'

Alison nodded. It was a conversation they'd had many times. What would people think? What did it matter? Whose business was it but hers and John's anyway how they chose to live? At times she felt defiant. The village would have to get used to them; that was all there was to it. Great Paxford was her home, the place where her friends were, and her new godson, too. And she was stubborn, as well – not about to be dictated to when it came to deciding who she could or could not love. In a week's time they would be married and she would be Mrs Smith. Alison had no intention of continuing the pretence that John was a paying guest. It was insulting when he had every right to be there.

Neither of them had anything to be ashamed of.

'I respect the man for coming here,' John said, 'but Jim Morton having an attack of conscience doesn't change a thing, not in the long run.' He took Alison's hand. 'I still think we've made the right decision.'

She nodded. 'I agree.'

'As long as you don't feel I'm pushing you into something you'd rather not do. There's time enough to change your mind if you're having second thoughts.'

Alison shook her head. 'We've talked it through, haven't we? We've made the decision together. The *right* decision.' She turned to him and kissed him softly. 'I have no intention of changing my mind.'

Chapter 41

ON THE MORNING OF their wedding, John was up early. He took Elsa for a long walk in the woods, enjoying the cold air. He knotted his scarf and tucked it inside his coat while Elsa ran ahead, picking up some scent or other, chasing after quarry she was never likely to catch. He watched, amused, as she skittered towards a squirrel that shot away up a tree before she got anywhere near.

'Give up, they're too fast for you, girl,' he called after her.

They tramped on, the sun coming up, sharp winter light seeping through the canopy of oak and sycamore, Elsa returning to trot at his side.

'Big day,' he told her.

He had chosen the date, his mother's birthday, wishing she could see him. He wondered what she'd have made of his marriage to Alison. In his mind's eye, he imagined her nodding her approval. *I see I brought you up to have good taste.* She'd have been pleased for him, and proud too, unconcerned about so-called 'convention'. Hadn't she always urged him to follow his heart? She had drummed into him for as long as he could remember the importance of living life to the full. Had she still been alive, she'd have been in no doubt how much Alison meant to him, or of the joy that came from the love they had for one another. At times, he could not quite believe his good fortune. The thought made him smile.

Alison was in the habit of saying the same thing to him.

Back at the house, Alison was making breakfast. She cracked eggs into the frying pan, where thick slices of bacon were already cooking. 'I hope you're hungry.'

'I'm not sure I can eat,' John said, sitting down. The china teapot and the cups and saucers reserved for 'best' were out. There were folded linen napkins on gilt-edged side plates and soda bread, still warm from the oven. The centrepiece was delicate snowdrops from the garden in a jar. While he was out with Elsa, Alison had been busy preparing their pre-wedding breakfast.

'Don't say you're complaining about my cooking already,' she teased. She knew by now that John was a good cook, able to make something tasty out of a few uninspiring ingredients in a way she couldn't quite match.

She put the plates of bacon and eggs on the table and sat facing him.

'Nothing to do with the food, but my stomach's all churned up.'

'Must be nerves. As long as you're not having second thoughts . . .?'

John gazed at her. 'Not me. I've never been so sure of anything in my life.' He reached for her hand. 'I can't wait to marry you, you know that. I love you, Alison Scotlock.'

'You won't be able to say that for much longer.' John raised an eyebrow. 'The *Scotlock* bit, I mean. Not long to go before I'm Alison *Smith*.'

'I'll still love you the same,' he said.

She smiled. 'That's all right, then. Now, eat up before your breakfast goes cold.'

Pat had worked wonders with the dress. By the time she'd finished, it looked as if it had been intended all along as a bridal gown; there was nothing to hint at its former life when Frances had worn it in the ballroom at the Ritz Hotel. Alison stepped into it and studied her reflection in the full-length mirror on the back of the wardrobe door. The dress felt different. *She* felt different. During her fittings, she had spent a good deal of time marvelling at Pat's cleverness, and not so much considering how the dress might make her feel on the day of her wedding. Alison was a practical person, and had been more concerned than anything that she might be about to ruin a perfectly good (expensive) dress by a celebrated designer. After all, did it really matter what she wore?

Now, she realised it did. It was her *wedding* day and *everything* mattered, including a dress she would most probably wear only once. She felt suddenly tearful and plucked a handkerchief from the drawer of her dressing table to dab at her eyes. *Don't cry!*

The dress, with its hidden embroidery, *Alison and John, 21 January, 1942*, tugged unexpectedly at her heart. She took a moment to compose herself, straightened her shoulders and put on the earrings Frances had loaned her. *I am about to change my life.* In the spare room, John was busy dressing. She would need his help to do up the row of tiny buttons at the back. She heard him whistling, something she didn't recognise, and called out to him, 'When you've a minute, can you give me a hand?'

He knocked at the door. 'Safe to come in?' he said.

'You'll have to – I can't manage the buttons on my own.'

He stepped into the room, looking smarter than she'd ever seen him, handsome in a suit, white shirt and dark tie. A silk handkerchief jutted from his breast pocket. He stopped abruptly and gave her a long look.

'What do you think?' she said, suddenly self-conscious, afraid the dress, so different from anything he'd ever seen her in, might not suit her.

His eyes stayed on her. 'What I think is I've never seen anyone look so beautiful.' He went to her and took both hands in his. 'You ever see a grown man cry? Because you just might today.'

Alison held his gaze. 'It's not . . . too much?'

'It's perfect,' he said. 'Just like the woman wearing it.' He began fastening the buttons. 'All done.'

Alison turned to face him and he gave her another appraising look. They stood side by side in front of the mirror. 'Are we the finest-looking couple that registry office will ever have laid eyes on?' he asked.

Alison smiled. 'I think we just might be.'

'We're missing one small thing.' She gave him a quizzical look as he took a leather box embossed with Lowe & Sons from his pocket. 'This is for you.' Inside was a heart-shaped pearl on a delicate chain.

Alison was overwhelmed. 'John, I don't know what to say.'

'You like it?'

'I *love* it – it's a perfect match for the dress. Help me put it on.' He fastened the clasp at the back of her neck. The pearl sat at the base of her throat. 'It occurred to me this morning I didn't have my "something new" and I was wondering if it mattered.'

'Strictly speaking, it's not new.' He had found it in a pawn shop, he said, which was how he'd managed to afford it. 'As soon as I spotted it, I knew it was just right – at least, I hoped so. It looks even better than I imagined.'

'Thank you, I'll cherish it.'

They stood a moment longer, watching their reflections. 'Nearly time to go,' John said at last. 'Are you ready?'

Alison grinned.

They left the house hand in hand.

The ceremony itself was short, filled with promises and smiles, and Alison and John emerged into winter sunshine and a sprinkle of confetti. They led their guests, comprising Teresa cradling Nicholas, Annie, Frances, Sarah, Pat and Erica, the short distance to the Grosvenor Hotel, where a table had been reserved in a quiet corner of the restaurant. On the way there, John and Alison walked ahead holding hands, not caring who saw them or what people might think.

'I don't think I've ever seen Alison so happy,' Frances said.

Sarah nodded. 'She looks utterly radiant, and the dress is just right. I'm struggling to remember what it looked like before. Pat has worked wonders.'

'Did you see the way John was looking at her as they exchanged their vows?' Frances said, smiling. 'I thought my heart would melt. It's obvious he adores her.'

'I'd say the feeling is definitely mutual.'

At lunch, John thanked them all for coming. 'There will be no speeches today,' he said, 'but we do have something to tell you. An announcement, of sorts. For a little while now, Alison and I have been talking about the best way to build a future together, a home of our own.' He took a breath. 'And we think it makes sense to begin afresh, head for pastures new. It feels like the right thing to do.'

Pat's eyes widened. 'You're considering leaving the village?'

Alison placed a hand on John's. 'More than that. We've made up our minds.'

Frances started up. 'But I don't understand. Your home is in Great Paxford . . . it's what you know, where all your friends are.'

Alison sighed. 'And I've been happy here, I really have, but all of us know there was what you might call a mixed reaction to John moving into the village. The moment Jim Morton started losing sheep, John was blamed. I hardly need spell out why.'

'Only a few people thought like that, and those that did were soon proved wrong,' Sarah said. 'That at least should make those same people think twice before they go hurling unfounded accusations in future.'

'Sarah's right,' Frances said. 'The likes of Martha Dawson ended up looking extremely foolish.'

Alison caught Teresa's eye and smiled. She had already confided in her their plans to move, and Teresa now nodded her encouragement.

'It's not as though we'll never be back,' Alison said. 'We'll visit every now and then.'

'But it hardly seems fair that you should have to uproot yourselves and leave for the sake of a few petty individuals,' Erica said.

'We could stay and see what happens,' replied John, 'but it's a risk. The next time something goes wrong and folk want a scapegoat, I'm an obvious target. I suspect I always will be. That's why we want to move away before there's another . . . incident.' He aimed a tender look at Alison. 'The fact is, some of our neighbours might never accept us as a couple – and I might never find work. It's a recipe for frustration, if nothing worse.'

'Where will you go?' Pat asked.

'London,' said Alison.

'I won't stand out so much there,' added John. 'There are people I know, friends we can stay with until we get on our feet. And I'll be able to find work.'

'But . . .' Frances hesitated. '*London*. It's so busy and . . . *anonymous*. And is it safe? If the bombs start again . . .'

John nodded. 'We've thought about it all seriously. And the busyness is part of its appeal. There'll be less chance of attracting too much attention.'

'You'll be missed very much,' Frances said, 'but of course, you must do what you feel is right.'

'You absolutely must,' Teresa echoed, 'as long as you *promise* to come back and visit us. I would hate it if your godson only rarely got to see you.'

Alison beamed. 'Of course, I don't want Nicholas growing up not knowing who I am.'

'That will never happen,' Teresa told her.

Erica sighed. 'Is there nothing we can say to change your minds?'

Alison shook her head. 'It's not a decision we've come to in haste. We've talked it through at great length and we both think it's for the best.'

John reached across and squeezed his wife's hand. 'There's something to be said for starting again, as long as we go in the right spirit, with hope and love in our hearts.'

Chapter 42

A FEW WEEKS LATER, IN mid-February, just after Alison and John had packed up and left Great Paxford with their dog, the first American GIs arrived. Among them was a contingent of black airmen whose impact on the village was sudden and dramatic. Overnight, black faces became commonplace. They were courteous, with money to spend, and were, mostly, well-received.

'What a pity Alison and John didn't stay long enough to see this,' Frances remarked to Sarah. 'They might just have changed their minds about going.'

Sarah wasn't so sure. 'I got the impression they were ready for a new adventure.'

'Wait until you hear this,' Frances went on. 'The other evening Claire and Spencer were in the Black Horse having a drink, and a few of the black GIs were in with one or two of the WAAFs from Tabley Wood. They're very popular with the local girls, apparently. Utterly charming and polite, Claire says. *Very* good-looking, and the uniform's rather fetching. And they have supplies of . . .

nylons.' Frances smiled. 'The girls they were drinking with appeared completely besotted.'

'Does this mean Trevor Dawson doesn't mind black men in his pub after all . . . as long as they've plenty of money to spend?' Sarah said.

'Well, this is the interesting bit. A group of white GIs arrived later in the evening and ordered the others to leave. Did you know, there's no mixing at all between them? I hear the black airmen are treated appallingly.'

Sarah nodded; she had heard about the policy of strict segregation within the American forces.

'So, the white GIs began name-calling, telling the black men to get out. Then Trevor Dawson squared up to them.'

Sarah's eyes widened.

'He only threw the *white* GIs out!' cried Frances. 'He told them that he runs a peaceful establishment and won't stand for any trouble. He refused to serve them.'

'*Trevor Dawson?*'

Frances clapped her hands in delight. 'I know! Can you believe it? Claire and Spencer saw the whole thing.'

Sarah looked utterly perplexed. 'I'm really not sure what to make of that.'

'We can only hope that what happened with John was a valuable lesson in treating others with respect, regardless of their skin colour.' Frances caught Sarah's look. 'I know it's quite a leap to imagine Mr Dawson thinking in those terms, but bear with me. It's just possible he's looking to make amends in some small way for his dreadful mis-judgement where John was concerned.'

'Or it may be something to do with the extent to which the black GIs had already boosted the pub's takings that night. They're certainly a lot better off than our servicemen.'

Frances gave her a reproachful look. 'You may well be right, but on this occasion I wonder if we might adopt a less cynical approach and at least give Mr Dawson the benefit of the doubt. Wouldn't it be something to think that John had somehow left a lasting and positive impression on him, that the unfairness he experienced may have helped pave the way for these new arrivals – who might otherwise have been met with suspicion – to be treated with far greater tolerance?'

Sarah smiled. 'Perhaps. And you're right, it's uplifting to think that all John went through, with great dignity too, might not have been in vain.'

Frances looked pleased.

'Actually, I called on Teresa the other day,' Sarah went on. 'The baby is completely adorable, by the way.' He looked like his father. Sarah had carried the sleeping Nicholas up to the nursery, which Nick had decorated before his death. Buttercup-yellow walls and stencils depicting scenes from the nursery rhyme 'Hey, Diddle Diddle'. 'You've reminded me, Teresa mentioned she'd had a visit from Martha Dawson.'

'Really? I wouldn't have thought they were friends.'

'They're not, but Mrs Dawson was asking after Alison and John. Apparently, she was sorry to hear they'd left the village and wondered if Teresa had an address for them, as she wanted to send a note of congratulations on their marriage.'

Frances was wide-eyed. 'Well, that does surprise me.'

'I got the impression Teresa gave her short shrift – she still feels rather raw about John being accused over the sheep killings.'

Sarah had later made a point of going to see Mrs Dawson and found her full of remorse over her treatment of Alison and John.

'I've a feeling Martha Dawson is keen to smooth things over with Alison and John.' Sarah, having finally embraced her role as vicar's wife, was already fully engaged doing all that she could to assist Mrs Dawson in her efforts.

She smiled.

At last, she seemed to have found her calling.

The arrival in Great Paxford of American servicemen with money in their pockets had transformed the fortunes of the Brindsley family. Trade at the once-struggling emporium picked up as the GIs homed in on sweets and chocolate – candy, as they called it. Every type of boiled sweet went down well. When Joyce Cameron came in for two ounces of pear drops, she found them temporarily unavailable. Bars of Cadbury's Dairy Milk, Turkish Delight and Fry's Chocolate Cream were snapped up. Expensive boxes of Milk Tray were in great demand. The GIs bought quantities of evaporated milk and stacks of the Nescafé tins that Joyce hadn't been sure would sell. Sales of Marmite unexpectedly soared and word soon spread that the salted potato crisps (or chips) that Miriam had started making were every bit as good as the best brands available in the States. No sooner was a fresh batch ready than it was sold out.

Miriam found all the GIs unfailingly polite. They tipped their caps, addressed her as 'Ma'am' and held open the door for other customers. And they never seemed concerned by the price of anything.

'What did I tell you?' Miriam said as she and Bryn cashed up one night. The GIs had been in the village for a week and business had improved with each passing day. 'I knew all we had to do was hold steady and that in time things would come right.'

Bryn smiled. 'You're always right, love,' he said. 'You must have a sixth sense.'

'I've been thinking about the sign over the shop,' she said. 'Brindsley and Son. When it was just the butcher's and we were expecting David to take things over eventually, it felt right, but now we've a much bigger business and there's Vivian to think about. Once she's older she'll be part of it, too. I don't know, Bryn – it feels as if we need to change that sign.'

The same thought had occurred to him. 'What did you have in mind – Brindsley *and Family*, perhaps?'

'How about just Brindsley's? It's what everyone calls it anyway, and it tells you right away it's a family business, one that includes all of us.'

Bryn nodded. 'I like it. Brindsley's. It sounds . . . *posh*. Like that fancy London store on Oxford Street.' He frowned, trying to think of the name.

'Selfridges,' Miriam supplied.

Bryn nodded. 'Or the other one, Harrods.'

'Brindsley's – purveyors of fine foods.'

'*By Royal Appointment!*'

They both laughed. 'I'll look into getting a new sign made.' Bryn chuckled. 'Brindsley's . . . the Harrods of the North!'

David was spending the evening at Jenny's. Her mother was away, visiting her sister in Nantwich, and was not expected back until later. She'd promised to telephone before setting off, so that Jenny knew when her bus would be arriving.

It was a rare opportunity for the pair to enjoy some real privacy and David was feeling nervous. All he could think about was what, if anything, Jenny was expecting from him. In all the time they had been seeing one another, he had kept the scarring on his back hidden from her. They'd finally spoken at length about his injuries, but he sensed she had little grasp of just how terrible they were. She didn't care about his scars, she said; she loved him anyway, and he believed her. But all the same – even he winced at their appearance. He had tried so hard to hide the thick red welts that cracked and split and left his shirts bloody, the skin that was forever puckered and angry-looking. No amount of time would make them disappear. He would never forget the look of horror on his mother's face the first time she'd caught sight of them.

How Jenny would react, he could only imagine.

Which was why he had no intention of letting her see them.

As they sat on the settee at her mother's house, Jenny curled into him, the wireless playing some dance tune, he began to panic. 'Shall we go to the pub?' he suggested.

Jenny sat up, surprised. 'I thought you might . . . want to stay in, since we've got the house to ourselves.'

'I do,' David said, 'it's just . . .'

She kept her eyes on him. 'Mum won't be back for ages, and she'll phone anyway.'

'I know, but . . .'

Jenny cupped his face in her hands. 'We can go upstairs.'

His heart lurched. It was what he wanted more than anything. And yet—

'Maybe we should wait.' He winced to hear himself sounding so feeble, especially when he saw the look of hurt on her face. 'It's not that I don't want to,' he said. 'It's just, I . . .'

I don't want you to see me. I'm afraid that once you do, I'll lose you.

Jenny bit her lip. 'David, I thought you wanted to be with me. Properly.'

'I do. I *do*.' He reached for her hand, and she pulled it away.

'Then tell me why you're being like this, blowing hot and cold, making me feel as if you don't even *like* me.' She sounded as if she might cry.

'I *love* you, you daft thing.' He gently turned her to face him. 'You're smart, you're beautiful, you're resourceful and kind and . . . Well, you're the best thing that's ever happened to me.' He bit his lip. 'I'm scared, that's all. I'm not like you. I'm . . . ugly. And once you see . . . everything, I'm just worried that's going to be the end of us.'

'Stop it,' Jenny said. 'I've told you, I don't care about the scars.' She held out a hand. 'You can't keep hiding, shutting me out, because that's what will kill us, not the scars on your back. You need to trust me, and if you can't, well . . .' She shrugged.

'I can,' David said. 'I can.'

They made love on the narrow bed in her room. When Jenny saw his back, she wept. Although she had heard about his heroism on the ship, seeing what it had cost him made her realise the full extent of his selflessness. The bravery he had shown, in risking his life to save others, made her love him even more.

As they lay facing each other, she stroked his face and told him he was perfect.

David shook his head. 'I'm not.'

'Perfect for me,' she said, gazing at him. 'I never want to be without you. I want to be your wife, David. I want to marry you.'

He blinked.

'Why not?' Jenny said. 'We love each other, don't we?'

He nodded. 'It's just, the last thing I was expecting was . . . a *proposal*.'

She looked serious. 'I'm not playing – I mean it. After everything you've been through, the heartache and loss and pain this war keeps on dishing out – what's the point of waiting? What exactly are we waiting for?'

David shook his head. 'I don't know.'

She kissed him. 'I'm still waiting for an answer.'

David laughed. 'Yes,' he said. '*Yes!*'

Miriam was knitting a V-neck slipover for Bryn using wool unpicked from an old cardigan of hers and a pattern for something with sleeves that she had managed to adapt. It wasn't the best colour, a kind of brownish orange with purple flecks, but the wool was soft and it would do. She stretched out her legs and rested her feet on the pouffe. Bryn was in the armchair facing her with his copy of *The Modern Grocer*. At his side, lying peacefully in her pram, was Vivian.

'Gold lettering or green?' Bryn asked, back on the subject of the new sign.

Miriam finished counting stitches before she replied. 'There's a grocer in Chester, he's been there years. All traditional, very high-class. Maybe we should take a look at what he's got.'

Bryn nodded. 'Good idea, we'll have a trip.'

He had his nose back in his book and Miriam was tackling the tricky ribbed edging around the arm of the jumper when David and Jenny arrived. 'Had a good evening?' Miriam asked, without looking up.

'Not bad,' David said. He grinned at Jenny, who gave him a playful dig in the ribs.

Miriam nodded, her eyes still on her knitting. 'Let me get to the end of this line and I'll make you a drink.'

David glanced at Jenny. 'In a bit.'

'Just *tell* them,' Jenny whispered, beaming at him.

Miriam, in the middle of a line, caught the excitement in her voice and looked up.

David took a breath. 'Ma, Dad ... we're getting married.'

For a moment, Miriam was too startled to speak. She let go of the knitting, dropping several stitches. '*Oh!*' she managed.

David laughed. '*Oh*. Is that all you've got to say?'

For once she seemed lost for words. Her eyes shone, and she felt as if she might burst with happiness. 'It's the best news,' she managed. 'Isn't it the best news, love?'

Bryn was grinning. 'It is, Mim, the best we could have wished for.' He got to his feet and shook his son's hand, planted a kiss on Jenny's cheek. 'Congratulations to the pair of you. I'll get that bottle of vintage port I put aside for a special occasion. If this doesn't warrant opening it, I don't know what will!'

'When's it going to be, then?' Miriam said, scooping up Vivian, who remained fast asleep, and going to congratulate them. 'What about May, when there's blossom on the trees? Or June, to be sure of decent weather? And you'll want St Mark's, now the vicar's back . . .'

'Give them a chance, love,' Bryn said, laughing.

'We've not decided anything yet,' David said.

Jenny caught hold of his hand. 'We wanted to tell you straight away,' she said.

'Well, we couldn't be happier for you,' Miriam told her. 'Welcome to the family.'

'Tell you what, Mim,' Bryn said. 'I reckon we'd better get cracking and change that sign over the shop.'

Chapter 43

PAT COULD NOT QUITE bring herself to give up on Marek. On the walks she took into the countryside surrounding the village, she felt his hand in hers, urging her to be strong. 'We must trust one another to endure periods of silence,' he had said. 'I will be thinking about you. You must believe it.'

Writing about him helped. It made her feel more closely connected to him. Each word she wrote anchored him ever more securely in her heart. As the months went by she promised to wait, to be there on his return. *For as long as it takes.* Whenever she felt hope fading, she took a leaf from Miriam's book, trusting that her prayers would surely one day be answered. It was simply a case of keeping faith. If she believed, she could make it happen.

Until. One morning she woke feeling overwhelmed by despair, tears running into her pillow. She felt less hopeful about the world than she had since Bob's death. Under cover of darkness as she slept, it seemed that every fragment of hope she'd been clinging to so resolutely had deserted her, simply fled into the night. Something had changed. Everything. Her prayers were no longer of any use; her faith had turned to dust. She must face the truth.

Marek was gone.

She knew it.

As she grieved, she wrote, more than ever, drawing inspiration from the love they'd shared.

I may have lost you, my love, but I will never forget you. You are forever in my heart.

On the day word finally came, she was not at home. The night before, she'd completed the alterations to Frances's Dior evening gown and decided to take it round first thing after breakfast. Frances barely recognised the dress. In its original state it had been sleeveless, with a plunging neck and back and a generous skirt with a short train. Now, the hemline ended an inch below the knee and the bodice had been reworked to include a neat little keyhole effect. Pat had used fine tulle from the generous underskirt to fashion sleeves. As she had anticipated, there was enough fabric to make a short boxy jacket to complete the outfit.

'Pat, you're an absolute genius,' Frances said, turning this way and that to check her reflection in the mirror in her bedroom. 'You should set up a dressmaking business. I'm quite serious. Think of all the perfectly good evening gowns hanging at the back of wardrobes, worn once or twice and then abandoned, all crying out for you to get your hands on them. Once word got round, you'd have women from miles around beating a path to your door.'

Pat laughed. 'Do you know,' she said, 'I might just do that. Nothing too formal – I wouldn't want too many demanding clients, and what with the money left from Bob, it's not as though I need to work . . . But there's something wonderful, isn't there, about taking something forgotten and making it good as new?'

'From a purely selfish point of view, I wouldn't want to lose you,' Frances said. 'But it would be a real shame not to exploit to the full your extraordinary talent.'

It was almost lunchtime when Pat returned home. A letter had arrived with the second post and lay face down on the mat. She picked it up and at once knew the handwriting. A rush of heat went through her. The envelope bore her name and old address.

After all this time. After I lost hope.

The walls in the dark little hallway seemed to shift and press in on her.

Marek.

She tore at the envelope, afraid of what it might contain. A single sheet of lined paper torn from a notebook.

Patricia, my love.

Her heart was beating fast, hammering against her rib cage. She berated herself for having given up.

You must wonder at my silence. All these months without a word. Forgive me.

Tears filled her eyes and blurred the next few lines. Odd words leapt out at her. *Wounded. Unconscious. Close to death.* She wiped at her tears.

The doctors tell me I have no business being here, that I died and somehow came back to life, that I survived against all the odds.

She let out a sob.

It's almost a miracle, you might say. None of the doctors here is able to make sense of it, or offer an explanation. Of course, it makes complete sense to me, Patricia. I know you will understand when I say that what saved me was you. How could I die when I have so much to live for, when I have you? How could I leave you after the promises I made? I know that you are the 'miracle' the doctors spoke about, the reason I am here.

He was in a military hospital on the south coast, recuperating – 'each day becoming stronger' – and would not be returning to action.

She took the letter into the kitchen and sat at the table still with her coat on, tears streaming down her face, the news slowly beginning to sink in. She had resigned herself to a different life. She had let go her dream of a future with Marek. *No happy ever after.* But now. *Now.* Her hands shook as she read the letter again, taking time to linger over each word.

Almost a miracle, you might say . . . I know you will understand . . . what saved me was you.

She closed her eyes and heard his voice, the soft Czech accent saying that she was the reason he had survived.

They had lost so much time.

She knew what she must do.

It was dark when she left the house the following morning. All she had was one small bag; it was all that she needed. The first bus was due in a few minutes. As she waited, she said her silent goodbyes to the sleeping village and the memories it held. The good she would cherish; the bad lay buried with Bob in the churchyard.

It was time to move on, and she was more than ready. In her pocket was Marek's letter, spurring her on.

What saved me was you.

He had saved her, too.

The life they had dreamed of together, one she feared was lost forever, was at last about to come true. *We are the lucky ones. We found that most elusive and rare of things, enduring love.*

In the darkness a blackbird began its song. A faint rumble signalled the approaching bus. Pat felt a surge of anticipation, a surge of joy. *This is the start of a journey, an adventure that could lead anywhere.*

When the bus arrived, she took a seat next to the window and gazed out as her old life grew ever more distant. Behind her was the past. Ahead was a new beginning filled with promise and possibility.

The best was still to come.

Marek.

My happy ever after.

Woolton Pie

Woolton pie, also known as Lord Woolton Pie, is a vegetable pie that was popular during World War II. Lord Woolton was the Minister of Food, and his pie was among several recipes recommended to the public by the Ministry of Food during the war, when rationing made many other meals hard to create. It includes a little Marmite, Alison's addition to the recipe.

You will need:

For the pastry:
- 150g potatoes, diced
- 250g wholewheat or plain flour
- 2 tsp baking powder
- ½ tsp salt
- 100g margarine
- 1 tsp water
- 50g cheese, grated
- 1 tbsp milk, for glazing

For the filling:
- 300g cauliflower, cubed
- 300g parsnips, cubed
- 300g carrots, cubed
- 300g potatoes, cubed
- 300g turnip or swede, cubed
- 2–3 spring onions, chopped
- 1 tbsp rolled oats
- 2 tbsp Marmite
- ½ tsp salt
- ½ tsp pepper
- ½ tsp parsley, dried

Method:

1. Pre-heat the oven to 200°C.
2. First, make the pastry. Boil the 125g potatoes until very soft, then drain and mash them until smooth. Leave to the side to cool.
3. Mix the flour, salt and baking powder together, then rub in the margarine.
4. Mix in the mashed potato, water and grated cheese. Then mix and knead to form a dough.
5. Next, make the filling. Put the chopped vegetables into a pot and fill with water to just cover the vegetables. Simmer for 15 minutes.
6. Add the Marmite, rolled oats and seasoning, then cook for another 15 minutes, until the vegetables are soft and most of the water has been absorbed.
7. Pour the vegetable mixture into a deep pie dish.
8. Roll out the pastry and place neatly on top of the dish, then glaze the top with milk.
9. Cook in the oven for 30 minutes until lightly browned.
10. Enjoy!

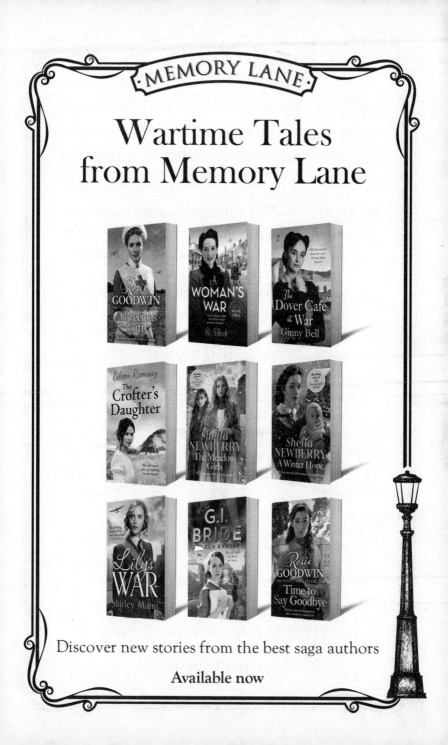